Dedication

This book is for Brennan and Madison. You are my world, and I couldn't imagine my life without you. You two are my greatest gifts from God.

I'm so glad you're experiencing this journey with me. You will see what it means to pursue your dreams and know that it is never too late to pursue what you want in life.

I love you to the Moon and Back!

Contents

AMNESIA

at the

ALTAR

Misty Jae
OGERT

Acknowledgments

There are so many people to thank this time around!

To my daughter, Madison, who took my vision of re-designing the cover and made it come true! I love it! Thank you for your precious time.

For Mark Jordan, who painted the original cover for Amnesia at the Altar.

To my Beta readers, Courtney Sweeney, Vivek Mehta, Ashley Wilson, and Heather Fournier.

To my AMAZING editor, Juli-Ann Carico, she bailed me out of grammar jail more times than I could count!

To all that participated in the contest to name the fictional town in this book. Especially Tasha Vohlken, the winner that came up with Willows Cove. (I love it!) Runners-up: Travis Vann (Cassam), Colleen Brunelle (Oakwood), Roland Bell (Harbor Bay), Kimberly Adelle Mollet (Berly), and Courtney Sweeney (Meadow Brook)

Last but certainly not least, to my amazing, super supportive, forever romantic, do-it-all dad and husband. For all the times, the dishes and laundry piled up around us as I worked. I love our crazy, busy life together!

Also By This Author:

See You Never

A Long Love Ago

Brides of Willows Cove Series:

Amnesia at the Altar

Honey Without the Moon

CHAPTER ONE

B eep...Beep...Beep...

What's that noise?

Beep...Beep...Beep...

There it is again. She was slowly becoming aware of her surroundings. Her long eyelashes fluttered open, and almond-shaped, emerald-green eyes glanced around the room.

She was tucked neatly in a twin-sized bed. There was no comforter, just a crisp white sheet and a thin blanket covering her lower half. A large window to her right revealed rain streaking down the pane.

What a miserable day.

Beep...Beep...Beep...

She turned her head to the left to locate the sound. The quick movement gave her a splitting headache. When she put her hand to her forehead, she found a bandage and an I.V. in her arm. That's when she noticed she was hooked up to a machine, which was the cause of the incessant beeping. This can't be good.

When the pounding in her head began to ease, she noticed a man sprawled across a chair adjacent to the machine. He was handsome, with thick, black hair falling over his forehead. He had a five-o'clock shadow on his chiseled jaw. He wore a black bow tie, which was unraveled and hanging loosely around his neck.

The door behind him opened, and an older gentleman with salt and pepper hair walked in. He was wearing a long white lab coat and carrying a tablet. A big smile spread across his face when he saw her awake.

Weakly, she returned the smile.

"How are you doing this morning?" he asked. His voice seemed to fill the room. The booming sound made her wince.

"Fine," she managed to croak out. Her hand reached for her throat, which felt like sandpaper.

"Would you like some water?" he asked but was already heading to a stand at the foot of her bed. He picked up a paper cup and a beige pitcher. She watched greedily, her thirst becoming more apparent as the water slipped out of one vessel and smoothly into the other.

She gladly accepted the water and drank all there was in the cup, allowing the cool liquid to coat her throat. Sitting up now, she set the cup on the bedside stand and folded her hands primly in her lap. Then, clearing her throat, she asked, "Now, this might sound like a dumb question, but who are you, and where am I?"

The man gave a slight laugh before thrusting his hand out for her to shake, "I'm sorry. I'm Dr. Peter Chandler, and you are at St. Vincent's Hospital. You were involved in a serious car accident yesterday morning." He watched her for a reaction.

A frown marred her perfect heart-shaped face.

"A car accident?" she whispered. "Was anyone hurt?" she asked, concerned.

"The woman that hit you was 78 years old. She just has a couple of bruises. She was wearing her seatbelt. Unfortunately, you were not."

Her frown deepened, "Okay, one more question?" She held a finger in the air.

"Of course," Dr. Chandler assured her.

The finger she held in the air pointed to the man in the chair, "Who is he?"

The shock on Dr. Chandler's face was unmistakable. Her mind started to scramble; she was supposed to know.

"That's Blake Duncan, your fiancé." He said slowly, "You were supposed to get married yesterday but with the accident..." his voice trailed off.

The man in question began to wake up as if he sensed he was the topic of conversation. When Blake saw her awake, he rushed to her bedside and picked up her hand, giving it a big kiss.

She immediately noticed his striking blue eyes. "Hey babe," he gave her a wicked grin, "I'm so glad you're awake. I've been worried sick." Blake leaned forward to kiss her, and her hand came up immediately, blocking his face.

She looked up at Dr. Chandler and over at Blake and asked, "Are you sure?" She had seen the ring on her left ring finger so she knew the answer but why didn't she feel it? Shouldn't she know this gorgeous man was her fiancé?

"Sure about what?" Blake had pulled his rejected face away from her hand. He glanced from one to the other.

"Excuse me," Dr. Chandler all but shoved Blake away from the bed. He pulled a penlight from his pocket. "Follow this, please." She did what she was asked with no problem, except her head started to hurt again. "Can you tell me your name?" His voice had grown serious.

Her heart beat wildly in her chest, and her palms were instantly sweaty. "Of course, I can," she said confidently, but her mind was blank, a deep void as if no information was there for her to retrieve.

She searched Blake's face, but he was no help. He looked as lost as she was beginning to feel. She glanced desperately at the doctor, needing answers. Anxiety welled up inside her, as tears stung her eyes but she chose to ignore them, "I don't know," she said in a whisper, willing it not to be true.

Blake finally found some words, and this time, it was his turn to push the doctor aside as he sat on the edge of her hospital bed. "Julie, babe, tell me you remember me." It wasn't a question.

"Julie? That's my name?" Not ringing any bells, she thought. "Julie what?" she asked.

"Julie Alexis Hart," Blake supplied her full name.

"What do you remember, Julie?" Dr. Chandler asked.

Remember? I can't even remember my name, and he thinks I'm supposed to remember my life story.

"Nothing," Julie said, frustrated, her hands hitting the bed, "Not one simple thing."

"Doctor, how long is this going to last?" Blake demanded as he stood to face him.

"You can never tell with amnesia. It can be hours, days, months, even...years." He said with a shrug and then continued, "In certain cases, memories are never regained, but that is a worst-case scenario."

Was he trying to be encouraging? Years! Never? Julie became frantic. Suddenly, she couldn't catch her breath. She pressed her hand to her chest, which had grown tight.

Seeing this, Dr. Chandler suggested that Julie sleep and called her nurse to give her some medication. Agreeing, she took the drug without question, hoping that she would discover this had all been a bad dream when she woke up. Dr. Chandler ushered Blake from the room as he promised to come back soon.

Julie eventually fell asleep with troubled thoughts.

Just outside the room, in hushed tones, Dr. Chandler and Blake discussed Julie's amnesia.

"How can she regain her memory?" Blake asked, his arms folded defensively across his chest.

"Sometimes people and places help. Getting her family and closest friends involved would be a good idea," Dr. Chandler suggested.

"They are here now in the waiting room."

"I'll go talk to them. You go home, get cleaned up, and get some rest. You can come back tonight at six when visiting hours start. I'll tell her family the same."

"Okay, I'll go," Blake's shoulders slumped, and he walked opposite the doctor and waiting room towards the elevator.

Dr. Chandler walked into the lounge, where seven worried people waited to hear some news about Julie. Like Blake, they were also dressed in formal wear from the wedding. Mr. and Mrs. Hart, Julie's parents, stood when he entered, and a young man stopped pacing.

"How's my baby?" Mrs. Hart asked anxiously. "Is she going to be all right?"

"Well, she just woke up." Dr. Chandler explained.

Mrs. Hart cried out of relief before she threw herself into Mr. Hart's arms.

The young man who was pacing moments before rushed forward. "Can we see her?" he asked.

"Not now. She's resting. But there is more....."

"What?" asked one of Julie's sisters, who was standing next to her parents.

"As a result of the car accident and trauma, she has suffered some complications. It appears Julie has a case of amnesia." Dr. Chandler stated bluntly.

Mrs. Hart began to cry on her husband's shoulder while he patted her back. A dark-haired young lady stood up next to the young man. Dr. Chandler assumed she was a friend because she did not possess the red hair of Julie, her mom, or her sisters.

"She doesn't remember us?" she asked.

"She didn't even know Blake or her name." Dr. Chandler tried to explain. He noticed the young man look at the dark-haired friend. Briefly, he wondered what that was about before continuing, "As I explained to Blake, familiar people and places will be crucial to Julie to successfully regain her memory. She needs to rest right now. I suggest you all go home and do the same. You can come back at six when visiting hours start."

They all conceded, and Dr. Chandler watched them leave disheartened.

CHAPTER TWO

J ulie was dreaming. She saw a woman running. In her
eyes, there was pure fear. First, she was inside, running
down a long hallway. The next thing she knew, she was
outside and still running. What was the woman running
from?

Julie woke up drenched in sweat. Her heart was
slamming against her chest. She collapsed back to the bed,
realizing she had bolted straight up in her sleep. She looked
to the window to see that the rain had stopped. Well, at
least that's something. Before she knew it, she had drifted
back into a fitful sleep.

Meanwhile, Julie's two best friends in the world
were driving back to the hospital in Cooper's black Jeep.
Melissa's feet were on the dashboard as she stared out the
window.

"Penny for your thoughts," Cooper asked, glancing
at Melissa.

"I think we should tell her before she remembers her
side of the story." Melissa was chewing on her fingernails.

"Melissa, I don't know if that's a good idea or not.
She seemed happy." Cooper sighed heavily, "I just don't
know."

"Cooper, we have to tell her. You know how miserable we have been, especially you." Melissa said, trying to convince him.

"I'll think about it," he said, hoping it would end the conversation. It didn't. Melissa continued to hound him the rest of the way to the hospital. Cooper's plan to beat everyone there didn't work. Pulling into the parking lot, he saw her family was there with the same idea.

Sandra Hart rushed into the room to see her oldest daughter sitting in bed, staring longingly out the window. The sun had finally broken through the clouds, and sunlight bounced off the water droplets on the cars in the parking lot.

"Julie, my poor baby," Sandy rushed to the bed.

"Mom?" Julie asked.

"Oh," she clutched her chest, "She remembers me. My baby remembers me. Jack, I told you we didn't need the photo albums."

"No, No." Julie rushed to correct, her hands outstretched, "I'm sorry, I was assuming." Julie hated the look on the woman's face, who obviously loved her. Her face was stricken with grief. Julie assessed this woman, who was her mother. She was tall and slim with dark red hair that was done flawlessly in a French twist.

The man coming in the door behind her was only a couple of inches taller than his wife, who was wearing heels. He had a portly belly, thinning blonde hair, and kind baby blue eyes. Julie liked him instantly. Her dad, Jack, her mother had called him, was holding a royal blue tote bag filled with family photo albums.

On his heels entered three girls. The first thing she noticed was the hair. All of them were redheads of different shades, from dark red to strawberry blond. Julie reached behind her head and pulled her hair across her shoulders, just as she suspected. It was a rich, dark auburn shade with a hint of blonde highlights. The logical conclusion was that these were her sisters.

Her mom came over and sat on her bed, holding her hand. Her dad came over with a large tote bag and a kiss on Julie's forehead. Sandy took the tote bag monogrammed with a big cursive "H" from him and started pulling out the contents. Jack stepped aside and let his other daughters come forward, each with a kiss on Julie's cheek and a squeeze of the shoulder or a small hug as if they were afraid she would break. Then, each one introduced herself in turn.

"I'm Kathryn, but everyone calls me Katie. I'm the baby of the family." Katie was cute; there was no other way to explain it. She had strawberry blonde hair pulled up into a high ponytail and beautiful blue eyes like their father. Julie guessed her to still be in high school, perhaps sixteen. Katie wore tight jean shorts and a black tank top with hot pink writing that hung loose and flowed around her hips.

"I'm Shannon, and I'm a couple of years younger than you." Shannon had long, fiery red hair that she wore loose and hung down her back in a massive wave of curls. She also had beautiful emerald-green eyes, like their mother, and while Shannon was taller than their mother, she wasn't blessed with their mother's bosom as she was rather flat-chested. Shannon, however, had an air of intelligence and confidence no one could deny.

"My name is Megan. I'm somewhere in the middle." Megan had copper hair that she straightened in a stylishly short bob. If she had to guess, she was an older teenager, or in her early twenties. Megan seemed quiet and somewhat reserved. Maybe it was because she was a middle child? Julie wasn't sure yet, but Megan had a warm smile that reassured Julie that there was more behind her exterior.

Julie was overwhelmed. She had three wonderful sisters and loving parents. How could she not remember them? "Wait, I'm the oldest?" Julie was surprised by this revelation. The girls giggled.

Her mom patted her shoulder, "Yes, dear, but you will always be my baby."

Julie's mom opened the first of many photo albums and began reciting all the people and places she should know. Finally, after about twenty minutes, her dad sank into the chair, Blake vacated, two of her sisters moved to the table to sit, and one took a seat by the window.

After another twenty minutes, there were more visitors, for which Julie was thankful. Her mind was spinning with all this new/old information. The door to her private suite opened, and everyone looked up to see who had arrived. In rushed Melissa, one of her best friends from high school. Julie knew this because of all the pictures she had just flipped through with what seemed like a five-minute description of each.

Melissa had moved to town at the start of their freshman year of high school and had immediately joined the ranks, becoming the third musketeer, as her mother had put it.

Melissa had long, dark, extremely curly hair she wore pulled away from her face but allowed the rest to cascade down her back. She was shorter than all her sisters, but that wasn't noticeable when she smiled because her whole face lit up, and that's all you could see. She wasn't afraid to hug Julie. She rushed into the room, gripped her in a big bear hug, and rocked her back and forth. She squealed with laughter, "Only you, Jewels. This could only happen to you."

Julie didn't think it was funny, but she had a feeling she would if she weren't in this situation. She smiled at Melissa.

Behind Melissa, standing at the door, was a pair of smoldering eyes that seemed to be searching her soul. Julie looked away quickly. Her heart had started to race, and her palms began to sweat the second her eyes made contact with his. Julie wondered if the machines she was hooked up to would start going off. Luckily, they behaved and didn't give away her inner distress.

Julie managed to cast a discreet glance his way again. It was Cooper Jackson, her best friend for life, or so she was told by everyone in the room. He lived next door with his grandma, whom everyone called "Nana." His parents had died in a tragic boating accident, and Cooper moved in with his grandparents when he was only three.

He wore a black polo shirt with white and gray plaid shorts. He had scruff on his chiseled jaw, and his hair was a thick mop on top of his head, light brown with warm blonde highlights from the sun. She even noticed the hairs on his arms. She swallowed hard as she watched his muscled forearms flex. That's when she noticed the bouquet of wildflowers he was carrying. They were all different shapes and colors, pinks, purples, and yellows, in a lovely arrangement.

A huge smile spread across Julie's face. Melissa moved out of the way for Cooper.

"Are those for me?" Julie asked, knowing full well that they were.

That's when she noticed that everyone had gotten quiet and was looking back and forth between them as if expecting something, but she wasn't sure what.

"Yes, they are," was the first thing she heard him say. His voice was deep and rich, sending little shivers down her spine. She prayed that no one would notice.

Julie held her arms out to Cooper. Then, as if she might change her mind, he made it to her bedside in three long strides. He handed her the flowers, his arms wrapping tightly around her back, enveloping her in the embrace she had offered.

His hug and the flowers swallowed her up and obstructed everyone's view of exactly what took place next. His lips grazed across her temple, and she automatically returned the kiss on his cheek. She inhaled the scent of him deeply. She could get lost in his aroma of clean cotton.

He pulled away, and the moment was gone. Was she crazy? She felt as if she had just cheated on her fiancé with her best friend. Pull it together, woman. Her cheeks flushed, and she prayed she wasn't as red as she felt.

"Thank you for the flowers. They're lovely. Where did you get them?" Julie gushed over the flowers and noticed the puzzled look on everyone's face. "What?" she asked, beginning to worry that they had witnessed the exchange between Cooper and herself.

"You hate flowers," Shannon offered dryly.

"Really?" Julie was looking at everyone in the room as she inhaled deeply the intoxicating scent of the bouquet.

"You think they're too girly," Katie stated. Everyone nodded in agreement.

"Well, then, why did you get them for me?" Julie looked accusingly at Cooper. "Is this some kind of trick?"

Cooper chuckled. "No. These are from my Nana's garden. We used to play hide-and-seek there as kids. I thought it might spark something."

"Oh," Julie couldn't think of anything else to say.

Just then, Blake came sweeping into the room with a big bouquet of red roses.

"I hate flowers," Julie said.

That stopped him in his tracks, and the smile on his face froze. Everyone in the room laughed, including Julie.

"Julie, what has gotten into you? You loved it when I brought you flowers." Blake felt at a loss standing just inside the room with everyone staring at him.

"I have amnesia. That's what's gotten into me. Maybe I was just being nice?" She shrugged her shoulders. "Apparently, the old Julie didn't like flowers...but I do! Hand them over."

Relief flooded Blake's features. He rushed around her hospital bed, and her mom begrudgingly gave up her spot. Blake went in for a kiss, and all he got was her cheek because that was what she offered him. Taking what he could get, he gave her the flowers.

"Well, maybe I need to get amnesia more often so I can get more flowers." Everyone in the room laughed except Cooper, and Julie wondered why.

After another hour of visiting, everyone left Julie's room except Blake. Cooper didn't hug her goodbye but waved to her from the door. Oddly, she was both relieved and disappointed.

Blake sighed, "Alone at last."

Julie gave a weak smile and assessed her fiancé. He looked great, well dressed in khaki pants and a navy blue short-sleeved collared shirt neatly tucked.

"Where were we going on our honeymoon?" Julie asked.

Blake flashed a dazzling smile, and she noticed perfect white teeth. "Aruba, for two whole weeks."

"Mmm...sounds nice."

"How are your parents taking the news?" she asked, changing the subject.

"My dad ran off when I was a baby, and my mom died five years ago. She had cancer."

"I'm sorry to hear that. Do you have any other family?"

"No, it's just me and, of course, you. That is when I can convince you to walk down the aisle again."

She didn't want to discuss marrying a stranger, so she quickly changed the subject. "Why don't you tell me how we met?"

"Oh! I'm your family's lawyer."

She raised an eyebrow, surprised she was marrying a lawyer. Okay, promising career...check. Good-looking...check.

"We've known each other for a few years. Your dad introduced us at a fundraiser. It took me quite a while to get up the nerve to ask you out."

"Awe, that's cute. Was I hard to talk to?"

"No, actually, you were easy to talk to. You were just so beautiful. I was intimidated."

She smiled at him.

"One day, when I was leaving your parent's house after having your dad sign some paperwork for me. It was during a blizzard. Your car had gone off the road-"

"Wait," she held up a hand to interrupt his story, "Seriously, this is my second car accident? I'm a great driver," she said sarcastically. "How long ago was this?" Julie wanted to know.

"Almost a year and a half ago."

"I've been in two car accidents in a year and a half? My insurance must be through the roof. Are you sure you want to marry me? It sounds like this is going to cost you big time."

Blake chuckled. "Absolutely. Babe, I was in love with you the moment we met."

She blushed, "So then what happened?"

"Well, your car had slid off the road, and I stopped to help. You were upset, so I offered to take you out for coffee after we called the tow truck, and you agreed."

Blake was a good storyteller. He used his hands and had a multitude of expressions. Julie began to see why she had been interested in him.

"How did you propose?"

"It was a little corny."

"Tell me," she pleaded.

"It was Thanksgiving weekend I proposed at dinner in front of your family."

"That sounds perfect," she told him and was rewarded with a huge grin.

"You wanted to get married on your summer break. You're a teacher."

"I am? What grade do I teach?"

"You're a professor at the community college in town. We planned the wedding for the start of the summer. This way, we could go on our honeymoon, and you could have plenty of time to set up the house before school starts in the fall. You didn't want to wait until next year." He shrugged. "So, we didn't wait." He noticed a wince on Julie's face. "Let me get you some painkillers, and then I'll let you get some sleep." He leaned over her, pressed the nurse's call button on her bed, requested meds for her, and then fixed her pillows. He was so sweet, she thought, and he smelled good too. Whatever cologne he was wearing was stimulating.

After the nurse left, Blake said his goodbyes. He leaned in for a kiss, and Julie didn't turn away this time. Blake brushed his lips against hers and stood.

"I'm going into the office tomorrow. They heard you stood me up at the altar, so I have to go in and take care of some stuff. I'll be by tomorrow night," and with that, he was gone.

CHAPTER THREE

They were letting her go home, kind of. Her mom had insisted that she move back in with them for a while, at least until she regained her memory. She thought the familiarity would help Julie. Her parents picked her up, and it felt a little nerve-wracking getting into a car with strangers. She didn't know these people who had given birth to her and raised her. It must be weird for them too. She didn't talk but stared out the window on the ride home.

They passed several businesses and came to a four-way stop. In front of them was a beautiful quaint town square. In the center was a gazebo surrounded by benches, trees, and a clock on a pole. Around the square, she could see cobblestone-lined sidewalks with businesses in all different shapes and sizes of buildings squeezed together. Flags lined up outside with open signs and bistro menus. She noticed an old-time movie theater with a big light triangle sign above the cashier window promoting two films.

Turning left, they passed a pizza place and a supermarket. Crossing a small stone bridge, Julie noticed the sign advertising the road named Meadow Brook Lane. Soon enough, she found out why. On the other side of the bridge were trees to her right, and on her left was a beautiful meadow that followed the natural curve of the river. The road coiled its way past a farm on the left, a road on the right, and down a hill. The car slowed as it turned right into what she assumed was her parent's driveway. They navigated through a large wrought iron gate and down the long-paved driveway, lined with large elm trees. A small gasp escaped her lips as the view opened up and she saw the monstrosity her parents called home. She was sure it had its own zip code. She hadn't anticipated that. In front of the house was a circular drive with a substantial water fountain in the center surrounded by flowers and shrubs.

The front of the house had four white columns and a nice big wrap-around porch. There were several seating areas, even boasting a hammock and swing seat on the ten-foot-wide porch. Double doors with glass and iron led to a two-story entryway. In the center of the foyer was a round table with fresh flowers, and centered above was a massive chandelier. There were hardwood floors throughout, and she could see an intricate compass inlay with differing shades of wood peeking from beneath the entry hall table in the middle of the room. To the right, Julie spotted a formal dining room. To the left, was a formal living room, and straight ahead was a staircase that curved up to the second floor.

Her parents ushered her through the rest of the house hoping to stir any kind of memory. They took her upstairs and showed her to her bedroom. It had its own fireplace. The furniture was all mahogany a beautiful four-poster bed, armoire, and dresser. She even had an attached bathroom. Why would she ever move out? This was wonderful.

They told her that Melissa had gone to her apartment to pick up her clothes and had already put them away for her.

"Come on I want to show you the rest of the house." Sandy hadn't let go of her hand since getting out of the car.

Downstairs the kitchen was large cream-colored cabinets and cream-colored granite with dark brown veins running through it. It looked beautiful on the enormous island in the center of the kitchen with six stools lined up. Stainless steel appliances gleamed including a six-burner gas range at the center of it all. On the back wall of the house, there were floor-to-ceiling windows and French doors leading out of the kitchen. In front of them was a long rectangular kitchen table. From what she could see the French doors led to a huge deck and off of that was an in-ground pool surrounded by extensive stone patios. On the far end was a built-in barbeque and fire pit and beyond that, she could see that there was a pond.

To the left of the kitchen and breakfast nook was a family room. Unlike all the other rooms in the house, which were decorated in French colonial antiques, this room was designed for comfort. A flat-screen TV was above the stone fireplace, neutral colors of beige and sage green made the room inviting and the couch and chairs were overstuffed, at least twice the normal size with tons of accent pillows.

"We have one more room to show you," her dad said with a twinkle in his eye.

"I can't wait." Julie was wondering how many times she would get lost. They led her through a hallway in the back of the house, past the kitchen. The door at the end of the hall stood open and she could see the room was bright. She didn't know what to expect but the emotion she felt was overwhelming. She gasped when she saw what was inside. A two-story library with revolving ladders one on the first story leading to a balcony that went all around the room and massive floor-to-ceiling arched windows on two of the walls.

"This is my favorite room," Julie tried to absorb it all.

"This room is the reason your father bought this house. He passed his love of books on to you," Julie's mom explained as she brushed her hair off her shoulder.

In the middle of the room was a sturdy table surrounded by chairs. Around the room were several seating areas each with a round side table and reading lamp. Several oriental rugs softened the room. There was even a fireplace on the right-hand side with a dark cognac leather couch facing it. Her parents were positively glowing at her reaction. Julie released her mom's hand as she walked to the bookcase on the nearest wall and ran her hands reverently over the books.

"I teach history!" Julie exclaimed.

"Honey that's wonderful," her mother rushed forward and took her in her embrace. "Do you remember anything else?"

Julie shook her head, "I don't remember... I just know." Knowledge flooded her brain, "I can tell you the dates of any war and what great leaders the world has had. Why can't I remember my life?" Julie threw her hands up in the air in frustration.

"It will come to you." Julie's mom tried to reassure her. "Come on I will make you your favorite dinner tonight." She ushered her back down the hallway. Julie looked back at her dad.

"Thanks for the room, Dad. I love it." Julie was rewarded with a huge grin.

CHAPTER FOUR

That night Julie gushed over her mom's homemade chicken pot pie. Julie had sat in the kitchen with her mom while she made the crust from scratch. Sandy made the filling while Julie peeled and boiled potatoes. Her mom baked the crust in the casserole dish and then added the filling. Her finishing touches were mashed potatoes on top and then in the last ten minutes, she added shredded sharp cheddar cheese. It was to die for.

"Mom how come we aren't all fat," Julie asked between bites.

Her mom laughed, "Well you have lost a lot of weight since you moved out."

"Really? Are you trying to fatten me up again?" Her fork clattered against her plate a smile still on her face.

"She worked so hard to get into her wedding dress that she ran like the devil was chasing her." Blake's comment brought everyone back to reality. Julie sobered quickly. Blake had joined them for dinner along with Cooper from next door.

She wondered what Blake was going through. She wouldn't know she hadn't asked him how he felt about all of this. He has no family. I'm all he has now and am I even here for him? She resolved to ask him tonight before he left.

The rest of the meal was filled with nice conversation that seemed to flow naturally. Julie realized that Cooper was a part of her family, having grown up next door with his grandparents he had spent a lot of time at the Hart family home.

Julie studied him while he ate. He was polite and always had a story to tell. Cooper had gone to college to be a landscape architect and worked designing gardens for the rich and famous. He had built his company from the ground up and didn't need to work but it was a passion for him. He had a warm smile and when he smiled at her it made her want to smile back. He had a strong jawline and a little dimple in the cleft of his chin and his nose was straight and slim. Julie felt herself drawn to him. Was it because they had been best friends for years?

Cooper looked up at her as if sensing the intense scrutiny, she had him under. The corners of his mouth curved up in a smile revealing perfectly straight white teeth, even his eyes sparkled. He ducked his head and she noticed he had the longest lashes. Did she just imagine that moment? Julie didn't think so. When she looked over at Blake he was watching her. Julie simply smiled and returned to her dinner.

After the table was cleared and the dishes were done Blake asked her if she would join him on the front porch. He said his goodbyes to everyone before he took her hand and led her outside.

The frogs were croaking, the crickets were chirping on the pond and the fireflies were out in full force. It was a warm night with a soft breeze.

Blake walked her over to the porch swing and waited for her to sit down. "I wanted to talk to you about something."

"Okay," Julie sounded a little hesitant, but Blake didn't pick up on it.

"I think we should get married."

Julie laughed, "Of course Blake, we've already had this conversation." She lifted her engagement ring hand.

Blake took her hand. "No, I mean reschedule the wedding... soon. I called the airline we had insurance on the tickets so we could still go. I talked to the priest, and he is willing to do it anytime under the circumstances. We would have already been married if it hadn't been for the accident. I know this seems sudden for you but really when you think about it you will be glad, I talked you into it when you regain your memory we will have had the whole summer together already."

Julie tried hard not to rip her hand from his, but she could feel the sweat forming on her palms. "I'm sorry Blake. I need more time. This is all still so new to me. Give me until the end of the summer. I'm sure that is all the time I need to fall back in love with you if I haven't already regained my memory by then. I want to make this decision based on myself now. I hope you understand that?" Julie pleaded with him.

"Two weeks from the end of the summer so we can still go on our honeymoon?" Blake seemed relieved with convincing her so easily. Julie was glad to get a small reprieve. Maybe she had nothing to worry about, maybe she would wake up tomorrow and all would be cured, and they could get married as planned.

"That sounds reasonable," Julie agreed with the timeline.

Blake swept her up in his arms and for the first time since she woke up in the hospital bed, he gave her a real kiss. Their lips met and he pushed gently with his tongue, she opened to him. Her hands slid up into his hair and his arms tightened around her back. The kiss ended and Julie felt good about the decision they had come to. She walked him to his car, gave him another goodbye kiss, and waved as he drove out of the driveway.

As she walked through the foyer Julie noticed a mirror on the wall. She went cautiously to the mirror not knowing what to expect. She had seen the photo albums, had seen pictures of herself at different ages but it still wasn't the same as going face-to-face with yourself. Julie stared hard into the mirror, hoping, praying it would all come rushing back to her. Disappointment flooded her features as all it revealed was a stranger staring back.

She had dark auburn, shoulder-length hair that fell in layers framing a heart-shaped face, a button nose, a full mouth, and perfectly sculpted eyebrows set above almond-shaped emerald-green eyes. She had seen those eyes before, and then she laughed at herself, of course, you have, silly! They're yours.

Shaking her head, she walked away from the mirror and headed back toward the kitchen. Julie's sisters were dispersing from the common area. Shannon was heading home, and Megan went to call a boyfriend. Katie had to study for an upcoming test for a summer course at the college.

"Want to go for a walk?" Cooper suggested.

"Sure, where too?" Julie asked.

"Come on you'll see." Cooper opened the French doors leading to the back deck as he waved goodnight to her parents.

They walked in comfortable silence through the garden, Julie was pretty sure her parents had gardeners to maintain the property. They continued towards the pond at the back of the house, the noise of the crickets and bullfrogs much louder back here than they had sounded from the front porch. They walked past the pond and approached another gigantic home.

"This is my Nana's place." Cooper gestured to the house that could be seen over the hedges. If at all possible, Nana's house was even larger than her parent's home. The house was all gray fieldstone and gorgeous, what little she could see of it.

They walked up to a little wrought iron gate with lanterns on either side of two stone pillars. Opening one of the gates he allowed her into a walkway of hedges, once inside and walking through the tall dark green manicured shrubbery she realized Cooper had taken her inside a maze.

"We used to play in here as kids. The only way our parents were guaranteed our return was our appetites." Julie laughed she believed that. Occasionally, they would come to an intersection where there would be a fountain or a statue in the middle with several openings around the circle.

"So, it's just you and your grandmother now?" Julie asked.

Sadness filled Cooper's eyes, "Granddad died last winter, and Nana hasn't been the same since. She has been moping around the house, refusing to take her meds. I find them everywhere, under her pillow and in the couch cushions. She doesn't eat. I had to hire full-time help for her." He shook his head wearily.

Julie stopped and put her hand on his arm like she must have done a hundred times before. "I'm so sorry," Julie said and she meant it.

Cooper glanced down at her and smiled warmly. Julie's eyes were held by his gaze, she felt her breath catch in her chest and was having a hard time breathing. Julie became all too aware of her hand on his arm and heat scorched her causing her to remove it quickly.

The spell broken, Cooper moved quickly away from her. As the air rushed back into Julie's lungs, she looked down at her hand to make sure it wasn't burnt then wiped it on her jeans. Realizing that Cooper resumed his walk, she hurried after him. It was starting to get dark.

"So...," she cleared her throat trying to think of something else to say. "Did we ever date?" That's the best you could come up with, she thought, ready to kick herself.

Cooper stopped dead in his tracks and turned to face Julie taking her off guard because she was running to catch up with his long-legged stride. Julie stopped and almost took a step backward he was so close, but the hedges were already at her back. Cooper grinned at her, and she thought her knees were going to buckle.

"No, but this is where we had our first kiss."

"Oh," Julie was again breathless, "I thought..."

Cooper smiled down at her again. "We were twelve and it was a dare."

Julie laughed. "Of course." She waved her hand forcing him to take a step back. She thought she saw a flicker of disappointment, but it was gone so fast she wasn't entirely sure she hadn't imagined it. Just then tiny lights at the base of the hedges lining the cobblestone walkway illuminated the garden.

"We better get back," Cooper suggested.

"Lead the way." Julie stood back to allow him through, she had no idea how to get back.

CHAPTER FIVE

Her heart was pounding she could see a woman running down a hallway. There was a mirror on the wall, the woman glanced into it. There was fear on her face.

Julie sat straight up in bed drenched in sweat and her heart pounding. She had been dreaming again. She climbed out of bed and headed for her bathroom. Stumbling a bit because she was shaking so violently, she made her way to the sink. She turned on the faucet and cupping her hands underneath, gathered some cold water to splash on her face. She grabbed the towel next to the sink and patted her face dry as she looked into the mirror, she dropped the towel. Julie gripped the edges of the sink. Recognition. The woman in the dream was her!

Was this something that had happened to her or was it symbolism for something else? Maybe she had glanced in the rearview mirror before the crash? Could that explain the fear in her eyes? Maybe it was something that happened a long time ago. It could be a recurring dream she had all the time. She had no way of knowing.

In the pit of Julie's stomach, she wondered if this was the real reason, she couldn't remember anything, and not the car accident that had caused her amnesia.

As Julie climbed back in bed and pulled the down comforter over her, she began to think about Cooper and Blake. She was now more confused than ever. Julie didn't know what her life was like before or what had led her to make certain decisions. Certainly, Blake was handsome and charming, she could see why she would be interested in him. Cooper, on the other hand, had been her best friend for the past twenty-two years. Were they so close that she couldn't see the attraction? Being around him tonight, well, she was having thoughts an engaged woman should not be having about another man.

She had just told Blake that she would be willing to marry him at the end of the summer. Now she wondered if she would have to break that promise or if the original Julie would pop in before then. She hoped so then she wouldn't have to make such hard decisions. Julie laughed at herself. It was she who had to make the decision she just didn't have all the relevant information. All she knew, all she had to go on were her feelings and they were a mixed-up mess right now.

Frustrated, Julie got back out from under the covers and grabbed her robe from the foot of the bed. Sneaking downstairs she made her way to the library, only to find her dad asleep in one of the chairs with a book opened in his lap. He was snoring softly. Julie stood in the doorway and watched her dad with a true sense of love. No mixed feelings there she thought. Walking over to her dad she took the book from his lap, marked his page, kissed him on the forehead, and shook him gently awake.

"Why don't you go to bed?"

His blue eyes shined, "Julie, my girl, I'm so glad you're home."

"Thanks, Dad." She helped him up and sent him on his way.

"Goodnight, My Girl."

"Goodnight."

Julie settled into the warm vacated chair after selecting a book on Egypt from the shelf.

Julie's dad found her asleep there the next morning.

CHAPTER SIX

After a big pancake breakfast, Julie decided to go for a run. Once she found a jogging outfit and sneakers, she walked out the front door with a bottle of water. On the front porch was Cooper decked out in his running gear. He was stretching using one of the columns for support. Julie glanced back at the door and wondered if her mom had given him a heads-up.

Julie noticed the chiseled legs covered in blonde hair. Cooper's arms were muscled from physical labor, and he was tan from being in the sun all day.

"Don't you have a day job?" Julie joked.

Dazzling white teeth flashed a grin. "I have people to take care of things. I want to spend time with you."

She flushed.

"Anything to help you remember. Your parents thought that I could maybe jog your memory by showing you around."

"Oh," Julie felt a twinge of regret at his later statement.

Of course, her parents would want their neighbor and her friend to show her around. Swallowing her disappointment, she began her stretches, and when she was

29

done, they started at a slow pace down the driveway. The gate had already been opened, so they ran through and turned left. It was a nice crisp morning, the sun shining, but it must have rained overnight because the pavement was wet.

Julie could hear their feet hit the ground simultaneously, they seemed to be jogging in unison. The road was a narrow country road, so there was not a lot of traffic. They were about ten miles from town, the road began to rise in front of them, and they started the slow ascent upwards. Julie began to get a stitch in her side but didn't say anything. At the top of the hill, Cooper leads her down Lovers Lane.

Julie started laughing, "Are you kidding me?"

"What?" Cooper seemed unaware of the cause of Julie's humor.

"Lovers Lane?"

"Oh," Cooper chuckled, "that. My grandparents named this road. They thought it would be romantic."

Julie's breathing was becoming more labored, and she began to fall out of stride with Cooper's pace. Finally, she could take the pain in her side no more. She stopped abruptly and put her hands on her knees while Cooper jogged back around behind her.

"Lift your arms above your head." He guided her arms over her head, holding her just below the elbows.

"I'm sorry, my side is killing me."

"Waffles?" He guessed.

"Pancakes. Mom is going to kill me with all this wonderful food."

"I'll be sure to tell her you enjoyed the food... at your funeral." He chuckled.

Julie laughed. She turned her head to look at him. Their eyes met briefly before he bowed his head. He was so close. Dropping her arms to her sides, he moved around her.

"Let's walk it off, okay?"

"Yeah, sure."

They meandered down the tree-lined road. Cooper led her down the next driveway. The lawn was beautifully landscaped with trees and shrubs surrounded by fresh black bark mulch. The colors were stunning. Dark greens with a multitude of light lime greens mixed in and a red Japanese maple to pull it all together. Annual flowers were everywhere in an array of colors and designs.

They had a cobblestone driveway that led to a three-car garage separate from the house, done in gray stone to match the house, with big beautiful black lanterns hanging between the doors. "That used to be a carriage house, but my grandfather converted it."

"Pretty." The real beauty was in the house itself. It was a grand two-story home with cream-colored paned arch windows. Balconies lined different areas of the house. Julie could count five different fireplaces just from her current vantage point. The house had several angles and peaks in the roof line and a round turret.

"Did you do this?" She was referring to the beautiful landscaping.

"No, this was all entirely my grandfather's influence. That's where I got my green thumb. I just help maintain it. Come on in. I want you to uh...introduce you to my Nana." Cooper held one of the heavy oak front doors open. The inside of the house was dark and quiet.

"Nana?" Cooper called.

"In here," came a voice from the living room. Out walked an older woman with gray hair in a short stylish haircut. She was a vision dressed in pale pink slacks and a matching short-sleeved blouse. Not what Julie would have pictured for a grieving Nana.

"Julie, Darling." She held out her arms, and Julie smiled, glancing at Cooper before going in for a hug. Nana was shorter than Julie by a good six inches, but that didn't stop the gripping hug she received.

"Where have you been? I haven't seen you in ages. You used to be over here every day, then-poof you disappeared into thin air!"

"Nana, don't you remember? I told you Julie had an accident and was in the hospital?"

"Oh. You did? I get so confused," she said the last to Julie. "Well, you're here now. Cooper, will you bring us girls some lemonade from the kitchen?"

"Yes, Nana." Cooper winked at Julie as she was being ushered into the family room. There was a couch facing the fireplace on the left, a sofa facing the door they just walked through, and two chairs, one on either side of the fireplace with a coffee table in the middle. Behind the couch near the window was a small table with four chairs.

Another woman sat at the table. She had short, curly brown hair, was about forty years old, and was wearing a pair of lavender scrubs. She was holding playing cards, and there were cards spread out on the table in front of her. "Julie, this is Carol. She's, my friend."

Julie walked over and shook the woman's hand. She was assuming this was whom Cooper had hired to help take care of Nana. Carol smiled pleasantly and shook her hand, "Nice to meet you."

"You too."

"Come sit," Nana pulled out a chair for Julie. "So, what have you been up to?" Nana questioned Julie.

She gave a short laugh, "Well, I was supposed to get married this weekend but with the accident..." she trailed off.

"Oh, I'm sorry to hear that," Carol supplied, "When is the wedding going to be rescheduled?"

Contemplating how much information to divulge to these women, she hesitated, but with a ragged breath, she jumped off the deep end, "With the accident, I seemed to have developed amnesia."

"Oh dear," was Carol's response.

Julie continued, "Unfortunately, I don't remember anyone, including my own family and fiancé."

Nana patted her arm, "That's okay. That happens to me all the time."

She smiled sweetly at Nana, she felt bad for this woman who went through life unaware of most things around her.

"I know!" she exclaimed before getting up from the table and walking across the room. She came back holding a photo album in her arms. She placed it on the table in front of her.

Picking one of them up, Julie flipped through the hundreds of pictures, and a good portion of them were of her and Cooper. Some were in the bathtub, some in the garden covered in mud, some of them in the pond swimming, and still more of birthday parties, holidays, proms, and graduation. Their ever-entwined life is laid out in photographs.

Nana leaned forward and placed a delicate wrinkly hand on hers before telling her, "He loves you, you know." Nana stated it more as a fact than a question.

"What?"

"Lemonade," Cooper announced at the door.

Go away! She wanted to shout. Julie couldn't be more frustrated. She wanted to growl at him, perfect timing. Julie looked at Nana, but she was shuffling through the pictures as if she had never made that startling comment. She looked up at Carol, but she just smiled and didn't say anything. Had she heard that right? Nana must be talking about a brotherly kind of love. Yes, that must be it. Was she relieved or disappointed?

Cooper poured the lemonade into tall glasses filled with ice as Julie looked over the pictures. The lemonade was delicious, with freshly squeezed lemons still floating in the pitcher and the perfect amount of sugar.

One picture she came across was of her and Cooper at about age fifteen, they were on his grandparent's yacht, or so she was told. Both were suntanned and their hair wet from swimming. They were sitting in their bathing suits, and Cooper's arm was casually thrown over her shoulder as Julie held up a big fish proudly. Julie was grinning into the camera, and Cooper was smiling at her. She glanced up, Cooper was in conversation with Carol and Nana and wasn't looking, so she casually slipped the picture into her pocket.

"Julie?" Cooper asked.

Wide-eyed, she looked up and across the table at him. Had he seen her hide the picture in her pocket?

"Would you like me to give you a tour of the house?"

"Oh!" feeling instant relief, "Yes, that would be great."

Julie jumped up from the table and followed him into the grand foyer after saying her goodbyes to the two women. Done in Italian Marble with white columns, the center of the room housed a hand-carved banister winding gracefully up a ten-foot-wide staircase. He escorted her past the stairs and down the hallway into the kitchen. Inside, she was surprised to find an older woman cooking away.

"This is Rose. She has been with the family forever. She does all the cooking and housekeeping for the family," Cooper introduced them.

Rose smiled warmly at Julie and shook her hand, "Cooper told me you have amnesia. What an odd thing. Would you like something to eat, muffins, bagels?"

Julie clutched her stomach and began shaking her head.

"Your mama, already got to you, huh?" Rose asked.

Julie laughed, and Cooper smiled at her, "Yes, she did. But thank you for asking."

They left the industrially equipped kitchen and headed to the other side of the house. Cooper showed her his study, which used to be his grandfather's. The room was done in dark oak paneling with dark hunter-green paint. A beautiful desk sat before the fireplace, and a new addition to the room, his drafting table, was set up in front of three arched windows looking out on the well-maintained gardens of the backyard. Cooper told Julie this is where his best inspirations came from. She could see why.

He showed her several more rooms, but her absolute favorite was the ballroom. Two stories high with gleaming hardwood floors, there was an area for the band to set up and a grand piano in the corner. Huge arched windows lined three sides of the room, and to the back was a full-length balcony overlooking the gardens that had an entrance to the maze.

Cooper took her up the grand staircase and headed to the right on that side, or wing as Julie was beginning to suspect, were Nana's rooms and some guest bedrooms, all with adjoining bathrooms and a fireplace. Then Cooper directed her to the other wing off the left side of the stairs. That's where Cooper's bedroom was.

Inside, it was decorated in shades of blue. Whereas the rest of the house had antiques galore, this room was all new furniture. A huge king-sized bed sat against the wall facing two windows. Between the two windows was a flat-screen TV mounted to the wall. On the other side of the bed was a fireplace with two chairs. On the opposite wall were dressers with a door to the bathroom.

As she walked into the room, she assumed she had been there multiple times before and looked around. She assessed his bed and wondered if she had ever sat there with him. Talking, watching TV, or doing homework? Shaking her head, she tried to remove the visions she was having because her brain was going elsewhere.

What caught her attention were the pictures he had placed and hung around the room, all in silver frames. Walking over to the ones above his dresser, she peered at each one. One was of the two of them at graduation in their cap and gown, arms around each other. Another was Cooper in a suit and tie with his Nana sitting at a formal function. The picture on his bedside was of his parents, who had died too early.

The feeling she got when she held the picture was to take him in her arms and hug him for the loss, he had suffered at such an early age. How had that affected him growing up? Instead, she replaced the picture to its rightful spot and walked to the window to look out.

What she saw was how immense the maze below her really was and her house across the pond. She heard Cooper approach silently behind her. "You used to flick the porch lights on your back stairs at night if you were going for a swim and wanted company." His voice was low and sent shivers down her spine.

She could see the in-ground pool he was talking about and began picturing those late-night swims. She wished she could remember all these memories he had of them. What if she never got those memories back? She would have to rely on the stories she was told. Would that even compare? She didn't think so.

"I should let you get to work," Julie told him.

"Sure," he seemed crestfallen, as he took a step back, "I'll walk you home."

Cooper guided her through their backyards and said goodbye when she climbed her back porch steps. "I'll see you tomorrow. I have a surprise for you." Cooper had a glint in his eye. She watched him leave, feeling...she wasn't quite sure.

Eventually, Julie turned and walked into the house to hear the phone ring. No one was around, so she picked up the receiver on the kitchen wall.

"Hello? Hart Residence."

"Hey, Beautiful, just the person I wanted to talk to," Blake's voice came across the phone. Her heart sped up.

"Hi!" she was surprised to hear from him, "Are you at work?"

"Unfortunately, I have a mound of paperwork piling up in front of me as we speak. I would love to take you out tonight. Are you free?"

Julie had pulled the picture of her and Cooper out as Blake spoke.

"I'm free."

"Great. Pick you up at six?"

"Sure, I'll be ready."

"I better get back to work if I'm ever going to get out of here on time. See you tonight. I love you."

A knot built instantaneously in the pit of her stomach at his words of love. She didn't know how to address it, so instead, she chose to ignore it.

"See you tonight. Bye, Blake." Julie put the phone back in its cradle. She walked upstairs and hid the stolen picture in her dresser drawer.

CHAPTER SEVEN

J ulie was waiting on the front porch at six when Blake pulled up in front of her house. She stood up and straightened out the front of her light blue sundress. She was wearing flat sandals with colored rhinestones on the straps.

He met her as she came floating down the stairs. She noticed he had changed out of his suit and looked casual in jeans and a graphic t-shirt. He looked damn good. Blake lit up when he saw her, "Hello, Gorgeous."

She smiled at his compliment. Her hand came to rest on his shoulder as he placed his hand on her hip. He leaned in for a kiss, and she offered her cheek which he accepted, but his lips lingered. She could feel his warm breath on her ear. His hand caressed down her bare arm and slipped his hand into hers.

He guided her to his car, a sleek shiny black luxury model, and opened the door for her. She slid with ease into the car, and he gently closed the door after her. When he got in, he buckled his seatbelt and glanced her way.

He looked so handsome, she felt so lucky that this man wanted to marry her. They would have beautiful children. She shook her head at the thought.

He grinned at her, and she melted a little more, "What?" he asked.

She didn't want to tell him what she was thinking, "Nothing."

"You sure?" he asked as the car purred to life.

She smiled at him, "Where are we going?" she asked, quickly changing the subject.

"Oh, you will like this. There is a fair in town I thought it would be fun to go to."

She was genuinely surprised. She had figured they would go out to a restaurant or a movie. This was much better. "That sounds like fun."

"Good." Blake seemed pleased with her response.

"How was work today?" she asked. "Did you finish everything you needed to?"

He laughed light-heartedly. "No, unfortunately, I did not, but I will."

"That's good."

About fifteen minutes later, they pulled into the fair parking lot and were directed into a spot. He parked the car and ran around to her side to open her door. They walked hand in hand through the gates.

Blake bought them tickets for the rides, and they rode the bumper cars. Then they shared a freshly squeezed lemonade, which didn't compare with the one she had at Cooper's house. While waiting in several more lines to get on other rides, he told her stories about his courtship of her.

Blake bought fried dough, "What do you want for a topping?"

A frown furrowed her brow. This shouldn't be such a hard decision, "I don't know."

"Sweetie, it's okay." He kissed her on the forehead, his arm around her back and pressing her towards him, "How about cinnamon and sugar?"

She nodded, feeling silly for being upset about not knowing the answer to such a simple question. "How about we take a ride on the Ferris wheel?"

She shrugged. "Okay." The sun had started to set, and the clouds had a pink hue. They walked over to the Ferris wheel and got right on. Julie broke off a piece of what was left of the fried dough on the white paper plate in Blake's lap.

"This is delicious," she said with a half-mouth full, giggling as she licked her fingers. She looked up at him as he stared back at her, mesmerized.

She held his gaze until the Ferris wheel stopped abruptly at the top, leaving their seat swinging in the air. The jolt startled her from the trance she had been in. Her hand went down to brace from sliding and landed on his thigh. It felt solid and warm beneath her hand. She looked back up at him. He smiled warmly at her, "You have sugar on your lips." His hand came up to her face his thumb rubbed across her lower lip. It felt gritty. She licked her lips.

He is going to kiss me, she thought. She closed her eyes a second before his lips grazed hers. She sank into the kiss, and his tongue eased into her mouth. His hand slid up her bare leg and under her skirt. While the feeling felt amazing, she wasn't ready for that at all. Her hand quickly grasped his wrist, pulling it down.

"I'm sorry," Blake's breath was ragged.

"It's okay," she reassured him.

"I just got a little carried away."

"I know. I'm sorry too."

He pulled away and searched her eyes. "Don't be. It's not your fault. I don't blame you. I hope you know that."

She nodded her head and then breathed out a sigh of relief. He did put her at ease. "Thank you." She kissed him again to let him know she appreciated his patience.

They stayed to watch the fireworks. It had been an incredible date. When he dropped her off at her parent's house, he kissed her at the door, "Can I pick you up again tomorrow night?"

Grinning, she agreed, "I'd love that."

CHAPTER EIGHT

J ulie was dreaming again... she saw people, their faces flashing before her eyes, her family, Blake, and Cooper. Blake and Cooper flashed in her mind on repeat. Blake was smiling, and she started walking toward him. Then Cooper was walking towards her, and she stopped, torn between the two.

"Julie," said a voice she recognized.

In her sleep, Cooper was shaking her. "Choose," he told her.

"I can't," she whispered.

"Can't what?" The shaking was becoming more persistent now.

Startled, sitting straight up in bed, she came face to face with Cooper. What was he doing in her bed? His hands were still clamped around her bare upper arms.

"What? What time is it? What are you doing here?"

Cooper released her arms but remained seated on the side of her bed, their hips touching, his hands falling to either side of her.

"I told you I had a surprise for you today. Get dressed."

Julie glanced at the clock on her nightstand through hazy eyes. It read four a.m. What the hell?

41

She threw herself back in bed.

"It's barely today! Can't it wait, at least until daylight?" She rolled onto her side, facing away from him, bringing the covers, as much as she could, over her head but found the task difficult with him sitting on the majority of her comforter.

"Nope. It'll be too late, then. Come on, sleepy head, roll out of bed." He started pushing her to the other side of the bed, towards the bathroom. She tried to put a pillow over her head, but it was a futile attempt on her part. He just flung it on the floor. He gave her a friendly tap on her bottom to get her moving. Managing to get her out of bed, she only went as far as he had thrown the pillow and curled up on the floor with it.

"Don't tell me I have to drag you into the shower myself because, believe me, I will." Somewhere deep down, Julie believed him, so she jumped up and ran into the bathroom, locking herself inside. She heard him chuckling on the other side of the door.

Turning on the hot water, she stripped down and climbed inside the glass-enclosed tiled shower. She wondered what a shower with him would be like. Would he scrub her down? Julie shook her head and tried to think of something else... like where in the world he was taking her at four in the morning!

As she climbed out of the shower, Julie realized, a bit too late, that all her clothes were in her bedroom. So, she wrapped a fluffy white towel around her body and peeked through the door. Seeing Cooper lounging on her bed, she asked, "Could you please step outside the door so I can get dressed?"

"No can do. If I leave, you will crawl back into bed. No way, I stay."

Julie sighed in frustration. She knew he was right, she would be tempted to crawl back between the sheets, and she wouldn't bother putting on clothing. But who knew what would happen if he returned to the bedroom.? She was sure he would come back to check on her. Only to find her naked and sleeping again, which could be a big problem.

Julie ran to her dresser under his watchful eye and pulled out a pair of designer jeans and a gray Boston Bruins fitted T-shirt. She grabbed a bra and matching panties (registered that these likely came from an expensive boutique) and ran back to the bathroom. Ten minutes later, she returned ready for who knew what. She had thrown some gel in her hair, scrunched it, then sprayed it with hair spray. She left it down to dry and chose not to put on makeup. She figured she had no one to impress at this hour.

Cooper seemed satisfied and led the way downstairs through the dark halls. She realized he must have done this several times because while he never bumped into a single thing, she stubbed her toe on a table and hit the corner of one wall with her shoulder.

"Ouch," she said, rubbing her shoulder.

"You okay?" he asked, turning around to see her fumbling. "Here, take my hand." Automatically she reached for him, immediately engulfed inside his warm and much larger palm. He led her, uneventfully, through the rest of the house and outside to his awaiting Jeep. Cooper didn't release her hand until he opened the passenger door for her. Once inside, he closed the door behind her and ran around to his side. As Cooper navigated the long driveway, Julie realized her parents wouldn't know where she was.

"We should go back and leave my parents a note to let them know where we're going."

"They'll figure it out. We used to disappear all the time together, and at this hour, they'll know." Cooper said it with such confidence that she believed him. Settling back in her seat, she began to drift off to sleep. Cooper let her, knowing they had a little bit of a drive anyway.

Forty-five minutes later, Julie was rudely awakened by being bounced around the inside of the Jeep. She had to brace her hands on the door panel and roof to avoid hitting it. They were on a dirt road with more potholes than the actual road. Julie glanced over at Cooper and got a sheepish grin.

"Sorry, but we are almost there."

Up ahead, she noticed a clearing through the trees, and it looked like a spot to park. Cooper pulled to a stop and got out. He ran around to her door and let her out. As Julie hopped out and looked around, she noticed it still wasn't light yet, but there was the hint of the night sky fading.

Cooper jumped up on the running board of the jeep and started taking the canoe down from the roof. When they left, Julie realized it had been so dark that she hadn't noticed it was there. When Cooper unloaded the canoe, he opened the tailgate and pulled out fishing poles and a tackle box.

"Do you want to carry this or put it in the canoe and help me carry the canoe down to the water?"

"I can help you." Julie realized he had already started throwing the gear into the boat, knowing what her answer would be.

They had a short walk down to a lake. Cooper put the boat in the water and held it for her while she climbed aboard. He shoved off the shore and jumped inside the boat, as it glided across the serene water. Grabbing the oars, he rowed out to the middle of the lake. When he seemed satisfied with the distance, he pulled in the oars and opened the tackle box, pulling out rubber worms and placing them on hooks. "Come over, and I will show you how to cast but be careful not to rock the boat."

Julie eased her way over to him, holding the sides of the canoe, crawling on her knees, not wanting to stand up.

"Here, turn around. Easy," he warned, as the boat swayed a little as she tried to position herself on her knees facing away from him. Cooper spread his legs apart, circling one arm around her waist to pull her back against him. Julie inhaled the scent of him, and he smelled delicious, sort of woodsy, and like clean cotton. His arms came around her shoulders and placed the pole in her hands as he gave her some instructions on how to hold the pole and the line. She cast out onto the lake, and it plopped into the water not far from their boat. He chuckled, and she cast him a sharp glance, one eyebrow raised.

"Not bad," Cooper took the fishing pole from her and set it behind him. He handed her the next pole to cast, and this time, doing much better, she sent her cast far out onto the quiet lake. Julie took her pole and, as quickly as she could manage, scooted over to her seat, needing to put some distance between them. Cooper instructed her on how to reel the line back in, and they both cast their lines out on the opposite sides of the boat.

The sun started to come up over the mountains, and Julie looked around. They were in the middle of a lake that was so serene. It looked like a mirror reflecting the mountains to her right, and the woods surrounded them on all sides. No houses dotted the shore or even campground sights as far as she could see. "This is beautiful," she told Cooper with appreciation. She no longer cared that she had to get up at a god-awful hour.

Cooper smiled her way but said nothing. They had been sitting in silence, and she realized that it had been a comfortable silence, not really needing to talk. Cooper reached over to the backpack thrown in the middle of the canoe and opened it. Inside, he retrieved a book, and Julie's face lit up. Now it's perfect, she thought as she reached over and took the book from him, "Thank you so much."

"You're welcome. It's one you have read before, but I figured you wouldn't know that."

Julie laughed, "Sure, make fun of the amnesiac, I see how you are." Still, she opened the book and started reading, instantly getting engrossed in the storyline. About twenty minutes later, she realized her pole was moving. Book immediately tossed to the side and forgotten, she straightened and reached for the pole. "I got one!" She was so excited that she was having a hard time getting a grip on the pole.

Cooper set his pole down and came over to help her. He straddled the bench seat and put his arms around her.

Together they worked hard to get the line in. At the last minute, the fish got loose and the line went slack sending Cooper and Julie tumbling down in a heap of awkward limbs in the middle of the canoe.

They managed to keep the boat from tipping over by being extremely still. One of Cooper's muscular arms was under Julie's shoulders, and her legs were draped across his. Julie didn't notice the rocking of the boat.

What she did notice was that it felt good to be in his arms. His warm breath caressed her cheek, and she lost herself in the essence of him. She could spend all day lying in his arms at the bottom of that canoe and not get bored. If anything, she was having heart palpitations. It was wrong for a practically married woman to be having such feelings for another man, she scolded herself. What was wrong with her, and how was she going to fix this?

Cooper was looking down at the woman in his arms, his lifetime best friend. Her red hair, which was a big, beautiful mass of curls, looked like fire with the morning sun dancing off of it. As he smoothed her hair back, his big warm hand caressed her face. His hand lingered a little too long, then slipped down to her neck, where he could feel her pulse racing against his thumb. He wondered if she could feel his heart pounding in his chest.

Cooper's pole started moving behind Julie's head, and Julie jumped at the chance to retrieve it, having forgotten their tangled, limbed position. Reaching back to grab Cooper's dancing pole, it pushed her body forward, which in turn caused his hand to slip down and wound up cupping her breast. Eyes wide, Julie looked down at him. He instantly raised his hand with an apologetic look, then managed to crawl over her beating her to the pole.

Julie scrambled to resume her former position on the canoe bench and tried to compose herself. Her body was tingling everywhere Cooper had touched and even in some places he hadn't. She tried to settle her nerves and ignored what he was doing on his side of the canoe. This was her best friend, surely, she shouldn't feel like that when he touched her! Had he ever touched her like that before? Had it sent shock waves through her?

Cooper managed to get the fish reeled in with no problem but ended up throwing it back. "Why did you do that?" she asked.

"I didn't mean to. You moved, and my hand accidentally-"

She cut him off quickly. She did not want to talk about that. "No!" she exclaimed, then clarified, "Why did you throw the fish back?"

"Oh!" He looked a little chagrined and a little flustered, "If the fish aren't a certain size, you have to throw them back."

"Can I have another rubber thingy?" she asked, "I seemed to have lost mine in the struggle with the fish."

"They're called rubber worms," Cooper said, handing her one.

Julie shivered, "Well, at least they aren't real worms."

"I've seen you hook a real worm with the best of them," Cooper seemed impressed, "Not a lot of girls I know, like to fish." Julie digested this information and hooked her rubber worm, like she had seen Cooper demonstrate, then they simultaneously cast their lines out on opposite sides of the boat.

Not five minutes later, Julie had another bite. This time she was determined she would handle it herself. Cooper was just as resolved to let her. Julie pulled in a massive-sized fish and looked up at him in triumph.

"Is it big enough to keep?" she asked, unable to contain her excitement.

"That's definitely big enough. I don't even need to pull out the measuring tape."

The fish flip-flopped inside the boat.

"What kind is it?" It looked different than the fish he had thrown back.

"It's a rainbow trout. I think I know what your mom's going to cook for dinner tonight."

Julie was extremely pleased with herself, and over the course of the next hour, she managed to pull in two more, each bigger than the last. They wrapped up their fishing trip soon after, and Cooper rowed them back to shore.

Together, they put the canoe back on the roof rack and the rest of the equipment inside. He opened a cooler filled with ice and buried the fish in it. "Are you hungry?" he asked her as they both climbed back inside the vehicle.

"Starving," she admitted.

He grinned, "Good." He turned the key as she buckled up. Cooper entertained her with stories of other fishing trips they had taken together. One time Katie had stowed away inside Cooper's Jeep and fell asleep on the way there. Cooper and Julie were out on the lake when Katie woke up alone in the Jeep, she thought she could swim out to meet them... she was only seven. Cooper jumped in and swam back to save Katie. Julie loved the story about him rescuing her baby sister.

CHAPTER NINE

T he Jeep pulled into a quaint seaside town called Harbor Bay. They walked into the Crusty Crab and were seated on the veranda. Fresh salty air and waves crashing from the dark blue ocean met them as they took their seats. Julie glanced at the menu placed in front of her by their waitress. After a few minutes of scrutinizing the menu, she sighed and put it down.

"What's the matter?" he asked.

"I don't know what I want," she confessed.

"Well, tell me what you are thinking about, and I'll help you."

She put her head in her hands, "No, it's not that." She told him about her conflict with the fried dough the night before.

"Oh," he sat back, "That's rough. I didn't realize that was part of the amnesia."

"Me either. It's so frustrating."

"I can imagine." He picked up his menu.

The waitress came over to take their order. Julie began to tell her they were going to need a minute when Cooper started talking. "I am going to have a bacon cheeseburger with onion rings," he looked at her, "because she is going to steal them off my plate, and she is going to have the lobster mac and cheese with a side salad with balsamic vinaigrette dressing. Oh, and two sweetened iced teas, please."

The waitress looked at Julie to confirm, and she just nodded her head, handing her the menu. As soon as she was gone, Julie turned to Cooper, "So I steal your onion rings?"

"Every time," he grinned.

"Thank you," she said.

"Anytime. Oh, and you like strawberries and cream."

"What?"

"On your fried dough, not many people carry it, but if they do... you love strawberries and cream."

"Good to know, thanks. I'll have to file that away in the memory bank. It's quite empty up there, you know." She laughed at herself. He leaned over and squeezed her hand, trying to reassure her everything would be all right, and she desperately wanted to believe him.

When their meal came, she first helped herself to one of his onion rings. Then she picked up her spoon and dug into her lobster mac and cheese. Shoveling a large bite in her mouth, she stopped and looked at him wide-eyed. He watched her intently as she grabbed her napkin, spit into it, and then took a long drink of her iced tea.

"That's disgusting!" she whispered because she didn't want to offend the restaurant.

"Well, that confirms it. You weren't lying when you said you don't like shellfish."

"You tricked me!"

"Sorry, I thought it would be worth the experiment." He was laughing.

"What am I going to eat now?"

The waitress walked over with a chicken wrap and set it down in front of her. Taking the lobster mac and cheese, she said, "I'll wrap this up for you."

"Thank you," he told her.

Julie was watching in awe. "You had this all set up?"

"Of course! I wasn't going to let you go hungry."

She leaned over and punched him in the arm, he rubbed his arm because it wasn't a light tap. He was still laughing, "That's my Jewels."

Her heart skipped a beat when he called her his. She looked down at her plate then, hoping she wasn't being awkward, she stole another onion ring from his plate.

Cooper kept talking, and she enjoyed his company. She asked him questions she had about her parents and sisters, and he told her about them. Julie asked about high school and college, and Cooper had lots of stories from the good old days.

Afterward, they walked the town and went into all the little businesses. They went into a fudge shop and were offered samples. Walking out ten minutes later, with a five-pound variety of fudge because they couldn't decide on just one flavor.

They entered a jewelry store next. She strolled up and down the glass cases, eyeballing the sparkle inside. "See anything you like?" he asked, coming up behind her.

She pointed, "That's kinda cute."

Cooper signaled a woman to come over and pull it out for her. It was a sterling silver bracelet, nautical-themed, with dangly anchors, ship wheels, sea horses, starfish, and a compass. She lifted her wrist and twisted it, watching it jingle. "How much is it?" she asked.

"Two hundred ninety-five dollars."

Unclasping it, Julie handed it back, "Thank you for showing it to me. It's beautiful."

"You don't want it?" Cooper asked.

"I was just looking," she said lightly but eyeballed the piece of jewelry as it was being put away. They wrapped up their outing for the day after that.

Back home, Julie's mom was coming out of the kitchen, "Did you catch anything?"

Cooper nudged Julie's shoulder as he stepped past her letting her know that her parents had been aware of where they had been all day. He proceeded past her holding the cooler. He leaned down to kiss Sandy on the cheek. "I didn't."

"But I did!" Julie burst in behind him, grinning ear to ear.

"Well, if you kids can clean it, I'll cook it for dinner tonight."

Cooper turned around and mouthed the words, "Told you so."

Julie's mom disappeared somewhere in the huge house as Cooper sat the cooler down on the kitchen island and walked to the wall, where he turned on the built-in custom stereo system. He started dancing around the kitchen while he retrieved the knife and cutting board, he would need to clean the fish. Julie laughed and decided to join in thinking, this must have been what it used to be like, and she smiled at the thought. They used to dance around the kitchen together. She was sure of it.

Cooper offered her the honor of cutting off the fish's head, but she politely declined, "No thanks." Julie held up her hands and stepped backward.

He followed her, no... more like stalked her through the kitchen. "Oh, no, you don't. The rule is you catch it, you clean it. Come on, I'll show you how."

Julie reluctantly stepped up to the cutting board with Cooper close by, giving her step-by-step instructions on chopping off the fish's head and slicing it down the belly, then pulling out the insides. Julie was seriously grossed out.

Julie's mom came bustling into the kitchen as Julie was washing her hands. "Good heavens, child! How did he ever sweet-talk you into that?" Julie glared at Cooper and saw he had that glint in his eyes about two seconds before he bolted for the door. Julie was fast on his heels, not bothering to shut off the water.

"The rules!" she ranted as she chased after him. She caught him, but then she didn't know what to do with him, so she punched him in the arm. It didn't seem to faze him one bit. He just laughed and rubbed his shoulder where she had struck him.

"Do you know how long I have been trying to get you to gut a fish?" He didn't bother waiting for an answer when he said, "Forever!"

"It's not funny," Julie cried, which only caused Cooper to laugh harder. She couldn't help it. She cracked a smile, but not before she turned around and headed toward the house.

CHAPTER TEN

B lake showed up at the doorstep that night dressed for dinner. Julie answered the door, still dressed in her jeans and t-shirt.

"Oh, shit," she said as she saw him.

Blake barked out a laugh, "Not the greeting I was looking for." He eyed her up and down, "You're not ready yet?"

"I'm sorry, Blake, I completely forgot about dinner tonight. I caught a fish, and Mom is cooking it. Would you mind if we stayed here for dinner? Please?" She pleaded, holding her palms together in her request.

Blake smiled at her enthusiasm, "That's fine." She grabbed his hand and dragged him through the threshold. He tugged on her hand, stopping her before she returned to the kitchen and kissed her. "You caught a fish?" he asked.

"Three," She was bouncing up and down on her toes. She was proud of herself, "I even cleaned them."

They walked into the kitchen together. Her mom was behind the island working on red bliss baby potatoes, tossing them with butter, dill, and parmesan cheese. She had fresh green beans with toasted almonds, homemade rolls, and a tossed salad on the table.

"Would you like me to open a bottle of wine?" Blake asked, stepping around to the wine fridge built into the cabinets.

"Yes, please," Mrs. Hart said as she pulled the baked fish from the oven and walked it over to the table. "Dinner is served," she said as she removed her apron.

Blake poured the white wine and watched everyone coming in from the living room. Julie's sisters, her dad, Cooper, and his grandmother joined the long table set in front of the floor-to-ceiling windows overlooking the pond.

Cooper pulled a chair out for his Nana and waited for her to sit. Blake came bearing wine glasses handed one to Julie's mom, and offered one to Cooper's grandmother.

"Nana, you're not supposed to drink with your medication," Cooper reminded her.

"Oh, pooh. Who asked you anyway? You know..." she said, addressing the crowd, "in my day, there were none of these health warnings. Everyone smoked, drank, did a little pot too."

"Nana!" Cooper exclaimed.

"Don't get all stuck up on me now. You know I was young once, and I could party with the best of them."

"I know Nana," Cooper said in an almost sing-song voice, as though they'd played this tune before.

"You know, your grandfather was quite the dancer. That's how we met. Henry swept me off my feet." Nana seemed to get all wistful, and she took a sip of her wine. Cooper went to the fridge and grabbed himself and Julie's dad a beer. Blake had distributed the rest of the wine to everyone of drinking age. Katie and Megan were sipping sodas.

Everyone sat down for dinner, and grace was said. Julie got compliments on her catch of the day and how well it was cooked by her mom. The night was filled with stories courtesy of Nana. Laughter and wine flowed until well into the night as several bottles of wine were opened and polished off. For dessert, Cooper and Julie set out all the fudge they had bought on a nice platter, and the after-dinner liquor was poured.

Blake had to admit it was an enjoyable evening. Leaving that night, he pulled Julie in his arms. She was giddy and relaxed and slid easily into his embrace. She pushed his hair back off his forehead and looked into his eyes, searching for answers. Before she found any, his head had dipped, and he kissed her.

Blake released her and gave her a light pat on the bottom. "I'll call you tomorrow. Goodnight, Shannon," he called, waving to Julie's sister on the porch. She said nothing but raised her wineglass to indicate she had heard him.

Julie's gait back to the porch was slightly unsteady from the alcohol. She smiled and waved to Blake's retreating car as he drove down the driveway.

"He's a really good guy, you know?" Shannon said when she reached the porch stairs.

"Yeah, I'm beginning to think so, too," Julie said.

Shannon walked over to the porch swing and sat down. Julie walked over and sat down next to her. She wanted a little insight into what her sister might think. "I've never seen you as happy as you are when you're with Blake." Julie mulled over that statement for a while.

"You know Blake told me you wanted to wait until the end of the summer to make a decision, and he is being so good about that. What man do you know wouldn't be frustrated? Not him, nope, cool as a cucumber. You're lucky. Most women would give anything to get a guy like Blake, it's too bad he doesn't have any brothers."

Shannon patted Julie's knee and stood up. Julie's hands were holding the swing next to her arms, her head down, looking at her feet. "Don't leave him hanging too long, okay?"

Julie looked up and smiled at her sister, "I'm trying hard not to."

Shannon smiled, "Good. Are you coming inside? I think I might spend the night. I've had a little too much to drink."

"Coming." Julie hopped up and wrapped her arm around her sister's waist to walk inside with her. Shannon seemed a little taken aback by the gesture but didn't comment.

Inside the house, they found their mom cleaning up the kitchen. Megan and Katie had retired hours ago, and Cooper had walked his Nana home through the back door. Their dad gave each of the girls a kiss on the cheek and headed off to bed.

"Shannon, I assume you will be spending the night? It's late." He didn't mention her alcohol consumption.

"Yeah, I was planning on it." Shannon went over and kissed her mom on the cheek, and headed to her old bedroom.

"Can I give you a hand, Mom?" Julie asked.

"No, no. I'm finished. Go get some sleep."

Julie had been dreading sleep lately. It always seemed to be accompanied by a nightmare she couldn't quite figure out, but she wouldn't tell her mom that. She kissed her goodnight and headed off to bed.

CHAPTER ELEVEN

The following morning Julie awoke to find Melissa in her room. "Rise and shine," Melissa sang as she flung open the curtains and let the morning light come flooding in to blind any that dared to be still sleeping.

Julie realized her friends had no boundaries. They came and left as they pleased, probably had keys to the house! She glanced at the clock. It was quarter after nine. Julie sat up in bed. How had she slept that long? Then she remembered all the wine the night before and the late hour at which she had fallen asleep trying to avoid the inevitable nightmares that plagued her.

Last night, for whatever reason, they had eluded her, and for that, she was grateful. She wondered if it was the alcohol that had kept them at bay. Julie's thoughts were interrupted by Melissa as she talked and moved around the room.

"I talked to Cooper this morning. He had to go to work today. I decided to take the day off and we, my friend, are going to the spa. I've already called and made reservations. They're expecting us in an hour." Melissa never missed a beat as she continued pulling clothes out of Julie's drawers.

Melissa was beautiful. She was wearing no make-up and had a freshly scrubbed face which left her skin glowing, and her long, dark, curly hair was pulled back into a high ponytail. She was wearing a white bodice tank, showing off her amazing curves, and a beautiful white high-waist flowy skirt, embroidered with a coral paisley pattern. Julie could see flat brown sandals peeking out from underneath the skirt when Melissa moved. Completing the modern gypsy ensemble, she was wearing dangly, reverse V-shaped earrings and a large gold medallion necklace.

"What's this?" Melissa asked, holding up the picture Julie had hidden in her dresser of her and Cooper when they were teens.

Julie jumped out of bed and tried to snatch the picture out of her friend's hand, but Melissa just sidestepped her. "Well...well...well," Melissa said as she danced around the room with the picture.

Julie snatched the clothes Melissa had picked out for her instead and headed towards the bathroom like she didn't care about the picture her friend was studying. "That must have been in there from before," Julie tried to sound casual and failed miserably.

Melissa had a wicked grin on her face. "Well, that, Jewels, I know for a fact wasn't there from before because your mom sent me to pick up your clothes at your apartment. I put them away myself, and no picture was just lying around in the bottom of the drawer. And," she said with a shrug, "You can't lie worth a damn."

Shit, she forgot her parents had told her that. Julie looked at her friend pleadingly. "Please don't say anything."

"I promise. As good a friend as Cooper is, we girls have to stick together. Now get dressed. We have a long day of pampering in front of us." Melissa handed over the picture to Julie and the clothes she had picked out for her.

Julie took the picture into the bathroom with her and closed the door. She propped the picture on the mirror and stared at it, she hadn't dared to pull it out since she had snuck it home. Sometimes she would catch a glimpse of it in the bottom of the drawer, and out of guilt, she'd cover it over with more clothes. Now that it was out in the open, so to speak, she took a good long look.

Cooper had changed since this picture was taken about ten years ago. He had filled out nicely. He didn't have that baby face anymore. It was now more manly and rugged. His eyes, a warm honey brown, shone brightly ten years ago. Now often, she witnessed a more reserved look in his eyes, not showing what he was thinking or feeling.

Julie wished she possessed more of that trait, wondering if all her feelings were out in the open and if anyone saw through her conflicted thoughts. With a heavy sigh, she tore her eyes away from the picture and started the shower.

Getting out and toweling herself off, she started to get dressed. She loved the outfit Melissa had pulled together for her. It was a navy blue tank blouse with ruffle layer after layer and a pair of bright coral shorts. She had included a long necklace to compliment it. When Julie walked out of the bathroom, Melissa greeted her with silver earrings and bangle bracelets to complete the ensemble. "You're great at this!" she told her friend.

Melissa grinned at her. "Thanks."

The day at the spa was wonderful. They were given warm fluffy robes to change into when they arrived and spent the entire day in them. Julie was a little bummed people wouldn't see her in the adorable outfit Melissa had put together for her, but she had already asked her friend to put a couple more outfits together for her. Melissa was more than willing to help. "I'd love to!"

The first thing they did at the spa was a seaweed wrap, then a wax. Julie and Melissa enjoyed a nice lunch on the veranda, talking about their high school and who was doing what now. Even though she didn't know any of these people, the description Melissa gave her, she felt like she did.

Julie ordered ice water without lemon, and Melissa ordered water with no ice and with lemon. They both ordered a salad, Julie's a Caesar, and Melissa a garden salad, which looked like the weeds from the backyard, with a raspberry vinaigrette dressing. Melissa had half a turkey sandwich on focaccia bread, and Julie enjoyed a turkey and wild rice soup. They both shared a fresh fruit salad.

"Julie? Julie Hart, is that you?" Came a woman's voice from behind them.

Julie saw Melissa duck her head and mutter something under her breath but she didn't get a chance to ask before a leggy blonde was headed their way.

"Hi," she said sounding chipper and giving Julie a fake kiss on each cheek with great flare.

"Hi," was all Julie managed to get out before the woman was gasping and grabbing her left hand in hers.

"Oh my God, look at this rock! Who's the lucky man? Do I know him?" Gushed the bleached blonde, kissy face as Julie mentally dubbed her, disliking the woman immediately.

"Blake Duncan," Julie was thankful she remembered his last name.

The woman dropped her hand. "I can't say that I've heard of him. Does he belong to the Country Club? No, of course not. I'm on the committee. I would know." She rushed on. Did this woman take a breath? "We are having a summer dance this Friday. You two should think about coming. Introduce him around." She switched gears fast, "How's Cooper doing these days? I haven't seen him lately. I've sent him an invitation. Do tell him I send my best. You still see him, don't you?" At Julie's nod, she continued, "Well, it was so nice to see you, Julie," and to Melissa, "And you too, Melanie." And with that, she was gone.

"Who was that?" Julie asked when the woman was out of earshot.

"That is Courtney Champlain. Her father owns a pharmaceutical company, and her mother is a hotshot lawyer. They're worth millions, and Courtney just loves to flaunt the fact. She doesn't even bother with me. My parents don't belong to a Country Club, so we aren't worthy."

"That's ridiculous. Why was she asking about Cooper?"

"They dated in high school, you know, the prom queen/cheerleader with the all-star quarterback. Cooper broke up with her when they went to college, but if you asked Courtney, she would say she was the one who broke it off." Melissa said with a shrug, but she was watching Julie closely.

Julie managed not to let Melissa see how the news of Cooper's ex affected her. They went back to their lunch, although Julie only pushed the food around on her plate as Melissa tried to fill the silence.

After lunch, they enjoyed a full body massage and finished off with a manicure and pedicure. Melissa chose a soft pink for her nails, and Julie chose a classic French tip.

The day wasn't over because Melissa took Julie shopping. Melissa helped put together several more outfits. They arrived home at six that night laden with bag upon bags of treasures they had purchased.

Melissa stayed for dinner. Blake called and said he couldn't make it something had come up at work, and he had to stay and take care of it. Julie asked him about attending the function at the Country Club on Friday, and he was thrilled. He also told her he would take her out the following evening to make up for his absence tonight.

"Sounds great. See you tomorrow night," Julie said before hanging up the phone. Megan and Shannon were out with other plans. So, it was just Julie, her parents, Katie and Melissa. Cooper hadn't come over either. He had called earlier and said his Nana wasn't feeling well, so he was going to stay with her. ☐

Julie's mom had already sent Katie over with dinner for the two of them. It was a nice wind down to the day. Julie sat back and observed her life. She wondered if she ever appreciated how lucky she was to be surrounded by such loving people.

Chapter Twelve

As Julie crawled into bed that night, she stubbed her toe on something under her bed.

"Ouch," was muffled into her plush comforter as she fell forward, trying to grab her throbbing manicured toe. She slid off the edge of the bed, massaging her whole foot when curiosity got the better of her. Lifting the dust ruffle, she spied a large box.

Pulling it out, she opened the lid feeling like she was snooping. Inside the box was a stack full of black and white composition notebooks. Picking up one of the ones on top, she rubbed her hand across the faded writing "Julie Hart 7th Grade." She took a deep breath before opening the first one.

"August 23rd, 1st Day of 7th Grade. Today was great! Cooper and I got all the same classes."

Julie flipped through a couple of other pages, and stuck inside one of the pages was a picture of her and Cooper in front of a cake. This time it was Cooper smiling for the camera and Julie looking up at him with adoring eyes. There was an entry behind the picture dated September 12th. She read what she had written.

"Holy moly! Cooper just kissed me! Well, not just now, like five hours, seventeen minutes, and four seconds ago. Ok, so I made that last part up about the time, not the kiss. Sigh...

Ok, let me start from the beginning. Today happens to be Cooper's 13th birthday. Lucky twit- I hate that he is older than me. Anyway, his grandparents threw him a big birthday bash. Everyone who's anyone was invited, not that Cooper cares.

So anyway, we were in the maze playing Truth or Dare. We were sitting in a circle. Cooper was sitting directly across from me. Brooke and Lauren were sitting next to me on my left, and Josh and Cameron were next to Cooper.

Lauren went first. She chose truth. Josh asked her if she had ever been kissed. She got beat red in the face and said, "Yes." Surprisingly Cameron looked a little flustered as well.

Lauren then asked Brooke truth or dare. She asked truth, and she asked if she had a crush on anyone. She lied and said, "No." I know for a fact that she likes Chris Anderson, but no one called her out on that.

Then Cameron dared Josh to moon the girls. We screamed and covered our eyes, pretending to be grossed out but secretly trying to look between our fingers to see. Well, at least I was.

Sigh... now the wonderful dare. Cameron asked Cooper, "Truth or dare?" Cooper looked right at me when he said, "Dare."

This is going to be good, I thought as I leaned further into the circle. Maybe we would get a chance to see his butt!

"Hmm..." Cameron said as he pondered his dare, "I dare you to...kiss Julie!" he said with great flare pointing his finger at me. I almost jumped out of the circle.

"What!" My shocked eyes met his smiling ones. Did he want to kiss me? I looked around the circle for an ally and found none. All of the girls were giggling, and the boys were practically leering at me.

"Not in front of all you perverts." Cooper stood up, walked through the circle, and held his hand out to me. I looked at Brooke and Lauren, they couldn't contain themselves. They were holding their hands against their mouths. Josh and Cameron were grinning ear to ear.

I stood up on my own accord and walked past all of them and behind some shrubs. Cooper followed me into the maze.

"Hey, wait up. I think you're far enough. They aren't going to follow us."

I walked around one more corner just to be sure and turned around to face him. I had never even considered kissing him before. He was my best friend. We made fun of people kissing. At least we used to. I couldn't think of any time recently that he had. When had that changed?

Cooper had practically grown a foot over the summer and towered over me. I had to strain my neck to look up at him.

"You don't have to kiss me, you know. We could pretend, and you could put your hand on my mouth, then kiss your hand. I won't tell anyone. Swear."

Cooper seemed to be considering it. He put his hand over my mouth. "Like this?" he asked, taking a step closer to me. I nodded. My heart was racing. He put his other arm around my waist. I inhaled deeply. We didn't touch each other like this, ever. He bent down and kissed his hand covering my mouth.

His head was too close to me, and I was getting cross-eyed trying to look at him, and his eyes were closed, so I closed mine too. My hands were down at my side, not knowing what to do with them.

"I can see them. They're kissing," I could hear being whispered in the shrubs behind us. That's when it happened. Cooper removed his hand from between us and kissed me on the lips! Oh my gosh! I couldn't breathe. His lips were soft. No tongue. That would have been gross. It was the perfect kiss.

"Time to cut the cake!" shouted his grandfather somewhere close.

Cooper released me, and I almost fell to the ground. I could hear the other kids giggling and running. Cooper looked down at me and grinned. I have never seen him grin like that. His eyes were filled with mischief.

"Come on, let's get some cake." He said as he punched me in the arm like his old friend and took off running, leaving me stunned. But not for long I ran by him and punched him in the arm, beating him back to the party."

Julie closed the diary and held it up to her chest. She let out a big sigh. Cooper was right when he told her their first kiss had been a dare. Taking the entire box, she stood up, put it on her bed, and crawled in next to it. She read the first notebook cover to cover, coming across nothing as juicy as the entry about the kiss. She felt like she was gaining a little insight into her world. After reading several, she put them back under the bed, careful to mark the ones she had read, so she could continue where she had left off.

CHAPTER THIRTEEN

The following morning Cooper stopped by, and they went for a jog around the block, which happened to be a three-mile loop. Julie was getting back into shape and skipping her mom's huge breakfast, which was a big disappointment to her mom.

Cooper and Julie didn't talk much, keeping pace with each other. She didn't know why, but she kept the fact that she had found her diaries a secret. Everyone, including Cooper, knew so much more about her than she did that she wanted to keep this to herself.

After the run, she felt exhilarated, and she realized she got an adrenaline rush from the activity. "Hey, do you want me to take you to your apartment today?" Cooper asked her.

"Yeah, that sounds great. I bought a whole bunch of stuff yesterday I would like to get it put away. I think it's also time to consider moving out of my parent's house and maybe back into the apartment. Hey, I don't have a cat or anything that's not being fed, do I?" Julie seemed panicked at the thought.

Cooper chuckled, "No, no pets. I'm going home to get showered. I'll meet you back here in, say, a half hour."

"Twenty minutes!" Julie shouted, running towards the house.

"You're on!" Cooper said as he ran towards his jeep.

Twenty-three minutes later...Cooper stood outside leaning against the jeep, showered, dressed, and looking at his watch. He had already packed all the bags she had lined up on the front porch into the jeep. Julie came bursting through the front door, still buttoning the front of her shirt as she went. Cooper smiled at the sight as he ran around to his side and hopped in.

"How'd I do?" she asked breathlessly as she jumped into the passenger seat of the awaiting jeep.

"Right on time," he lied and was rewarded with a huge grin. Cooper started the jeep and headed down the driveway, then took a left and headed toward town. Crossing the bridge, they drove past the town square, but instead of turning right past the hospital, they continued straight, where she saw more shops, including a florist and corner hardware store. On their left, she saw a park and a pretty single-steeple white church. On her right were old impressive historical homes. Straight ahead, he pointed out the college where she worked.

Julie perked up and tried to get a look at the campus. It had sprawling lawns and walking paths lined with big trees. There were several massive brick buildings in a U shape facing a courtyard. "Would you like to stop and take a look around?" Cooper asked her.

She nodded. So, he pulled into a parking lot, and they got out. Walking towards the buildings, she asked him, "Do you know which classroom was mine?"

"Yes, you had a lecture hall. I'll show you... and I know where your office is."

"Great. Lead the way."

They were walking down the sidewalk, and she was looking around. "Did we go to college here?" she wondered aloud.

"No. You went to Ohio State, and I went out to California. I made a lot of contacts out there and because of

Hollywood East, a lot of stars have several homes around here, and I take care of them."

"That's exciting. Who is your biggest client? Are you allowed to tell me?"

He grinned, looking down at her, "Elizabeth Lucas." When she gave him a blank stare, he laughed. "She is only your favorite actress!"

"Oh! Did you meet her?"

"I did. She had a lot of input in the design."

"What was she like?"

"She was down to Earth, super sweet, and beautiful."

"Is she married?"

"No."

She digested this information as he opened one of the glass doors so she could enter the building. She narrowed her eyes at him. "What?" he asked, noticing her concern.

"Hmm..." was all she said.

"Hmm....what?"

"Are you interested in her?"

"Why do you ask?"

She shrugged her shoulders, "Just asking. Are you dating anyone?"

"No," was all he said. "Stairs or elevator?" He changed the subject.

"I would like to take the stairs," she said.

"I figured," he responded.

"That's normal for me?"

"Yup."

"Huh," she responded.

They raced up the stairs, and she laughed as she realized this was another thing they did together. On the third floor, he stopped and opened the stairwell door for her out into the hallway. He opened a door across the hall, and they walked into a huge lecture hall. They were in the back of the classroom, and there were three sections with twenty or more rows of stadium seating with stairs in the aisles in between. The front of the class had a desk and a podium with a giant dry-erase board behind it.

"Wow, this is impressive."

"You're impressive," he stated, his voice low, his head bent close to her.

She blushed at the compliment as he nudged her and then walked ahead of her down the stairs. She was slow to follow him. About two-thirds of the way down, he took a seat in the center of the row, and she continued down to the podium.

"Teach me something," he said from his seat.

She took a deep breath and looked around the room. It looked even scarier from down here. She looked at Cooper Jackson. He looked so relaxed, arm hanging loosely on the small wooden desk attached to each chair. His hips were thrust forward in a slouch like he didn't have a care in the world, hanging out in her lecture hall, waiting to hear whatever was ready to come out of her mouth. She cleared her throat.

"Good morning, class. My name is Julie Hart, and...That's all I know!" She threw her hands up in the air, and they came down hard on the podium, making a loud thud that reverberated around the room.

Cooper stood up and gave her a standing ovation. She stepped sideways away from the podium and took a bow. Grinning, he hopped down the remainder of the stairs. "Come on, I'll show you to your office."

He led her through a maze of hallways, finally reaching her office, which was shared with another professor. There was a row of seats and two cubicles. Hers was the one to the right. There was a window in the waiting area and a window in each cubicle looking out into the courtyard.

When she walked into her cubicle, she was surprised to see someone there. A young man was shuffling through some papers on her desk. "Excuse me? Can I help you?"

He whipped around, and the notebooks he was carrying scattered to the ground. His eyes rounded in surprise. "Professor Hart, I'm sorry. I was trying to leave you a note," he sputtered, then bent down to pick up his papers.

He had black hair that was gelled and sticking up all over the place and dark eyes. Julie felt Cooper come up behind her protectively.

"What can I help you with?" she asked.

He stood with the papers and notebooks in his arms, going in opposite directions. "Umm..." he looked nervously at Cooper, "I wanted to talk to you about your European History class."

"I'm not teaching this summer," she told him.

"I-I know, it's actually about the grade I received last semester." He put his notebooks down on her desk, retrieved a paper, and handed it to her. She took it and looked it over.

At the top of the paper, it had a large, red, circled D minus at the top. "I can't have that kind of grade, especially at what you evaluated it at. It dropped my grade point average, and I'm going to lose my scholarship. I was wondering if you could reevaluate it. Or maybe grade on a curve? Something? Anything would help."

She looked at the paper again. The name at the top said, Andrew Miller. "I'm not sure what I can do for you, Andrew."

"Just read it again. I did everything you asked for, please, Professor Hart?" he pleaded.

"Sure," she agreed.

He seemed relieved, "Thank you so much! I really appreciate it. That's great. I look forward to hearing from you." He said as he rushed out of the room.

When he was gone, Cooper stared at her. "What?" she asked.

"You're such a softy," he told her.

"Apparently not," she said as she held up the kid's paper.

"Touché." And with that, they left.

They drove out of the college parking lot and, three streets down, took a right. They passed huge Victorian houses close to the college that were once single-family homes and now housed college students. They came to a

"T" intersection, and brick townhouses lined either side of the street facing inward to a grass median with trees. Cooper turned right again and pulled up to the curb in front of one of the townhouses. They got out, and Cooper started pulling bags from the backseat. As they approached the front door, Julie realized she didn't have a key. Cooper pulled out his keys and reached around her, unlocking the door and pushing it open.

Julie stepped inside, not knowing what to expect. She was met with the old world versus the modern. There were hardwood floors throughout, the stairs were straight ahead leading to the second floor, to her right was a modest-sized living room, the wall to the left was original exposed brick, and the rest of the room was drywalled. There was a couch, two chairs, a glass coffee table, and a TV on a stand against the wall and between the front two windows. Through a large opening, she could see a table and chairs. To the left of that, she saw an ultra-modern kitchen. She walked through the archway and could see a bay window and French doors leading out to a patio and garden area.

Julie walked to the window and looked out at her little English garden. "It's beautiful," she whispered.

"I designed it, especially for you. I even did the work myself. We spent the whole weekend out there." Julie could picture in her mind both of them in shorts, t-shirts, and gardening gloves working together to make the space appear inviting.

"Thank you," Julie said and turned around so she could face him when she said it. He was right behind her. Cooper smiled down at her, making the little dimple in his chin stand out more.

"You're welcome. You should have seen it. When you moved in here, there were broken bricks buried in the mud and overgrown shrubs taking over a rotting fence." Cooper was pointing over her head to show her where things used to be.

"Well, it's just beautiful."

Julie walked around the rest of her apartment, finding a half bath with a laundry room on the first floor down a little hallway off the kitchen. Upstairs she found two bedrooms. Cooper helped her carry her bags upstairs to be unloaded.□

Julie turned left into her bedroom, where she discovered a queen-sized bed to her left, tucked in the corner up against the wall facing a balcony window. To her right, was a nightstand and dresser with a mirror and two doors revealing a closet and bathroom. She walked into the bathroom and found that it was remodeled to include a marble Jacuzzi bath, tile flooring, and stainless-steel fixtures.

Julie walked across the hall to the other bedroom and smiled when she found a mini library. There were books from floor to ceiling, a desk sat in the middle of the room with a state-of-the-art computer. This must be where she graded papers at night, she thought, with maybe a glass of wine nearby.

After unpacking all her goodies from the day before, they headed back downstairs. Looking around, she got the feeling of home. With her things surrounding her, it makes her feel comforted. "I can see the charm of having my own place," Julie said as she walked into the kitchen, Cooper following her.

"It's going to seem strange not having you so close anymore. I'm going to miss you," the last he said quietly. Julie turned to look at him, having heard him. Realizing he was expressing his feelings. She responded quickly before she gave it a second thought.

"I'll miss you too," Julie said, looking directly into his eyes. Cooper took a step towards her, one hand outstretched. Her eyes darted away from his. She wondered what it would be like to be home and away from him. Would they continue to see each other as often, or would life take over?

"Do you hear that?" his voice broke her chain of thought.

Looking up, her emerald eyes questioned him. Did he hear the thudding of her heart in her chest? He strode purposefully towards her. She swallowed hard as he approached.

He brushed past her and walked to the sink. Opening the cupboard, he announced, "You have a leak."

"What?" she asked, dumbfounded.

He turned around, only to find her trying to peer over his shoulder.

"Can you go out to my Jeep? I have a toolbox in the back. I'm going to shut off the water."

Grateful for something to do, she ran for the front door. She needed a second to breathe and distance herself from Cooper. Julie didn't know what was wrong with her. She liked Blake. She did. He was beautiful to look at, and so was Cooper, but Blake was whom she had chosen to marry. She had so many questions and none of the answers she sought.

Back inside, she found the kitchen empty, hopefully, Cooper knew where the shutoff valve was because she didn't know. Water that had, moments before, been trickling was now gushing from under her sink. Quickly she put his toolbox on her granite kitchen island and ran to assess the damage. The puddle was growing bigger by the moment. She ran down the hall to the laundry room and found a basket full of towels. Taking the whole basket with her, she met Cooper back in the kitchen. The water had stopped gushing. He must have managed to get to the shutoff valve. He squatted down, evaluating the damage.

"We are going to need to go to the hardware store," he told her.

She was laying towels down on the tile floors trying to soak up the water. "Okay," she agreed. She piled all the heavy, saturated towels back into the laundry basket.

They went to the store, and she trusted he bought everything they needed. When they got back, he went to work replacing the rusted pipe, and she worked around him, finishing wiping down the floor. She removed cleaning supplies she had stored under the sink and dried them off. Kneeling next to him, she wiped up under the sink. "All right, I think we are good," he said, looking up at her. "Go ahead and turn on the water." He told her where the shutoff valve was in the front hall closet. She walked back into the kitchen she found him still under the sink.

Walking over, she turned on the faucet. The water sputtered and then drained. "Stop! Stop!" he called out from under the sink. Quickly she pushed the lever down, shutting off the flow of water. Cooper sat up, sputtering water dripping down his face and drenching his shirt.

Squatting down next to him, she laughed, "What happened?"

"I forgot to tighten this bolt."

"Well, that's a problem."

"I'm soaked," he stated the obvious.

"Give me your shirt. I can throw it in the drier."

He looked at her for a minute, she swallowed hard. He put his hands down to his waist, then lifted his T-shirt over his head and handed it to her. As much as she tried to avert her eyes from his chiseled bare chest, it was really hard. Standing up quickly, she handed him a couple of paper towels to wipe down with.

"Thank you," he said.

"Yup!" she called nonchalantly from down the hallway. She sped-walked as fast as she could to the laundry room.

Melissa showed up with beer and pizza a half hour later. Cooper was, thankfully, back in his dry T-shirt. Melissa and Cooper hopped up on her kitchen island and sat cross-legged to eat. Julie smiled. She really did love her friends. Jumping up on the countertop, she joined them. They sat around eating and drinking, Cooper was telling the story of the epic water leak, and it was hilarious. Afterward, Melissa told them she needed to get going, and they walked her to the front door.

"Goodnight, Melissa. Thanks for dinner," Julie called out to her friend as she made her way down her front steps. Melissa waved on her way to her car parked behind Cooper's Jeep. Cooper stood behind her leaning on the doorjamb, watching their friend leave. Melissa called out one more goodbye before getting in her car and driving off.

They walked back inside. Cooper beat her to the kitchen, where he started throwing away paper plates and collecting beer bottles to rinse them out.

"I'm going upstairs to make sure there aren't any lights on," she informed him.

He turned, looking over his shoulder at her, "Okay," was all he said, but it sounded like he was conveying so much more.

Julie ran up the stairs two at a time, she was pretty sure there were no lights on upstairs, but it gave her an excuse to settle her heartbeat. Walking into her office, she turned on a light, strolled over to her desk, and sat down. Settling back into her chair, she evaluated the cozy office and tried to imagine herself working there.

Sitting up, she touched her mouse, and the computer jumped alive. It was asking for a password. Well, that could be a problem. What would she have put in for a password? She started looking in drawers, wondering if she had written it down anywhere. Ten minutes later, Cooper found her sitting at the desk, holding up her keyboard and looking underneath it. "What on Earth are you doing?" he asked.

His voice caused her to jump, the keyboard clattering to the glass desktop. "You scared me!" Her hand went to her chest. She laughed when she realized it was just him. Again, he was casually leaning against the doorjamb, watching her with a lopsided grin.

"Any idea what my password is?" She was joking, but he sauntered into the room and leaned over the desk. He was so close she could smell his cologne and feel the warmth of him. Quickly, his long fingers tapped across the keys, clicked enter, and then stood, "There you go!" he said triumphantly.

She sat up amazed, "Wow! What's my password?"

"Cooper is my favorite person in the world."

Was he serious? Clearly not, because he burst out laughing. "Oh man, you should see your face."

Julie could feel the heat rising in her cheeks. She glared at him, and he just laughed harder. "I'm sorry I couldn't help myself."

"Seriously, what's my password? I need to know."

"I heart Wes Morgan."

"What? Who is that?"

"You really do have amnesia."

"Pretty sure we've established that." She continued to glare at him, her arms now folded over her chest. He pointed to her computer screen where there was a screen saver of a football player. He was gorgeous, with broad shoulders, his arm cocked back, ready to throw the ball. He was dressed in a Dallas Cowboys uniform. "Wes Morgan, I'm assuming?"

"Correct, he is the star quarterback for the Dallas Cowboys, your dream man. No one can compare."

She got up and shoved him out of the way, "Oh, be quiet. Who asked you anyway?"

He chuckled as he let her by, "I believe you did." She shut the lights off on him on her way out.

He followed her downstairs. "God, I miss teasing you. You're so easy." He walked into the kitchen where she was standing and stopped abruptly when he saw her face. "Jewels, what's the matter? I'm sorry."

She shook her head and couldn't look at him, "This sucks! I don't remember anything!" She wailed.

"It's just temporary," he said softly.

"Is it?" she demanded.

Damnit, he didn't know. He strode towards her. She could see he wanted to sweep her up in his arms, and she wanted that to happen so badly but instead turned around and walked to her fridge. Cooper was left standing dejected in the middle of the room.

Julie opened the refrigerator door, bent over, and stared inside at what she didn't know. The insides were cleared out of most everything. Cooper came up behind her placing one hand on the closed freezer, then slowly covered her hand that was resting on the open fridge door. Julie had nowhere to go. She didn't want to turn around to look into the eyes she knew would reflect her own thoughts and emotions.

"Don't," Julie pleaded.

"Don't what?" Cooper's warm breath was near her ear.

He was standing as close to her as he could without making physical contact. It didn't matter. Julie could feel him, his warm hard, toned body anyway. She closed her eyes, but it only made it worse, becoming all too aware that she wanted to be touched.

She stood up straight, and Cooper moved in half a step, molding his body against her back. Julie's eyes popped open, but her body seemed to melt into him. "Julie," Cooper's deep voice sent shivers down her spine. His arm slid around her waist, his big hand spreading across her mid-drift.

"Hmm..." was all she could manage. Cooper leaned down. She could feel his hot breath on her neck. He brushed her hair off her shoulder and kissed her neck. It was soft and exhilarating having his lips against her skin. Her heart was thudding inside her chest. She wanted to lean her head back for him, but she managed to turn around instead.

Big mistake, she thought, but it was too late as she stared into his intense dark eyes. There was no escape. She was surrounded on all sides by the refrigerator, door, and him. His look was overwhelmingly intense, and she knew she must have had the same look because he groaned before lowering his head. Julie met him halfway as his arms swept around her body, crushing her to him, her arms wound around his neck, drawing him in closer.

Their lips met in an open-mouthed kiss, hungry to discover one another. At first, the kiss was fierce and intense, their tongues thrusting and stroking, trying to get as close as possible. Then Cooper, with one arm still firmly behind her back, brought his other hand to her face to brush her hair back. He softened the kiss by sucking on her lower lip.

Julie let out a moan, and their kissing became frenzied again. Cooper's hands slipped down her body and cupped her butt. She grabbed at his shoulders, and in one fluid motion, he had lifted her, and she wrapped her legs firmly around his waist, locking her ankles. He pushed her up against the open refrigerator. Magnets and pictures fell to the floor unnoticed.

Cooper's hands roamed up until they reached her arms, and he pushed them up against the freezer door and kept going until he was holding her hands in his. His lips broke free from their kiss, and Julie let out a little whimper until his lips met her neck. She couldn't stop herself from pushing herself shamelessly toward him as he worked his magic, kissing, nibbling, sucking, licking, and even gently biting.

All of Julie's blood flow quickly rushed from her brain to between her thighs aching for more. Her nipples hardened and began to tingle. She managed to break one of her hands free and tugged at his hair before thoroughly kissing him again.

The phone rang, shattering the little world they had created for themselves.

"Oh, My God. I'm so sorry." Julie's eyes pleaded with Cooper to understand.

He let her down gently but held on to her until he felt she was steady enough to stand up on her own. Julie was grateful for the support but embarrassed that she needed it and that he knew she would need it. Cooper walked away, not looking at her. She could feel his frustration. She felt it too.

Julie didn't make it to the phone before it stopped ringing. The machine picked up. "Hi, you have reached Julie. I'm on my honeymoon! Leave me a message! Beep..."

Cooper put his hands on the kitchen island, and his head fell forward in defeat. Julie shut the refrigerator door and began picking up the magnets and pictures that were on the floor. Cooper came over and knelt beside her to help.

"I'm supposed to be a married woman," Julie sounded forlorn.

Cooper didn't comment.

"What am I doing? What am I supposed to do? I have to marry Blake by the end of the summer! I gave my word."

"You don't have to," Cooper said softly.

"This is all happening so fast. I feel like I'm living someone else's life. I worry that I will make some life-altering decision, and the real me will pop in and wonder why the hell I screwed everything up."

"Julie," his voice was a husky whisper.

"What?" she asked, refusing to look at him.

Cooper's big warm, bronzed hand came down to cup her face.

"Look at me," he pleaded. This time, she did. "Just follow your heart" He hoped her heart would lead straight to him.

Cooper and Julie drove back in silence. Neither noticed because they were both deep in thought. However, Cooper was so excited he could barely sit still. This is everything he was hoping for and more.

That night Julie continued her mission to uncover past secrets by reading through her diaries. She wanted to know why she had chosen someone else.

CHAPTER FOURTEEN

The next night Julie had dinner with Blake. He picked her up at seven. Julie was already out on the front porch waiting for him. They drove in silence into the neighboring town, Oakwood, to the restaurant. Julie couldn't help but remember how she'd felt in Cooper's arms. She shivered.

"Are you cold? I'll turn down the AC." Blake was already reaching for the control panel.

Julie blushed that she had been caught shivering, knowing full well it wasn't the temperature that had her shivering.

They arrived at the fancy restaurant, and Blake handed over his keys to the valet. He ushered Julie inside, placing his hand on the small of her back. They were seated in a private booth in the back, and for that, Julie was grateful. After drinks and appetizers were served, and Julie was sure the staff wouldn't return for a while, she decided to broach the subject of Cooper with Blake.

"I kissed Cooper last night," Julie held her breath. Nothing like jumping into the deep end. She sat back and waited for his reaction.

Blake set down his glass of wine before responding, "I see." He was trying hard to compose himself before he spoke. The waitress was walking towards them, and he held his hand up, indicating they didn't want to be disturbed. The waitress getting the hint, turned around immediately and walked away from the table. Blake let out a big sigh.

"Well, I can't say I'm surprised." Was not what Julie expected to hear.

"What?" She leaned forward, sure she hadn't heard correctly.

"Well, you told me once that he had broken your heart. He had betrayed you. At least that is the story you told me. You didn't go into much detail, and I wasn't one to pry. I figured that whatever you once had was over.

Apparently, having amnesia, you just have your feelings to go on and not a recollection of a past that was obviously painful for you." Blake reached for his wine letting her mull over the information.

Julie took a long time to digest this new information. Why had no one told her? She realized she must have voiced this thought because Blake was answering for her. "No one knew. You said that you had been friends for so long that you wanted to see if it would go anywhere before getting anyone's hopes up. It looks like you made the right call."

Julie was shocked.

Poor Blake, he had lost his parents when he was young. He had found love and possibly lost it on the day of his wedding. He had a fiancée who didn't recognize him or feel the same way about him. Now here she was breaking the news to him that she had kissed another man, and he was taking it all in stride.

Blake reached across the table and took her hand in his. "Julie, I love you. More than anyone can love another human being. I don't care that you kissed Cooper-well I do. But I will get past that if you will just, please marry me. I beg you. I know you are confused, and that is understandable, but Julie, I'm not confused. Please let me call the priest, and we can get married as early as tomorrow. We can have our reception at your parent's Fourth of July bash."

"I'm sorry, Blake, I'm just not ready yet. Please tell me you understand. I know this is frustrating for you. It's frustrating for me!"

He reached across the table and squeezed her hand. "Let's enjoy our dinner, shall we?" He tried to sound upbeat, but it fell flat. The appetizers sat untouched and cold when the dinner arrived. Julie picked at her plate as Blake tried to keep up the conversation. They decided against dessert, and like the ride there, the return was driven in silence.

"May I still accompany you to the Country Club Dance tomorrow night?"

Julie nodded. "Of course."

He leaned over and gave her a warm kiss on her cheek, she was grateful that seemed to satisfy him.

Julie watched from the porch as he drove away. She didn't hear any activity inside the house, so she chose to take a walk. With her shawl wrapped around her tightly, she walked down the driveway, not wanting to be spotted at the back of the house. She took a right out of the driveway wanting to avoid Cooper's house. It was just starting to get dark outside, and she was thankful. She felt safer wrapped in the darkness. She didn't like that others saw her when she couldn't even see herself.

Julie took a shortcut through the woods, and before she knew it, she still wound up in front of Cooper's house. Amazed, she wondered why all roads seemed to lead to him. In the distance, she heard coyotes howling at the full moon. All of a sudden, walking through his lighted backyard seemed like a much better option.

Julie tried to stay close to the edge of the property, hidden in the darkness. When she reached the backyard, she found herself wandering through the lit maze of shrubs. She was lost in about two minutes. She kept ending up in the middle of the maze with the big fountain, which is how the maze was designed. On her third attempt, she found Cooper sitting on the bench waiting for her.

When Julie looked up and saw him, she started to cry. It seemed the whole world just came crashing down around her, and she couldn't take the weight of it anymore.

The adorable lopsided grin Cooper had on his face vanished and was instantly replaced with concern. He jumped to his feet and rushed to pull her into his arms. After a few minutes, still crying, he picked her up and carried her to the bench. Settling her on his lap he waited in silence as she let it all out.

Cooper was massaging small circles on her back, and he could feel her begin to relax. Julie was spent going limp in his arms. Finally, the crickets and bullfrogs began to penetrate her consciousness, and she lifted her head to look at Cooper.

He wiped a tear off her cheek. "I've never seen you cry."

"Really?" A frown marred her porcelain face.

"No, never. Not when you fell down the stairs when you were little and got nine stitches. Not when your puppy got hit by a car or even when your favorite Aunt Gwen died last year. What can I possibly do to make it better?"

"What did you do to me?" Julie was suddenly reminded of why she was so upset. She felt him stiffen beneath her, and she realized it must be true. "You lied to me. You said we never dated-never kissed."

"I swear on my mother's grave it was all a misunderstanding. You wouldn't listen to me when I tried to explain, and before I knew it you were dating Blake. I thought you were just doing it to get back at me until you announced your engagement. I was trying to give you your space. You have been mad at me before, but we always worked things out.

We never went out on an official date, and I said our first kiss was when we were twelve. I never specified that we hadn't had others after that."

Why didn't you tell me? What was so bad that I was marrying Blake and not you? Maybe he didn't want to get married but wanted his freedom more. These were all questions racing in rapid succession through Julie's head.

"Julie, you didn't talk to me for months, and then, by some miracle, you forgot that you were mad at me. These past few weeks have been the best days of my life. I go to bed thinking of you and I wake up thinking of you and dream of you in between. I have to see you every day to prove to myself this is real. God has given me a second chance. Please, won't you do the same?"

Cooper spoke with such passion that it was hard not to get swept away in it.

"I can't think right now." Julie waved her hands in the air. She stood up, and he did too.

"Will you go with me to the Country Club Dance tomorrow night?"□

"I already told Blake I would attend with him."

"You're still seeing him?" Cooper sounded incredulous.

"I told him I would, and I plan to keep that promise even though I broke a promise to him much greater than that."

"What about our kiss?" he exclaimed.

"What about it?" she shot back at him. "I'm engaged!" She held up her hand, showing him the ring he damn well knew was on her finger.

"I have never forgotten!" he shouted back. She took a step back. She had never seen him mad. Well, at least that she could remember.

He ran his hand through his hair. He seemed deflated, "Julie, I'm sorry."

"I have to go." Julie turned around and started down a different path. She came across a three-way intersection and turned right. Cooper came up behind her.

"This way," He tried taking her arm, but she managed to avoid him.

"Lead the way." She stood back to allow him by.

Cooper escorted her through the maze. "Thank you, I can see myself home," she ground out. Julie felt grateful that he didn't try to follow her. The further she walked away, the emptier and colder she felt like a part of her was missing.

Julie walked into the house through the backdoor, and no one noticed or, more likely, decided not to comment on it. "I'm going to bed," she announced.

"Goodnight, sweetheart," her mom called from the couch.

"Sweet dreams, My Girl," her dad waved.

"Yeah, right," she muttered to herself.

"Honey?" her mom called her back to the couch.

"Yes," she was careful not to sound annoyed.

"We are going camping this weekend we would love it if you joined us. It's a yearly thing we do as a family. Your dad likes to rough it once in a while to remind us how lucky we are."

Being around family only, sounded wonderful. "Of course, I'd love to go, mom." She kissed both her parents and headed off upstairs.

Chapter Fifteen

Julie took the stairs two at a time. She showered for a long time. When she stepped out, she put her hair in a towel and got into some comfortable pajamas. She sat on the bed, unwrapped her hair, and began brushing it. After about ten minutes of staring off into space, she grabbed her cell phone from her bedside stand and scrolled through her contact list. When she found the number, she had saved under favorites she hit send.

When the phone was picked up, all she said was, "I need you."

"I'll be right there," the response was immediate.

She clicked off put the phone back down on her bedside stand, and waited. Twenty minutes later, Melissa sat cross-legged on her bed in her borrowed pajamas and was hugging a pillow. She had come bearing gifts of Ben and Jerry's ice cream and two spoons.

"This is delicious," Julie said of the Chunky Monkey she was digging walnuts out of.

"It's your favorite."

"Good to know," she smiled at Melissa, who was licking Cherry Garcia off her spoon.

"So, what's up," Melissa tried to sound nonchalant, but it wasn't quite coming across.

"Have you ever seen me cry?"

"Never. Did you cry? Who made you cry? I'll kick their ass!"

Julie laughed even though she felt miserable. Melissa was definitely the right call. She decided to start from the beginning.

"I kissed Cooper-" That was as far as she got.

"Oh My God! That's wonderful! Isn't it? What was it like? Hot right? I knew it!"

Julie was staring at her with her mouth open. "You talk a mile a minute, you know that, right?"

Melissa giggled, "That's what you love about me," She slapped her on the knee. "So, tell me all the juicy details."

Julie decided to tell her what had happened with Cooper in detail. Melissa was practically drooling, and Julie felt like she was reliving the moment all over again.

Then Julie went into telling her about her date with Blake and her encounter with Cooper next door. "Do you know what happened between Cooper and me, before I had amnesia?"

Melissa looked down, "I do. I wanted to tell you, but Cooper..." her voice trailed off.

"What about Cooper?" Julie suddenly had a sinking feeling in her stomach.

"You thought that Cooper and I were involved, but it's not true!" her head snapped back up and looked Julie square in the eye, "I promise on our friendship. Please believe me." Julie did believe her as she had believed Cooper when he had told her earlier. Julie told Melissa about her encounter with Cooper in the maze what had been said, and the infamous "crying incident."

"So, what happened that I would think the worst of my two best friends?" Julie wanted to get to the bottom of this story.

"Well, we both lied to you, and that is never good because you can usually sniff out a lie faster than Sherlock

Holmes. We were planning a surprise birthday party for you. I told you I was sick and couldn't go shopping with you, and Cooper said he had a work emergency. Being the spectacular friend that you are you, made-well had your mom make me chicken noodle soup to bring over. When you showed up outside my apartment you saw Cooper's Jeep parked outside. You just assumed that something was going on. When you went to the door, you heard Cooper say something like, "Julie will never know..." and that was it. You thought the worst of us and, no matter what we did, you were hurt and didn't believe a word we said. You weren't taking either one of our phone calls or responding to our texts. We were devastated.

Then you show up with Blake, and it killed Cooper. You need to give him a second chance," Melissa begged. "You don't want to go through life wondering "what if."

Julie thought long and hard on that point.

Melissa spent the night, and the two of them fell asleep, curled up in her bed as they had done in years past, mid-sentence, at four in the morning. Not unlike countless other nights they had spent together.

CHAPTER SIXTEEN

The night was dark on the lonely road. A parked car was sitting in the breakdown lane with two occupants.

"This situation is getting out of control. I thought, at first, we could use it to our advantage...I think we need to move on to plan B."

"No. I just need a little more time."

"You have one week, otherwise I do it my way."

"You won't have to, I promise. Just give me some more time."□

CHAPTER SEVENTEEN

The night of the Country Club party Julie had Blake pick her up at her townhouse. She had gotten ready there because that's where all her formal gowns were.

She'd chosen a classic "little black dress." It had two thin spaghetti straps going over one shoulder, leaving the other bare, and had a dangerously low back. The front revealed the swell of her breasts, hugged her hips and showed off her flat stomach. The rest of the gown swirled around her legs, falling gracefully to the floor, and when she moved, the dress sparkled like it had thousands of tiny diamonds attached.

She wore black three-inch heels, making her feel more confident for the ensuing evening. Julie had gone to her hairdresser two hours earlier, and he managed to give her a beautiful arrangement of curls piled up on her head, showing off her creamy white shoulders.

Julie had found a matching purse in her closet, and she held it in her left hand, which had Blake's ring to adorn it. She had found a pair of emerald earrings that was the only piece of jewelry she added.

She was waiting outside when Blake pulled up in his Mercedes Benz. She came down the steps to meet him.

Blake was just walking around the front of the car as she reached him. He went in for a kiss and, with her hands on his shoulders, kissed him on the cheek. Julie could tell he was disappointed but didn't comment on it. Instead, he said, "You look beautiful tonight," as he opened the car door for her. Julie sank into the plush leather upholstery gasping slightly as her bare back touched the cold surface.

Blake reached inside the car across her lap and hit the button, instantly turning on the seat warmers. "Thank you," Julie said. Blake turned to her, still in the car only a breath away from her. She looked into his beautiful blue eyes and could see he wanted to kiss her. She didn't say anything, only lowered her lashes slightly. Blake, taking this as a sign, leaned in and kissed her. With one hand, he braced himself on the outside of the car, to keep from falling on top of her. His other hand came up and cupped her face gently. Blake applied just a little pressure to her chin, and she opened up for him, his tongue sweeping inside her mouth.

Julie's hand came up and found its way into his curls. Her other hand came up and touched his chest through his tuxedo. Julie kissed him back, and it was a pleasant kiss. It just didn't ignite the fire she knew she had inside. When it came to kissing-hell even looking at Cooper- she simply melted. Blake pulled away and seemed extremely pleased with himself. Julie didn't want to burst his bubble, at least for now.

Blake drove holding her hand the whole time, impressing her with his ability to shift with his left hand and controlling the steering wheel with his knees, never letting go of her hand. He talked to her about his day at the office, he had to go to court today, but she just wasn't paying attention.

"What are you thinking about," Blake asked with a knowing smile, sure that she was caught up in the kiss just minutes earlier.

"Just my life and what it used to be like," Julie answered honestly.

"Well, not much different from now, except you live with your parents, and right now, you're on summer break. You usually like to teach a class or two during the summer, but because of the wedding..." his voice trailed off.

"Ah yes, the wedding," was all Julie said. She turned and looked out the window watching the streetlights as they passed.

Blake stopped talking after that, and they rode in silence. Minutes later, they pulled through the stone gateway of the Country Club and up the cobblestone drives to the main house of the Country Club. A valet opened Julie's door, and Blake was forced to let go of her hand so she could step out of the car. He met her on the other side and offered his arm, which she took.

They walked up the wide grey stone stairs into the opulent marble foyer. To the right were double doors, which were thrown open in a magnificent fashion by two doormen dressed to the hilt in matching tuxedos. They entered the two-story ballroom on the second floor. The second floor consisted of the grand entrance and a balcony with private alcoves which skirted the ballroom.

People were lined up on either side, watching participants dancing below. Others were tucked away in little alcoves built into the walls with bench seats. Most everyone was holding a glass of champagne and were paired off into small cluster groups, some laughing at jokes, others discussing business and or money.

Blake escorted Julie down the staircase to the main level, where a live band played and people in the middle of the room were dancing. A wide circle of spectators observed from the sidelines. In front of them were two stories worth of windows, the bottom half of which were French doors leading out to a massive stone balcony.

Looking around, Julie noticed there was a century's worth of portraits lining the walls. She was suddenly extremely interested in who these particular people were and wondered if anyone knew.

Blake had taken two glasses of champagne from a waiter as he walked by and handed a glass to her. Julie started to feel self-conscious, not knowing anyone there and realizing that they more than likely knew her. She suddenly wished Cooper was there to help her through this. The music ended, and there was a collective gasp from the audience.

"She might as well be naked for all the good that dress is doing her," an elderly woman whispered loud enough for several people, including Julie, to hear. Julie turned around and stared at what everyone else had apparently noticed.

Standing on the top of the staircase was Courtney Champlain, wearing an almost see-through cream-colored dress. You could see she wasn't wearing a bra, and her perky breasts and hard nipples strained through the material of her plunging neckline, which almost reached her naval.

Julie watched as she hooked her arm through her escort and smiled up into the eyes of none other than... Cooper Jackson. It was a good thing the music began to play because it covered the gasp that escaped Julie's lips. She quickly looked around, trying to determine if anyone else had heard her. Realizing no one had or at least pretended not to, she began to relax.

Cooper was dressed splendidly in his custom-tailored tuxedo. She didn't know how she could tell from this far away, but she was sure it was no rental. He stood erect and smiled down at Courtney, showing off the dimple in his chin.

Julie was fuming mad. How could he come here with her? His ex-girlfriend looking like that! She was a rich heiress who was obviously still in love with him. Couldn't he see that? Maybe he did, and he preferred Courtney to her. Maybe old sparks were flying.

If Julie was able to be reasonable and acknowledge that she was here with her fiancé... but she couldn't see any of that, in her tirade as she was blinded by jealousy. All she saw was him kissing her in her apartment, him telling her she was all he thought about day and night, and she wondered why they weren't here together. Again, it was her fault. He had asked her, and she had refused, already committed to Blake.

"Well, hello there," Courtney practically purred from behind Julie. She turned to her now enemy for life, with a smile that killed her, glued to her face.

"Hello," she said with the same false tone Courtney had used. "I would like to introduce you to my fiancé, Blake Duncan. Blake, this is Courtney Champlain."

"Nice to meet you, Courtney," Blake shook the hand Courtney delicately offered to him.

"You two both know Cooper?" Courtney asked coyly.

"Blake," Cooper said, holding his hand out.

"Cooper," Blake said, accepting the handshake.

"Have you rescheduled the wedding yet?" she asked in a sickly-sweet voice. "Cooper was telling me what a terrible accident you had. What a shame!"

"We are working on it," Blake said smoothly as he slipped his arm comfortably around Julie's waist. Julie gave him a grateful smile, and he returned it pleased that he had made her happy. The exchanged look between the two was read differently... as an intimate moment and not for what it really was, a lie.

"Would you care to dance?" Cooper questioned Courtney.

"I'd love to. If you will excuse us?" Courtney didn't bother to wait for a response but sauntered out on the dance floor with Cooper.

Well, I never! She would have crossed both her arms in a pout if she wasn't holding the champagne glass. Cooper had never even acknowledged her presence once. Julie watched from the sidelines as the couple on the dance floor glided gracefully across the room, Courtney's hips swaying gently, one of Cooper's hands resting low on her hip. No wonder they were the prom king and queen. Just look at them.

"Would you like to dance?" Blake asked her.

"I would love to," Julie answered, downing most of her champagne and handing the glass off to a waiter passing by. Blake disposed of his and said nothing about Julie's obvious distress. Blake was an exceptional dancer, but it didn't matter to her. She was caught up in her anger toward Cooper.

Was he all about the chase? She was perfectly fine with Blake until he had come along and messed everything up. Making her question decisions she never remembered making in the first place. She knew deep down she was being unreasonable, but she didn't care. She was furious with him and if she looked close enough, at herself, and this stupid amnesia.

If she hadn't lost her memory, she would be a married woman now and she wouldn't be going through this turmoil; but would she have married the wrong man? Would she have come to realize she had made a mistake, or would she have never known what she was missing with Cooper?

Cooper caught her eye from across the room and held her gaze captive for a moment longer than was appropriate. As soon as the song ended, she excused herself saying she had to go to the ladies' room.

Julie left through the double doors on the side of the room and headed left down an empty hallway following the signs. The hallway was the width of a regular-sized bedroom. It had plush oriental carpet runners, big potted plants, and small alcoves lined up and down each side. Julie found the bathroom on the right.

Inside were several women powdering their noses and touching up their hair. Julie went into one of the stalls and waited until several women had gone from the room. Emerging when the other women had left, she washed her hands in the sink and stared back at her reflection.

Julie had her auburn hair swept up in a beautiful arrangement on her head showing off several curls, artfully placed. The only jewelry she wore was a pair of princess-cut emerald earrings the same shade as her eyes. She had found them in her jewelry box at home and instantly put them on.

When she walked out of the bathroom, she found Cooper leaning against the wall to her immediate right. "What do you want?" she snapped. Cooper grinned at her. "What are you smiling at? Oh, never mind I don't want to know." Julie turned to the left fully intending to go back to the party when she whirled to face him. "So, you're with Courtney now? I'm sure you enjoyed that thing she calls a dress!"

Cooper's grin widened with each word she spat at him.

"You're enjoying this, aren't you? Well, go to hell!" Julie said getting closer to him instead of running away from him. Her finger poked in his chest. The double doors down the hallway opened and a new flood of women came down the hall towards the bathroom. Cooper grabbed her wrists and swirled her into the nearest alcove. Pressing her up against the wall, his body curved into hers.

"Shh..." he said holding his finger to her lips. She was tempted to take it into her mouth and see what he did then, but she didn't, she was still mad. Her body was rigid against his and she refused to melt into him like she wanted to.

"You're jealous," he laughed.

"I am not!" She spat at him.

"You know, in high school, I tried everything to get you to notice me, as something other than a friend. I paraded around you, half-naked, I played every sport imaginable, knowing you liked sports. I took you to muse-ums, knowing your love of history. I tried taking the same classes as you, we worked on projects together. I even dated the prom queen to get you to notice me and... nothing!" His finger left her lips and went to her ear. "I gave you these earrings for Christmas one year and still nothing. If I knew all I had to do was kiss you I would have swallowed my pride in letting you come to me and done it a long time ago."

"Your kisses don't have that kind of effect on me," Julie lifted her chin to glare at him.

Cooper responded by kissing her. Julie stood tense, her mind protesting but her body had a different agenda. Her knees started to go weak, and his arms came around her to support her weight. Her arms went around his neck, and she kissed him back. Cooper's kiss was intoxicating making her whimper with pleasure.

"You better get back before Blake notices you haven't returned and starts looking for you." He kissed her one more time and shoved her out of the alcove with a gentle swat to her bottom. Julie, unsteady on her feet, made her way slowly back to the dance.

Cooper collapsed against the wall.

"Well done," a voice came from behind him. He turned around to face Courtney. She sat elegantly on the padded bench seat in the alcove. Cooper heaved a great sigh and sat down next to her. □

"Thanks for doing this for me," Cooper said, genuinely meaning it.

"Hey, what else do I have going on? My boyfriend, who my parents don't approve of, is skiing with his buddies in the Alps. They always loved you, but I knew you were in love with Julie, even back then."

Cooper faced her shocked, "How long did you know?"

Courtney laughed at the expression on his face, "Not at first, but it wasn't hard to see after a while. I saw the way you looked at her and you never looked at me that way."

"I'm sorry, Court," Cooper apologized.

Courtney shrugged her shoulders, "It's done and over with. I guess I was hoping if I could stick it out long enough you could come to love me that way."

"I did love you," Cooper swore.

Courtney patted his hand as if he were a child, "I know, in your own special way you did but you weren't in love with me like you are with Julie." Cooper looked down the hallway at the mention of her name, but she was already gone. "Let's see if we can put more icing on the cake, shall we?" Courtney said with a wicked grin.

Cooper stood, held out his arm for her and they walked arm and arm back into the ballroom. They found Blake and Julie in a group of people. Julie was asking if anyone knew the origins of the paintings.

"These are paintings of the Pembrooke family that began in England, they transported these portraits here and added the next generations over the years. This used to be a private residence until the 1950s when the grandson turned it into a country club," one of the older gentlemen began.

"That portrait over there is Lady Aislynne she was a rich heiress, and her father held a tournament in her honor, declaring the winner as her groom." Cooper provided.

Julie's eyes lit up at the story, so Cooper continued and pointed to one with an old man, "That one there had five young wives, all died giving birth to each of his five daughters. He refused to allow any of them to marry but he died when his eldest daughter Lady Grace was twenty-one, she inherited the estate found good husbands for her four sisters, and began a search for her own husband. Her only stipulation was they had to change their name to Pembrooke to carry on the family name. She was extremely beautiful and had many takers-she is that one down there," Cooper pointed.

Julie looked on in interest. Lady Grace was indeed beautiful, with high cheekbones, full lips with honey blond hair piled on top of her head, and big brown eyes. Cooper resumed his story, "She married a man named James and together they had eleven children, nine boys and two girls ensuring the succession of the name." On and on it went, Cooper telling the stories of many of the portraits on the wall.

Julie was in awe, trying to soak in every word. "How do you know all of this?" she asked. Some of the men in the group chuckled. Julie didn't know her question was so funny. "What?" she asked genuinely confused.

"Well, how could I not read the book my best friend wrote?"

"I would love to read it sometime," Julie was even more confused when laughter erupted from the group.

"Honey, you wrote the book," one of the men said.

"Yeah, and that's not all," added another guest.

"There's more?" Julie scanned the crowd of faces before her trying to determine what else she could be missing.

Cooper took a formal bow. "Cooper Pembrooke Jackson, at your service."

Julie's eyes got as big as saucers. She knew Cooper was well off and didn't need to work but this was crazy. How could he not tell her he owned this splendid place with all this history?

"I need some fresh air," she reported as she passed her empty champagne glass to the waiter. She hadn't realized she had drunk two glasses while listening to Cooper's story, she had just been so fascinated. Now she felt as if she was some big joke, and everyone was in on it.

She knew Blake had excused himself as well and was following her out to the veranda. She moved to a quiet spot near the end and waited for him. Julie was looking out over the perfectly manicured landscape of the golf course. No doubt it was Cooper's green thumb that had this place looking so spectacular. Blake came up behind her and wrapped his arms around her. She was stiff up against him as she allowed him to hold her.

She wished it could be this easy. He loved her why couldn't she have fallen in love with him again? Julie turned to face him and if it hadn't been for the three glasses of champagne, Cooper's kisses in the hallway, and the history lesson adding to her bad mood she might not have wrapped her arms around his neck.

"Kiss me," she demanded.

His hand caressed her face as he looked down at her. He obliged by lowering his lips towards her and this time she held nothing back kissing him willing herself to love him again. She slipped her tongue into his mouth and deepened the kiss. He groaned into her, his hands roaming down her back and settling on her backside.

Others came out on the veranda, saw the couple in an embrace, and walked to the opposite side to give them some privacy. Julie broke off the kiss anyway. She looked up at Blake, "Take me home please."

He grinned down at her, "Gladly." Blake led the way, holding her hand. Cooper was watching her from across the room as they made their way through the crowd. Julie slipped her arm in Blake's and smiled up at him. She knew it wasn't fair to tease Blake, but she wanted to get Cooper back for bringing Courtney here and making a fool of her in front of so many people.

On the way home, she fidgeted with the ring on her left hand. It was a gorgeous ring, a round diamond with several other smaller round diamonds that went in a V shape from the band to the center diamond on a platinum band. She wished she could remember the day he proposed and how she had felt accepting this ring. She thought about how she was going to broach the subject with Blake and tears stung her eyes as she looked out the car window.

Julie had Blake drop her off at her parent's house because they were going camping the following day. Blake put the car in park and turned towards her. Without looking at him she slipped the engagement ring Blake had given her off her finger and broke the promise the old Julie had made to him. She held it out to him, willing him to take it from her. Blake seemed stunned. He sat back in his seat not wanting to be close to the ring as if, if he didn't take it, they would still be engaged.

"This isn't working for me." She felt like there was a knife in her chest.

"I just don't understand how we got here." He said to no one in particular. "We were in love. We were getting married, now what? We aren't anything to each other."

She looked at him heartbroken.

Turning, he looked at her, "Why did you kiss me like that tonight?"

Her heart thudded in her chest, yeah that wasn't good. "I was hoping that if I gave it my all it would spark something and maybe I would remember how I used to feel about you."

He was quiet for a long time. He still hadn't taken the ring from her. "When you kiss me, you don't feel anything for me?"

She bit her lower lip. "You are a great kisser, and any woman would be happy to have you, I just don't think I'm that woman."

"You are breaking my heart."

"I'm so sorry Blake, I really am."

He held out his hand and she slowly placed the ring on his palm. His fingers closed over it. "Thank you for understanding," she said, her hand on the door anxious to escape the confines of the car.

"I don't understand."

She let go of the door handle, "I wish I could explain it to you better, but I'm not sure I know how."

He sighed heavily, "I know. I love you, Julie."

She leaned forward and kissed him on the cheek. "Goodbye, Blake." This time he let her leave.

Julie got out of his car and felt a sense of relief, relief she had finally ended it with Blake but at the same time, she felt guilty. She was also looking forward to getting away from Cooper for the weekend because she needed time to think.

She chose not to read the diaries that night. She was mad at Cooper and the young impressionable Julie who had written those memories was not disgusted with him like she was at the moment. She thought it better to wait than to dive into her past tonight.

CHAPTER EIGHTEEN

The following morning, with bags packed, Julie cheerfully headed down the steps and onto the front porch. Stopping dead in her tracks as she spotted Cooper's Jeep, fully loaded with camping supplies, in her parent's driveway.

□Sandy was coming out of the house with a cooler and Julie whispered loudly, "I thought this was a family trip."

"It is dear."

"Then why is Cooper coming?"

"Because he's family," Sandy replied rather matter of fact.

"I'm not going." Julie turned back towards the house.

"Did you and Cooper have an argument?"

"No. I just don't want to go anymore." Julie tried not to sound childish and failed miserably.

"Well, it seems to me that he must have won the argument."

"What!" Julie shouted.

Sandy ignored her outburst, carrying the cooler towards the vehicles. "It seems to me that if you had won you wouldn't care if you saw him and if you hid inside, he has most definitely won."

"Oh, no he doesn't," Julie said and flung her bags into the back of his Jeep. Sandy quickly turned around before her daughter saw her grin. Julie hopped in Cooper's vehicle and slammed the door shut behind her.

Everyone filed out of the house carrying something, loaded it up and away they went. Katie hopped in the backseat of Cooper's Jeep with her cell phone, wireless earbuds firmly in her ears, and still dressed in her pajamas, holding a pillow.

Megan and Shannon got in the back of their parent's car and the caravan pulled out of the driveway. The drive took about two and a half hours, and the views were spectacular. They drove along a windy road that seemed to teeter at the edge of a cliff. Julie stared out the window watching the sun rise over all the trees, drying the rain from the night off the ground.

Katie had fallen back to sleep in the back with her music playing softly in her ear. Julie turned towards Cooper and stared at his profile. He was wearing Maui Jim sunglasses to keep the morning sunlight out of his eyes while he drove. She wanted to ask him about the book she had written. That must have been quite an accomplishment she thought, only twenty-six, a college professor, and published author. She had enjoyed the stories he told her last night and she wanted to ask him if she had gotten all the stories from him or if she had to do a lot of research. Instead, she went on the attack.

"Why didn't you tell me you were a Pembrooke?" Julie asked so softly she wondered if he heard her.

Cooper turned to look at her, but she couldn't read his expression behind the sunglasses. "Why does it matter what my name is? I liked the fact you didn't know, and you didn't care. You always told me you didn't care if I was dirt poor, that it would be good for my ego."

"I wish you were poor," Julie said.

"I'd give it all away today if I thought that would make you love me."

His declaration took her off guard but only for a split second before she started in on him again. "Why were you trying to make me jealous? Did Courtney know you were just using her?" Are you going to use me? She thought the last to herself.

"It was Courtney's idea. She called me and I told her that I had asked you, but you refused. She thought she could help. She has a boyfriend."

Julie wasn't convinced that Courtney was the saint she claimed to be, and she probably didn't even have a boyfriend. "Well, I'm still mad at you."

"Not like it's not the first time."

"Good, then you know what to expect!"

Katie woke up in the backseat, "Are we there yet?" Neither answered, Julie turned to look out the window and Cooper stared straight ahead at the road.

Twenty minutes later, they pulled off the tarmac and onto a dirt road. The narrow lane was a hard-packed road they followed until they reached a deserted parking area. The family unloaded the cars, put on their backpacks, with all the equipment they would need for the weekend, and hiked another hour into the woods. They walked in pairs on the trail, carrying coolers and such in between them.

They stopped on a slope down to the lake and found a flat area to set up camping gear. There was a fire pit, from previous campers, in the middle surrounded by logs where they could sit. Julie's parents set up their tent easily, due to years of practice. Cooper had one of those new tents you threw in the air and it popped open ready to go. Julie's sisters were setting up the largest tent together when Julie noticed an extra tent that had been brought along.

"Can I use this one?" Julie asked.

"Sure, but there is plenty of room in this one," Megan offered.

"That's okay, I kind of want to be by myself." She turned to glare at Cooper, but her sisters took the look differently. Katie and Megan giggled, and Shannon made a snide remark under her breath like, "Sure you do."

The only spot left was between her sister's tent and Cooper's. She tried setting it up herself, but it kept falling on top of her. Cooper came over to offer his assistance, but she would have nothing to do with it. Frustrated, Cooper walked off towards the lake saying he would catch lunch.

Julie's sisters finally took pity on her and came to help. They didn't ask her, which was probably a good thing, they just jumped in and helped. At first, Julie was mad but it wasn't her sister's fault in any way so why should she take it out on them?

"Thank you," she said at last when they were all finished.

Cooper came back to the campsite two hours later with a line full of fish. Julie's mom began preparing them for lunch while Julie's dad started a fire. Julie's mom had a wire rack she placed over the fire to cook the fish. When it was done, she pulled out an arsenal of food she had made before leaving this morning from the coolers.

The girls set up napkins and plates on the picnic table and somehow everyone managed to grab a seat before Julie because the remaining seat was next to Cooper. Julie managed to sit stiffly by his side and did her best not to touch him. It seemed everything he needed was on the other side of her. Instead of asking which she would be hard-pressed to respond to, he reached across casually brushing up against her. One time he was so close she could feel his warm breath on her ear and smell his toothpaste.

She was so busy concentrating on ignoring him that she didn't see her family around her giving each other sly smiles of conspiracy. Her mom was the first to notice Julie was no longer wearing her engagement ring and without thinking she mentioned in front of the group, "Julie, what happened to your engagement ring? Did you lose it?"

Julie looked down at her naked hand. Everyone stopped eating, she heard Cooper's plastic fork hit his paper plate. She felt everyone's eyes on her, none more than Cooper's who seemed to be boring into her.

"No."

There was silence. She shoveled a spoonful of her mom's macaroni salad into her mouth. They were all waiting. She swallowed and wiped her mouth with a napkin. "I gave it back to Blake, last night."

There were several startled gasps around the picnic table. "Oh," her mom was the only one that responded.

The rest of the day went by without incident. After lunch Cooper volunteered to gather firewood and Julie quickly offered to help clean up. Julie's dad, Cooper, and Megan all went out to gather more firewood while Julie stayed to help her mom. Katie disappeared with her phone down by the lake and Sharon unpacked all the sleeping bags.

Katie came back in a huff, "You would think that just once we could find a spot with cell phone reception." Sandy just laughed as her youngest went storming into the girl's tent.

Hours later, they went out in inflatable rafts and caught more fish for dinner. Julie and her dad each caught one, Cooper caught two and Julie's mom caught three. Her sisters were just along for the ride because they didn't even try. They were in bikinis laying out, trying to get a tan.

They built the fire back up. Her mom made baked potatoes and corn on the cob over the flames. They had a nice dinner, and this time Julie managed to avoid sitting next to Cooper. Later that night they sat around the fire and told stories and made smores. Julie enjoyed listening to the wildlife around her, it was soothing to hear the crickets and bullfrogs down by the lake.

Her parents were the first to retire. Julie and Shannon sat on opposite sides of the fire as Cooper and Katie. Megan was sitting on the side closest to her tent. Julie missed the exchange between Katie and Megan, but Cooper didn't. Yawn. "Boy, I'm tired." Katie stood and stretched.

"Yeah, me too," Megan jumped up at the same time. "You're tired too right, Shannon?" Megan asked but it wasn't a question and the two practically dragged her to the tent.

Julie and Cooper sat quietly in front of the fire for a while. Cooper stood up to walk around to her side but just as suddenly Julie stood. "I'm going to bed," she announced.

"Julie," was all he said to her retreating back.

CHAPTER NINETEEN

J ulie could see two people talking, they were whispering to one another. What were they saying, she wondered? Was it about her? They were just dark figures. She didn't know what they were wearing or who they were. She must have made a noise because they both looked up. Could they see her? She didn't know but she didn't want to stick around to find out.

Julie was running down a dark hallway. She needed to escape but where? She saw the exit sign above the door and pushed it open. Were they following? Had they known she had overheard their conversation? She didn't think so, but she couldn't be sure.

Someone grabbed her by the shoulder, and she screamed. It was them they had come for her. Someone clamped a hand over her mouth, and she fought with all her might to be released. She bit down hard on the hand of her assailant and was rewarded with her release. She heard him swear and she smiled.

"Julie, please wake up."

Somewhere in the fog she began to realize she was dreaming again and woke up with a start. She couldn't see it was pitch black inside the tent. "Who's there?" she tried not to sound frightened. It was hard to do when her heart was racing so fast.

"It's Cooper. Are you okay?"

"Fine thank you," her voice was stiff.

She felt him tense, "Well I'll just be going now." He started to leave.

Panic rose inside her, she didn't want to be alone. "Wait!" This time some of the panic she felt was heard in her voice. "Can you just stay with me a while until I fall asleep?" She sighed heavily, "Please."

"Let me get my sleeping bag. Will you be all right for just a minute?"

"Yes," it was barely a whisper.

Cooper was only gone thirty seconds, but it seemed like an eternity. He set up his sleeping bag next to hers and crawled inside. Julie's eyes were growing accustomed to the dark with the help of the full moon. Cooper hadn't been wearing a T-shirt when he left but he was wearing one now.

It took her a long time to fall back to sleep but eventually, she did. Cooper fell asleep waiting for her to and awoke hours later, with Julie in his arms. She had snuggled right up to him and had her head on his chest. His sleeping bag was half unzipped and pulled down to his waist because he was usually hot when he slept, and it helped. Now he was hot for an entirely different reason. Julie was running her hand over his chest and down his belly. Cooper tilted Julie's head up towards him and kissed her lips, he soon realized she was enticing him in her sleep. He kissed her neck and across her face, kissing her lips once again. This time she started to respond. Cooper sucked in his breath when he realized he was rock hard, and her hand was now stroking him.

"Julie?" he questioned softly in the dark, kissing her neck again.

No response.

"Julie, wake up." This time he was more forceful.

"What?" she asked coming out of the fog of sleep.

"If you don't want me taking advantage of you while you sleep, I suggest you stop what you're doing."

Julie let out a startled gasp and promptly removed her hand, but she didn't move away from him. Her hand, instead, moved up more appropriately to his chest. Cooper realized he had already taken slight advantage of the situation but damn it if she hadn't started it first. Cooper raised himself up on his elbow and tried to see her face. Her face started to come into focus and the passion he saw in her eyes caused his heart to quicken he almost didn't realize why he could see her eyes.

Passion was quickly replaced with fear, and she was tugging on his shirt. Their tent was on fire at the front entrance. The inside was beginning to fill up with smoke and the fire was spreading quickly.

Cooper jumped up and unzipped the back window that was covered in mesh for a window screen. Julie began using the sleeping bags to beat out the flames, but they just caught fire. They were both coughing, and Julie started calling for help. Cooper managed to rip open the mesh with his teeth when Julie's dad appeared at the rear of the tent. Cooper grabbed Julie around the waist and fed her through the hole to Jack before climbing out behind her.

Sandy was standing in her robe and she and Katie were both holding buckets that contained water. They had tried to douse the fire, but it wasn't enough. Shannon and Megan had come out of their tent and were holding onto each other, everyone watched in horror as the small tent engulfed in flames burned to the ground.

A sickening feeling began to wash over everyone as they realized that had Julie and Cooper not been awake, they could very well have been seriously injured or worse yet dead.

"It must have been a spark from the campfire," Sandy whispered.

No one saw the look exchanged between Cooper and Jack they were both aware that the fire had been doused the night before. Rule number one in camping. This was no accident, but they kept their theories to themselves.

It was about two in the morning, but no one could go back to sleep. "Cooper and I are going back to the car to see what we can scrounge up for pillows and blankets," Jack announced. When they were out of hearing range Jack voiced his concern about the fire. They agreed to split up, did a perimeter search, and met back at the car twenty minutes later.

"Did you find anything?" Jack asked.

Cooper didn't know if he should be pleased with himself for finding something or scared out of his mind that their fears were confirmed. "Yeah, someone was traipsing through the woods all right. Broken branches and footprints lead down to the roadside. Did you find anything?"

He gave a heavy sigh and held up a transponder. "I found this under your Jeep. Someone intentionally followed us here. I don't think that they will be back tonight, and we'll be leaving in the morning. I don't want to frighten the girls. I have some connections in the police department maybe I can get someone down here to collect evidence." He pulled out a cell phone from his pocket and walked around the dirt parking lot looking for a signal. He made the call while Cooper pulled out an extra sleeping bag, a blanket, and one pillow.

They walked back discussing taking shifts the rest of the night to walk the perimeter. Julie's dad agreed to go first, seeing as Julie would more than likely be in Cooper's tent.

Cooper had unzipped the sleeping bag and spread it down on the floor of the tent like a bed and had the blanket down on top of that to cover up with. Katie had given up her extra pillow so Cooper and Julie could each have one.

They took their shoes off at the entrance and crawled inside. Snuggling down under the covers Julie felt like a schoolgirl with a crush. She decided that talking was a safe bet when she saw that look in his eyes. "So did I have to do a lot of research for your family history to write my book?"

Cooper grinned. "I thought you'd never ask, I wanted to give this to you sooner, but you were a little...what's the word I'm looking for?" he asked in mock innocence. He was rummaging through his backpack and turned around with a great show and presented her with her book.

Julie was immediately on her knees, "Oh, this is wonderful." She ran her hand reverently over the cover, "Pembrooke Manor, by Julie Hart."

Cooper sat up next to her watching her reaction extremely pleased he brought that shine into her eyes. The next instant he was being tackled to the ground. "Thank you, thank you, thank you," Julie said in between kisses spread across his face. Cooper laughed and his arms went around her waist hugging her to him. Her hands held his face as she gazed down into his eyes and the moment turned more serious. Julie leaned down to kiss him, stopping a breath away from his lips. A second passed before she pressed her mouth softly against his. Her tongue darted out to touch his lips and he opened up to her inviting her to deepen the kiss. She took him up on the offer, her head slanting back and forth trying to see what angle would be best to get the closest.

They made out like teenagers testing all types of kisses to see what was good and it was all good. They kissed softly and gently then ruff and biting. Slowly at first, then the kiss turned fast and passionate. They rolled around the expanse of the tent. When Julie began wiggling her hips against his he laughed and pulled back.

"Oh, no. Your parents are in the next tent."

Julie giggled then heaved a great big sigh. "All right, I'll just read my book." She found her book in the corner of the tent where it had finally landed after Cooper had rolled over it one too many times and that's where it had been tossed. She grabbed the flashlight and turned it on. Inside was an inscription written in blue ink, "To My Best Friend in the Whole Entire World, I couldn't have done this without you. Thank you. Love, Jewels." Settling down under the covers she began to read words she had written.

Julie fell asleep an hour later, the book on her chest and the flashlight still on in her hand. Cooper had been dozing next to her but when he knew she was asleep he shut the flashlight off and crept out of the tent.

Cooper found Julie's dad down by the lake.

"Have you seen anything?" Cooper asked.

Big sigh, "No. I don't like this one bit."

Cooper nodded his head in understanding. Why would anyone want to harm Julie? "Why don't you go back to bed sir? I'll stand guard for the rest of the night."

Jack patted him on the shoulder as he walked by, "You're all right, Cooper Jackson. I always liked you," he said with feeling.

"Thank you, sir," Cooper circled for the rest of the night but saw and heard nothing other than wildlife. At about six in the morning, Julie's dad came out to relieve him. Cooper crashed next to Julie. Feeling his warmth, she snuggled up next to him.

CHAPTER TWENTY

That day everyone packed up and drove home. On the ride home Cooper, without much convincing got Julie to agree to a date for the following night.

Melissa was at the house when they arrived, she was waiting with Nana. Together they had cooked a big Italian dinner for everyone. Julie got Melissa to spend the night so she could tell her all about the country club party and how she had finally broken it off with Blake. She also updated her friend on what had happened on the camping trip including her tent burning to the ground. Melissa was mainly interested in the part about Cooper and the date. They talked for quite a while before falling asleep.

Julie woke up to find a note from Melissa: "Had to go to work. Call me after your date! Love Always, Melissa." Julie hugged the note to her and smiled. Reaching across the bed she picked up her phone and pressed Cooper's number saved under favorites.

"Hello?" came a familiar voice that wasn't Cooper's.

"Hi, Nana. Is Cooper there?"

"No, I'm afraid not he is out planning your first date."

Julie was taken aback. "Oh, okay," was all she managed to say. "Thank you."

Byes were exchanged and Julie hung up the phone. He is out planning our first date. A huge smile spread across her face, she rolled across the bed and bounded for the bathroom she was so happy she didn't think her feet touched the floor. She sang in the shower at the top of her lungs and scrubbed and rinsed and shaved, wanting to look her best for her date tonight.

She got out of the shower and blew her hair dry then took her curling iron and used it to straighten her hair making all of the separate layers stand out with a slight curl on the end. She went to her closet and threw open the door, walking inside nothing seemed quite right. Julie threw on a pair of jeans and a fitted shirt and ran out of the room. She found her youngest sister Katie in her room on the computer. "Want to go shopping? You can drive," Julie promised.

Katie was downstairs with keys before Julie even heard a yes. Julie laughed and followed her sister downstairs. Katie was buckled inside the car doing a mirror check when Julie climbed inside. "Where to sis?"

"Well, I need an outfit...for a date."

"Oh."

"With, Cooper."

"Ohhh..." Katie looked at her sister, "It's about time!"

Julie started laughing she just couldn't help it. She was feeling giddy today. She liked the feeling. It replaced all the worry and stress she had recently faced in her life. Katie started driving to the mall, "Well, where is he taking you? That is important if you're going to pick out an outfit."

"I don't know, Nana said he was out planning it now."

Katie reached into her purse and produced her cell phone. She hit a speed dial number and listened for someone to pick up. "Hey, it's Kat. We need wardrobe info." She listened intently, "Uh huh. Uh-huh. Wow!" Katie looked quickly at Julie who was hanging on every word. Into the phone she said more seriously, "Uh huh." Julie was exasperated she was gaining nothing from the conversation. Katie hung up, "I think casual dress in this situation. We should drive into Oakwood, they have a mall. You'll have a better chance of finding something there."

"Okay." Julie agreed. They went into town, took a right as soon as they crossed the bridge, and followed the road out of town. They passed a restaurant that looked like it used to be an old mill. It had a wheel, which still worked, turning the water of the river over. She saw the sign that read "Oakwood est. 1858." Oakwood was a busy town, boasting store after store but it didn't have the charm that Willows Cove had. Julie commented on the differences between the two towns.

"Oh!" Katie said, "They are our archrivals."

"Really?"

"Oh, yes. We take it very seriously."

"Good to know."

Twenty stores later, they came up with a compromise on what to wear. Julie had tried on dresses, shorts, capris, and rompers. Katie was the one who actually found what Julie finally bought.

"How about this?" Katie pulled it off the rack waving the dress triumphantly to show it to her.

Julie gasped when she saw it. "Yes!" Grabbing the hanger from her sister she ran to the dressing room. Stripping down quickly she pulled the dress over her head, a big smile spread across her face as she saw her reflection. The straps were thin, the top folded over itself and hung down almost to her waist where it was brought together with a braided dark brown belt. The dress was blush in color, all lace with a hi-low hemline that landed just above the knee in front and the back hanging down to just above her knees. The color went beautifully with Julie's red hair and green eyes. Now if only she could find the right shoes to do justice to her long shapely legs.

She and her sister were walking out of one of the stores when her sister came up short. "Professor Hart?" Julie had to step around her sister to see the young man. What was his name?

"Andrew?" she guessed correctly.

He smiled, "Andy, yes, ma'am. I saw you at the food court eating and I didn't want to disturb you."

She smiled, "That's okay, Andy. How's your summer going?"

"Fine."

"This is my sister, Katie."

They shook hands, "Nice to meet you," he told her.

"You too," Katie said.

"I hate to bother you, but have you had a chance to reread my paper?"

"I'm sorry I haven't, it's been a busy summer." She pulled out her phone and handed it to him. "Here give me your contact info and send me a text so you can have my info and send me your paper again. I promise I will read it."

"Thank you so much, Professor. I really appreciate this."

"You're welcome. Try to enjoy the rest of your summer."

"Thank you, you too. Bye, Katie."

Katie grinned at him and waved bye. When he was out of earshot Julie looked at her sister and told her sternly, "No."

Katie looked at her, "What? No, what?"

"Don't play dumb with me, he is a college guy, and you are still in high school."

"So? Mom and Dad are eight years apart."

"That's mom and dad and they didn't meet actually I don't know how mom and dad met," she laughed, and Katie joined her.

"I'm sure Mom would love to tell you."□

Five stores later they found the perfect pair of strappy, dark brown, open-toed wedge shoes. They also found a gold bangle bracelet, dangly pink stoned earrings, and a dainty gold necklace with a pink glass bead and smaller baby blue and yellow stones. By the time they returned home, it was five o'clock.

"Hurry, he's going to be here at six to pick you up." Katie ushered her sister into her room and laid the clothes out on the bed while Julie went into the bathroom and turned on her curling iron. With all the changing of clothes, her hair had gotten a little static built up. Julie pulled her makeup case out from under the sink and began touch-ups as Katie rummaged through her panty drawer. "Ah ha!" She cried when she found the right pair of panties with a matching strapless bra.

Julie came out of the bathroom, her makeup done, her teeth brushed, and started undressing. She quickly put on the new outfit careful to step into it, so it didn't wreck her hair. "How do you feel?" Her sister Katie jumped up on her bed cross-legged and watched her put herself together.

"Nervous! Do you think that's weird? I've known him forever and yet I haven't."

Just then Megan burst into the room. "What's this I hear about a date with Cooper? It's true! Look at you!"

Julie looked at her, wondering what her thoughts were on the subject seeing as how she was supposed to be married to someone else at the moment. Julie didn't have time to worry about her because Shannon stormed through the door shouting, "How could you do this to Blake? He loves you and you threw that big, beautiful ring in his face after he stood by you. I think it is a disgrace. An outrage! -"

"Don't hold anything back do you?" Megan asked. She winked at Julie then and she knew not everyone was feeling that way, but it did dampen her spirits some.

Katie jumped off the bed, "Get lost. If you have nothing nice to say don't say anything at all." She made Megan smile. It sounded just like their mother. "If you don't leave, I'm calling mom."

Shannon glared at Katie, "Brat!" And with that left as quickly as she had come.

Megan joined Katie in cheering Julie on for the rest of her preparation and at six o'clock on the dot the doorbell rang.

The girls flew down the stairs and were greeted by the sight of their father shaking Cooper's hand. Cooper was in a hunter-green polo shirt that made his tan seem darker and his eyes were amazing, they almost had a hazel look tonight. He wore khaki-colored shorts, new white sneakers, and short socks so you could see his ankles. Julie didn't know ankles on a man could be sexy but his were. His golden hair looked wonderful on his tanned runner's calves.

Cooper was doing a similar inspection of his own and he approved, she could tell by the twinkle in his eye. "Are you ready to go?" He offered her his arm. She gave her sisters each a hug and thanked them for their help. Megan handed her a small purse she had retrieved from her room and filled it with lip gloss and other girly essentials. Julie then offered her dad a peck on the cheek and taking the hand Cooper offered, they walked outside. His hand felt warm and perfect. He opened the door for her and closed it after she was seated. Cooper ran around to the other side and got in and started the jeep.

"So, the suspense is killing me. Where are we going?"

"Good. Guess."

"Um..." and Julie guessed all right but never even came close to his big plans for the evening.

Twenty minutes later they arrived in a big field. In the middle of the field lay a hot air balloon. "Oh, Cooper this is so cool. I've never been in one before." Julie was so excited, "I think," she added as an afterthought.

An old man waited for them on the ground. The basket was lying on its side and the colorful balloon lay out on a giant tarp. Cooper shook his hand and clapped him on the back. He was introduced to Julie as Harvey.

Two younger men were using a giant fan to inflate the opening of the balloon. Then they turned on a burner and blew a flame into the opening. The balloon inflated and they tipped it right side up. Harvey hopped over the side like he was twenty years old and one of the younger men opened a door in the basket to let Cooper and Julie inside.

Cooper went to the back of the Jeep and pulled out a blanket and picnic basket. Julie held her hand out to Cooper and he gladly accepted it. They walked hand in hand into three-quarters of the wicker basket. It was sectioned off from Harvey and the tanks that controlled the hot air balloon. The man closed the basket and locked it, "Enjoy your evening sir, madam."

"Thank you," they said in unison. They untied the balloon and started their ascent.

It took a lot of work to get the hot air balloon into the night sky. Julie watched in amazement as Harvey manipulated the aircraft above the ground to a cruising altitude.

On two sides, instead of a wicker basket was clear plexiglass that allowed them to see out without leaning over the basket. Cooper laid out the blanket and set the picnic basket on it.

Holding onto one of the edges Julie slipped her shoes off and dropped three inches in height. She made herself comfortable on the blanket and Cooper joined her on the floor. The two of them sat with their backs against the divider between them and Harvey and enjoyed the view.

Cooper produced a chilled bottle of champagne and two long-stemmed glasses. He handed her the glasses and popped the cork. Julie held out her glass as he poured hers, then his. He put the cork back in and returned it to what looked like an insulated picnic basket and Julie handed him his glass.

"I propose a toast." Cooper lifted his glass and Julie did the same, "To sharing a beautiful sunset with a beautiful woman, to living every day to the fullest because we never know what tomorrow may bring." They touched their glasses together and their eyes held.

"Cheers," Julie said softly agreeing with the latter part of the toast. She had been living day to day, but she realized she had been putting too much emphasis on the future. She took a sip of the bubbly champagne.

They watched the world go by through the plexiglass in front of them. "Would you like to eat?" Cooper asked, "I got the best caterer in town, your mom."

Julie laughed, obviously her mom didn't have a problem with this date. Cooper grinned showing off the dimple in his chin.

"You look amazing by the way," Cooper said.

Julie smiled up at him. Cooper had knelt next to her to pull the food from the basket. Julie got up on her knees to survey the contents. When she did her arms were touching the hairs on his arms sending a shiver through her body.

"Are you cold? I brought jackets..." Cooper realized mid-sentence what caused her to shiver and he had to stop himself from experiencing one himself. Julie looked up at Cooper and willed him with her eyes to kiss her. She was so beautiful, her long red hair falling over her shoulders, her lips full and pink with a shine from her lip gloss. He knew he had been caught staring at her lips because she sucked part of her lower lip in and nervously worked her teeth over it. A habit she had developed in high school whenever she got nervous about something. Cooper couldn't resist he lowered his head and kissed her full on the lips.

Julie parted her mouth to him ready and willing for anything he had to give but his kiss, although intense, was quick. She glanced over her shoulder to see if Harvey had witnessed the kiss. When she realized he had given them some privacy she was thankful.

Cooper began rummaging through the food her mom had packed. It was a satisfying kiss, but it only made her want more. Julie decided to be bold and go after what she wanted. She placed her hand on his thigh. Cooper's breath caught in his throat, but he waited to see what her next move would be. He didn't have to wait long. Julie rose on her knees in front of him. He was on one bended knee the other leg was bent under him and he still pretended to be interested in what was in the basket. Cooper knew if someone offered him a million dollars, he wouldn't be able to tell them what was inside.

Julie contemplated what she should do to him to get his attention, not realizing she already had it. She placed her hands on his hips just below where his shirt fell and slowly worked her fingers under his shirt to touch his sides, his skin was warm and firm. Her fingers traveled inwards, and she could feel his springy chest hairs across his abdomen, he had a six-pack under there. Not only could she feel it, but she had a vivid memory of when he took his shirt off at her place after the water leak. Julie leaned closer and decided to lick his neck like he had done to her.

Cooper was surprised he'd lasted that long as he lifted her heart-shaped face and his lips met hers with intensity neither one knew they possessed. Cooper's tongue played with hers, she moaned and kissed him back. Without breaking the kiss, he sat back and brought her to sit across his lap. His free hand went down her throat across her collarbone and his other hand caressed her leg sliding up her thigh. Julie wanted to leap on him with the feelings that were coursing through her body, she also realized that, even with the privacy they were being given they couldn't continue on this path.

This time Julie pulled away and he knew why. He leaned his forehead against hers trying to regain control of the situation. "So, you want to try for dinner again?"

She smiled and kissed the tip of his nose, "That sounds like a great plan."

Dinner was delicious as always. There was bruschetta and sliced cucumbers as a starter, followed by chicken Waldorf wraps, a bean salad, and chocolate-covered strawberries for dessert. It was finger-licking good, so they were thankful her mom had remembered to pack napkins.

After dinner, they stood up to look around and experience a more 3D version of the hot air balloon experience. They watched as the sun got closer to the horizon, lighting up the sky with the most amazing shades of pink and orange. Cooper put his arm around her and together they leaned into each other their heads close, whispering things they saw to each other. They ended up landing on a golf course. "Why didn't we land where we took off?" Julie asked confused.

"The hot air balloon has a mind of its own it never lands in the same place. I'll take you folks back to your vehicle. I radioed ahead so my guys know where we landed," Harvey told them.

The owner's mode of transportation was a beat-up pickup truck. The two gentlemen who had helped get the hot air balloon in the air pulled up with a trailer attached to the back. They unhooked the trailer so they could pack up the basket and balloon while Harvey drove his passengers back to their vehicle.

Cooper helped Julie out of the hot air balloon holding on to her mom's picnic basket and blanket. He held the door open for her on the truck, put the basket in the back, and then climbed in beside her. Harvey was pleasant company and she felt guilty she hadn't taken the time to talk to him on the ride. She noticed all the deep lines in his hands as he wrestled the wheel of the truck on the dirt road they took back to Cooper's jeep. What a life he must've lived, the things he must have seen. They thanked him for the ride as he pulled up next to Cooper's Jeep.

Once inside the Jeep, Cooper turned the ignition and then held his hand out to Julie. A huge grin spread across her face as she placed her hand on his. This was a new start she thought to herself she was free from Blake and now she could start a life with Cooper.

She began to think that it wouldn't be so bad if her memory never returned. Her mind drifted and she began to wonder what a life with Cooper would be like. She was so engrossed in her thoughts that at first, she didn't realize what was going on.

Julie heard Cooper swear under his breath and when she turned to look at him, she saw the strain on his face as he was pumping the brakes that weren't working. She instantly let go of his hand so he could wrestle with the wheel. "Brace yourself," he warned as he tried to get the Jeep to slow down. They were on a dirt road and going downhill. He tried swerving the wheel and when that didn't work, he tried running the wheel off the beaten path to slow it down. They were approaching the main road and he could see traffic coming in both directions, even if they made it across the road without incident, there were woods and a ravine directly across the road. Cooper saw the embankment at the last minute and ran the Jeep up on its side.

CHAPTER TWENTY-ONE

H arvey Michaels had run his hot air balloon business for fifty-four years and had met and married his wife fifty years ago. He had been working at the county fair when she walked up to him with her friends, eating cotton candy. He fell head over heels the moment he had been introduced to Miss Kathleen and had asked her to marry him that night she said yes.

Together they had three beautiful daughters, seven grandchildren, and two great-grandchildren. Kathleen had been diagnosed with breast cancer six years ago and beat it. He had wanted to sell his business then, but she wouldn't let him, knowing it was a passion of his.

Tonight, when he had seen the two lovebirds on the hot air balloon ride, he realized that Kathleen was his other great passion, and he was going to sell the business. Harvey wanted to take her around the world like they'd always talked about. He wanted to start with Italy, where they had honeymooned.

The dusk had quickly turned to darkness, so Harvey flicked on his headlights. He started to slow down because he saw reflectors in front of him on the road. Crazy kids, he thought they hadn't even pulled off the road to go at it. He slammed on the brakes when he realized the vehicle was upside down. Throwing the lever into park he jumped from his old pickup truck.

Harvey hobbled over to the driver's side window and found the driver hanging upside down still buckled and bleeding from the head. "Please help him," he heard from the other side of the cabin. He let out a sigh of relief at least one of them was alive. Running around he found the woman hanging upside down trying to release her seat belt. He tried and found it stuck.

"I'm going to lift you and you unbuckle, okay?" Harvey was already climbing in on his hands and knees ignoring the glass shards imbedding into his hands.

"Okay," Julie also nodded her head even though he couldn't see her. Harvey pushed her up releasing the weight against the seat belt and when Julie tried again, she was rewarded by falling on top of Harvey, for an old man he was built like a tank. He never flinched under the extra weight, and he quickly pulled her to safety.

"You stay here," he wanted her away from the wreck, knowing he had smelled gas. Harvey was worried about how much time they had before the Jeep caught fire if it might blow.

"No, I want to help. If his belt is stuck too, you're going to need me to release the lever when you lift him." Harvey didn't want to waste time fighting with her, partially knowing she was right.

"Fine," Harvey said running around the other side of the Jeep. Julie crawled back in her side and got her hand on the seat belt. Harvey hoisted Cooper up and Julie pressed the lever. Nothing.

Harvey looked up into Julie's frantic face.

"It didn't work, it's stuck."

Harvey tried and it wouldn't budge. "Come on I have a knife in the truck." Harvey motioned for her to vacate the truck.

"No, I'm staying here with Cooper."

"Listen. I smell gas it's not safe for you in here."

Cooper groaned, "Go," before slipping back into unconsciousness again. That was all Harvey needed to hear to drag Julie from the Jeep. She struggled on the way to his truck.

"The more you struggle the longer it's going to take me to get back to him." This sobered her right up and she ran to the truck of her own free will. Harvey retrieved the knife and tossed his cell phone to Julie.

Kathleen was never going to believe this story and she would laugh knowing that was the only phone call ever made on his cell phone. Julie was thankful for something to keep her busy and dialed 9-1-1.

"9-1-1 What is your emergency?"

"There has been an accident. My...boyfriend has been hurt he needs an ambulance."

"Okay, I'm dispatching an ambulance now. Was there anyone else injured?"

"No, no one else."

"Can you tell me where you are?"

"Umm," Julie was looking around but all she saw were trees. "We had gone on a hot air balloon ride."

"In Essex County? Off of 128?"

"Yes." Julie was excited to have remembered the sign on the main road.

"What about you? Are you all right? Was there another car involved?"

"No, I'm fine. It was just us."

"Tell me what happened."

Julie let out an ear-piercing scream before dropping the cell phone to the ground. The Jeep had just exploded.

CHAPTER TWENTY-TWO

J ulie paced outside of Cooper's room. The ER had finally let her go after picking out what must have been
a million shards of glass from her hands and knees. She
had thrown her hands over her face during the accident so
luckily not much of her face had been scratched up. The
nurse came out of the room Cooper had been assigned.
"You can see him now, he's awake."

Julie rushed past the nurse and into his room, Cooper
sat propped up with pillows looking weak with his eyes
half closed. He had a 4x4 bandage on his forehead, above
his left eye, the doctors had told her that he needed nine
stitches. His left arm was in a sling. It wasn't broken, just
a minor sprain on his left wrist. His right hand had an I.V.
and lay still next to his side.

"Oh, Cooper," Julie rushed to his side and sat down
on the bed next to him. She picked up his hand and began
kissing it. "I'm going to take such good care of you," Julie
promised.

Cooper smiled then winced at the pain in his face.
"Honey, that's great but, who are you?"

Julie looked up in shock. This can't be. He can't
possibly have amnesia too. What are the chances? "Maybe

if you kissed me, I might start to remember something," he asked innocently.

"I'm your sister!" Julie said quickly and as outraged as possible.

It was Cooper's turn to look shocked. They both burst into laughter at the same time. "I forgot how quick on your feet you could be." Cooper was still chuckling holding his bruised ribs.

"Here's something else I don't want you to forget," Julie said before leaning in for a kiss.

"Is this how the accident happened?" Julie's dad demanded loudly from the doorway. Julie jumped away from Cooper and ran to her parents and sisters. Nana went to her grandson's side taking the hand Julie had just let go of.

"That's what I want to know," a voice from the hallway asked.

The crowd, aka her family, parted like the Red Sea to allow the police officer access to the small hospital room. He pulled out his notepad and flipped it open. "Hello, Mr. Jackson. I'm Officer Sinclair. I was told by your doctor that there were trace amounts of alcohol in your bloodstream but not even close to the legal limit. So, seeing as alcohol wasn't a factor and there wasn't another car involved what occurred to cause this accident?"

Cooper locked eyes with Jack when he answered, "The Jeep had no brakes."

Jack walked up to the officer and requested a moment alone outside. The officer, knowing Jack's good standing with the mayor and even the chief of police, readily agreed. Outside the door, in hushed tones, Jack confronted him with his worst fear. "I believe someone may be trying to kill my daughter."

"And what gives you that impression sir?"

Jack told him about the camping trip just a few days ago and now this. "Well, I will have them examine the Jeep but more than likely we won't be able to prove what happened because of the damage done by the explosion. Have there been any more attempts that you know of?"

He shook his head, "No, not that I know of. She was involved in a car accident a while back, causing amnesia, but I don't believe there is any correlation between these other incidents."

"I'll still check into the car accident if you don't mind," he continued with Jack's nod, "Does your daughter have any enemies? What about you, sir? Is there someone that may be trying to get to you through her?"

Again, he shook his head. "Call your supervisor. I've already approached him about what happened on the camping trip. We also might look into the fact that this could be an attempt against Cooper. It was his Jeep we found the transponder on and his Jeep that had the brakes cut."

The officer nodded, "I will do that, keep a close watch on your daughter sir." And with that, he left.

Inside the room, Shannon pulled Julie into a corner. "What happened?" she asked anxiously, looking at the cop talking to their dad out in the hallway.

☐"We were coming home and suddenly we had no brakes. Cooper ran the Jeep up an embankment to try to slow us down and it ended up flipping us over." Julie tried to keep her voice down as much as possible, to spare her mom the anxiety she knew would follow such news. "Luckily someone came along because we were trapped inside the Jeep and Cooper was unconscious. The Jeep ended up exploding just seconds after Cooper was pulled out."

"Oh, my God," Shannon whispered. She had been holding Julie's hand as she recounted the events of earlier that evening and when she was done took her into her arms and held her tight. "I'm so sorry," she whispered.

"It's okay. We're okay," Julie tried to reassure her. Jack walked back into the room and Shannon let go of Julie.

CHAPTER TWENTY-THREE

C ooper was released from the hospital around midnight. Nana took Cooper home and Julie went home with her family.

No one even considered letting Julie go home to her townhouse with recent events. Everyone fell into bed immediately, exhausted from the long night at the hospital. The following morning Julie wandered downstairs in her pajamas, green and pink striped cotton pants, and matching tank top. When she sat down next to her dad at the table, he handed her a section of the paper.

Her mom was cooking up a storm in the kitchen when the doorbell rang. Everyone looked at one another before Jack stood up to answer the door. He came back with a splendid floral arrangement. Julie's face lit up when her dad placed it before her on the table.

"Ohh...look at those," her mom stopped all progress in the kitchen to come and admire Julie's flowers. They were white lilies accented with purple irises that had a touch of yellow on their petals surrounded by dark greenery. It was simply elegant.

Julie pulled out the card and read it to herself.

"Jewels,

A shoulder separation, a black and blue eye, total demolition of my Jeep, near-death experience, and it was still the best night of my life. Then again, any night or day spent with you will be the best day of my life. I am counting the seconds until I see you again. Love, Cooper"

Julie smiled and held the card to her chest. "I have to go," she said as she jumped up from the breakfast table and ran out the back door.

"You're not dressed," her mother called after her, but it was a futile attempt because her daughter was already halfway to the pond. "Jack," she said exasperated, her fists landing on her hips, "she's not even wearing shoes!" Sandy looked pleadingly to Jack for his help, but he just pulled the newspaper back up to his face, not before she saw his smile. After a deep sigh, she looked back out the window and a slow smile began to spread across her face as well. Go get him, Julie, she thought and with that went happily back to the kitchen.

Julie had to run the long way around fearful she would get stuck in the maze her feet were wet from the morning dew. Her hair wasn't brushed, and she had no makeup on but she didn't care. Reaching the front door and without thinking she just opened it up and ran inside. No one seemed to be around this morning, and she was somewhat grateful not to have to explain herself. Note in hand she took the stairs two at a time to Cooper's bedroom. Outside his door gave her pause, was he awake? Realizing she didn't care she flung the door open. Besides he had let himself into her house and bedroom countless times, no questions asked.

Julie burst inside, hair wild, chest heaving, wet feet and all. Cooper looked like he had been waiting for her, propped up in bed reading a book-well maybe not-reading but it was open before him. His chest was bare, and the rest was hidden beneath the covers. She held the note out to him, "How many seconds?"

"Nine hundred and twenty-four," Cooper said without hesitation. "You look beautiful," he meant every word.

She didn't care if he had made up the seconds count or not but flung herself into his arms. He grunted when she landed, his arm was still in a sling, but the bandage was off over his eye. It was no longer bleeding but scabbing over the gash he had received was going to leave a scar and he was sporting quite the shiner.

"Oh, I'm so sorry." Julie started to pull away from him, but his good left arm just encircled her waist pulling her back.

"I'm glad you came to see me."

"You are?" It made her heart race to hear those words.

"Yes."

"Good," she said as she snuggled up against his side careful not to hurt him. They ended up watching TV in bed all day long with bouts of making out. It was perfect. They took a break to raid the kitchen at lunch. Rose made them macaroni and tomato soup with grilled cheese sandwiches.

Later that night she groaned stretching in bed beside him, "I have to go."

"Are you sure?" he asked, "You can stay here tonight."

"Yes." She told him, "I've been here all day. I'm still in my PJs for crying out loud." She kissed him careful not to hurt his shoulder. "I'll see you tomorrow?"

"It's a date."

CHAPTER TWENTY-FOUR

T he next morning, she found Cooper in her parent's kitchen talking with her dad. They were both enjoying a cup of coffee.

"Good morning, Sunshine." Cooper smiled from his seat.

"Hey," She went to her dad and kissed him on the cheek then looked at Cooper, not sure as to what to do next. He looked up at her, his eyes sparkling, he could see her internal distress and he was having fun with it.

Yes, her parents had come in on them kissing in the hospital, but she still felt uncomfortable showing public displays of affection, especially since she was supposed to be married to someone else.

"Julie, would you like any potato pancakes this morning?" her mom asked. Phew, saved by the bell.

"Yes, yes I would." She quickly joined her mom behind the kitchen island. She could hear Cooper, chuckling behind her but he didn't call her out on it. Thank goodness.

After filling her plate with two potato pancakes that were stuffed with cheese and bacon and adding a dollop of sour cream and chives, she sat down on the opposite side of the table from Cooper.

"So, what do you two have planned today?"

Julie looked up with a mouth full towards Cooper. "Well, I was going to ask Julie if she wanted to be my chauffeur today. I was going to go car shopping seeing as the Jeep is no longer." He sniffed, mourning the loss of his vehicle.

"Sure. Dad, can I borrow the car?"

Her dad smiled at her, "Actually, that reminds me, Doug from the auto body shop called me last week and I forgot to tell you. Your car is ready to go. If you want, I can bring you down there when I go to work this morning."

"Okay, when do you leave?" Her mom joined them at the table.

"In about twenty minutes."

She poured herself a glass of orange juice from the pitcher sitting on the table, "Great. Thanks, Dad."

Jack smiled at her. "You're welcome."

Julie looked to Cooper, "Do you know what kind of vehicle you want?"

"Yes."

She looked at him expectantly. "Another Jeep."

She laughed, "Seriously?"

"I might let you pick out another color if you want. It doesn't need to be black."

They finished their breakfast and followed her dad out into the garage. She let Cooper have the front seat. Jack dropped them off at the auto body shop in town. A man in a gray jump suit came out to greet them. The name on his shirt said "Doug."

"Cooper," Doug shook his good hand. "What the hell man? I heard about the Jeep. They tell me it was totaled."

"Sad but true," Cooper confirmed.

Doug turned towards Julie and smiled. "The good news is your car is as good as new, for you Jewels."

She looked at Cooper surprised at his use of her nickname. "We graduated with Doug," Cooper explained.

"Shit, yeah!" he said. "Awe man I forgot you forgot about all of us."

She laughed. She tapped the side of her head, "It's in here somewhere."

"It's probably good she can't remember you," Cooper teased Doug.

"I got her drunk one time!"

"Yeah, when she was sixteen!"

Julie was quite entertained by these two. She had gotten drunk when she was sixteen. She would have to remember to ask the story behind that.

"Let me get you your keys." Doug jogged off towards his office.

He came back and handed them over to her, "Lucy, is right over there." He pointed over where there were parked cars.

"Lucy?" she asked.

Cooper chuckled, "Yeah, that's what you named your car. Your parents bought it for you at graduation."

There were four cars lined up all facing out. There was a black Toyota Corolla, a red Nissan Maximum, a silver Honda Accord, and a blue Ford Fusion.

"Any guesses?"

"The red one?" The two men grinned at each other. "Am I right?"

Doug pointed to her keys, "Try clicking the unlock button to see," he suggested.

She held the keys out and pressed the button. She squealed with delight when the red car flashed. She signed some paperwork then after saying goodbye to Doug she and Cooper hopped in Lucy.

As they drove away Julie asked, "So how did my car get the name Lucy?"

"She's your favorite redhead." At her confused look, he explained, "She was a 1950s funny girl housewife. She had her own TV show called "I Love Lucy." We used to watch reruns."

He gave her directions to the Jeep dealership. They walked up and down the line of Jeeps looking at colors and options. Cooper's old Jeep was sporty and rugged, but they started looking at more of the luxury of the Grand Cherokee.

They took a couple of test drives. "So, what do you think?" Their salesman asked Cooper.

"Don't ask me. She's the boss." He deferred to Julie.

She looked up startled, "What?"

"Do you like any of them? Which color do you like?"

"I do like them, but it's your vehicle. You should pick."

"Well, can you help narrow down the colors for me? Which two do you like?"

She contemplated for a minute then said, "Well your last one was black and that really does look nice, but you should probably pick something different. I like the way the white and blue look."

CHAPTER TWENTY-FIVE

J ulie walked out on her back porch, it was pitch black outside and she could hear the crickets and bullfrogs in the pond. Everyone inside had retired for the night. She was wearing a blue bikini. She had found it in her dresser drawers among four other bathing suits. She tried them all on and liked this one the best.

Reaching over she flicked on the lights that illuminated the in-ground pool. Then she flicked on the back porch light and flicked the switch three times. She took her fluffy white towel down the steps with her and flung it onto a chaise lounge chair. Kicking off her flip flops as she walked around to the back of the pool where the diving board was.

Bending down she dipped her hand into the water realizing her parents had a heater installed because the temperature was just right for a night swim. Steam from the pool rose up in front of her like a light fog. Julie climbed up onto the diving board and dove gracefully into the pool. As a last-minute thought, that made her heart race she prayed that she could swim as she broke the plane of the water. She easily swam from one end of the pool to the other gliding through the chlorinated liquid under the surface. When she came up for air on the other side near the stairs, she ran her hands over her face and down her hair removing the excess water.

"Hey there," came a voice from behind her.

Startled, she turned around and was relieved to find Cooper standing there. He was wearing black swim trunks matching flip flops and a sultry smile. His sling was gone as of that morning she had driven him to the doctor's office and was told he was fine without it. His black and blue bruising had turned to green and yellow and was hard to see under his tanned skin. He took her breath away, his chiseled chest tanned from the summer sun and his muscled calves with golden hair made her want to swallow her tongue.

"Hi," she managed.

Cooper grinned at her she was wearing his favorite swimsuit. He couldn't get over how his life was turning out, madly in love with the girl next door. He kicked off his flip-flops in the direction of hers and walked into the warm water down the stairs. Julie was wading in the water and started to swim slowly backward as if she was being stalked, which she was.

Cooper took his time coming after her. She had a come and get me grin on her face that reflected in his don't think I won't grin. Julie ended up against the back wall of the swimming pool where the sides of the pool came up and her feet could touch. When he got to the deep end, he dove under the water and swam to her. When he resurfaced he came face to face with her. He wiped his face so he could see her green eyes.

Julie placed her hands on his chest, and she could feel the strong beat of his heart. Her hands slid up over his shoulders and his arms wound tightly around her small frame. She lifted her head for a kiss and he gave her one. It was a gentle kiss, not demanding just telling her how he felt about her. That he would always take care of her, that he loved her and no other.

After his accident, they had decided to take it slow. They had talked it over and decided it might be best to date first. They had gone to the movies, and out to dinner. They rode their bikes along the coast and stopped for a picnic. He had taken her to shows in Boston. Today she had taken him to the doctor's office. They had told him he didn't need to wear the sling anymore.

Stolen moments between them proved that it was getting harder and harder to resist.

CHAPTER TWENTY-SIX

J ulie had picked out a flowy dress with spaghetti straps it had a blue, green, and white swirl pattern that came down to just above her knees.

Her hand was firmly in Cooper's as they boarded his family yacht. Cooper shook the captain's hand and re-introduced Julie. "Julie, this is Captain Tom." He was an older gentleman with broad shoulders, a barrel chest, and a white bushy beard. He was dressed nicely in a white sailor's uniform complete with the captain's hat.

"Miss Julie!" his voice was booming and jovial as he clasped her hands between his two meaty ones. He leaned closer and spoke like he meant for it to be a whisper, but it was more like someone's normal tone, "I've heard about your troubles."

She smiled warmly at him, "Thank you, Captain Tom. It is nice to meet you."

He leaned back and let out a large belly laugh, "I'm sorry." He said wiping the corners of his eyes, "I don't mean to laugh but I've known you since you were just a little lass!" he gestured with his hand holding it flat and towards the ground as he spoke. He sobered some but still held a grin on his face, "Welcome aboard," he gave them both a salute.

Julie returned his smile, and they boarded the yacht. Melissa was there to greet them dressed in a long summer dress in a shade of coral pink that looked amazing against her dark hair.

The two women raced to greet each other arms outstretched like they hadn't seen each other in ages. After their embrace, Melissa took Julie's arm and ushered her over to a tall, good-looking man standing by a table that had refreshments and snacks. He held a beer in one hand and the other was in his pocket. He had short brown hair, and she couldn't tell what color his eyes were because he had dark sunglasses over them. When they reached him, Melissa introduced him, "Julie, this is my boyfriend, Chad. Chad, this is my best friend, Julie."

She looked at Melissa, "I haven't met him before?"

"Nope, we just recently started dating."

Chad pushed his sunglasses up on his head. His eyes were a nice shade of green Julie noted as he reached to shake her hand. Cooper came up behind her and Melissa introduced the two men. They shook hands. "Nice to meet you, Chad," Cooper said.

"Same here," Chad replied.

Cooper's arm slipped comfortably around Julie's waist. Melissa wiggled her eyebrows at Julie, and she tried not to giggle.

Julie loved being in a new relationship, everything felt amazing and was exciting. She often wondered about Blake and why she hadn't fallen for him again. She had before. People often said things were about timing, but it still made her nervous about the path she had chosen. Would she have been happy with either man? She didn't know. She felt like she was playing a game but didn't have all the right pieces. Could she win the game without them? The couples engaged in chit chat talking around her as she tried to process her thoughts.

When she finally tuned back into the conversation, she learned that Chad was in marketing and that's how he and Melissa had met. She also discovered what Melissa did for a living. "I work for a top publishing company in Boston."

"Oh really?" That piqued Julie's interest, "Did you publish my book?"

Her friend smiled, "I did."

"Well, if I haven't said it before, thank you!"

Her friend laughed, "You have told me like a million times."

"Well, I guess you know I mean it. What made you want to get into publishing?"

"You did actually. When I met you, I never saw you without a book in your hand. I started reading what you read. We took Journalism class together and joined the school newspaper. I fell in love with books."

"Well, I might not remember everything but I do know I have not lost my love of books."

Two more couples boarded the ship, and she was introduced to Lauren and her boyfriend Hudson. Lauren was a pretty brunette with blue eyes. Julie found out that Lauren had gone to high school with her, Melissa, and Cooper. She remembers her from the journal entries.

Melissa introduced Julie to Greg, her assistant from the publishing company. He was adorable with his spiky faux Mohawk hair and electric blue glasses. Greg introduced Julie to his boyfriend Todd.

After that several more people strolled in, and she started to lose track of all the names. There were friends of Cooper's and coworkers of hers from the college, soon the boat was full. The yacht pulled out of the dock and the music was cranked up. They laughed and danced. The food and drinks flowed freely. They watched the sunset and then twinkling lights strung over their heads with sphere-colored lanterns gave off a nice romantic glow.

The DJ on the upper deck changed the fast-paced music to something slower tempo and couples gathered together, swaying in each other's arms. Julie looked up at

Cooper as his hands caressed her down low on her hips that were swaying side to side. She thought back to a time, not that long ago when she had watched him dance with Courtney, it had made her so jealous, and had wished Julie could trade places with her. The look he had given her that night had been smoldering as if he wished the same thing. □She could feel a tightening in her chest as she looked up at him and that same look, he had given her that night reappeared. He lowered his head and she rose up on her toes desperate to meet his lips. She could feel his fist clench on her hips through her dress. People danced around them, and they were oblivious to anything outside of their embrace. Cooper was the one to pull away leaving her craving more. Gazing down at her, he knew she did.

His hand took hers, "I want to take you on a tour," and maneuvering between their friends, Cooper escorted her from the dance floor. He took her through the wide opening in the back of the yacht. There was a living room with white sectional couches that were occupied by several groups of people. Past that, they walked through a dining and kitchen area. Taking her down the corridor he showed her the bedrooms but there were people everywhere, not a quiet space to be found. She was amazed by the beauty of the boat and how elegantly it was designed.

Cooper retraced their steps back out on the deck and pulled her upstairs, nodded to the DJ as they walked by, and he took her into the yacht's wheelhouse. Inside was Captain Tom manning the boat, looking out over the wide expanse of windows she could see the lights of the city in the distance. When they left Cooper took her up one more level to an observation deck and found another couple had already occupied one of the benches up there. So back down two flights of stairs, they went. Cooper was starting to get frustrated and seriously considered throwing everyone overboard as he led her down the outside corridor that had been roped off. Cooper unclipped the rope letting Julie pass then re-clipped it behind him, there was decking above them and open to the sea on the left side with a hip-high railing. From here they could hear the party, but it was more muffled. It was dark and secluded and they could feel the gentle sway of the ocean slapping against the yacht.

Cooper leaned up against the railing and pulled her in close, she fit easily between his thighs. His hand grazed her chin, cupping it gently. Even sitting he was almost at eye level with her. She copied him by putting her hand on his face and lowered her lips to his. He sucked in a breath drawing her near and their bodies meshed together her breast was just below his neck. His free hand found the edge of her dress and worked his way slowly up her thigh, she moaned into his mouth. His hand squeezed her rear end. He could feel the outline of her panties they felt like lace. One of his fingers deliberately slipped just under her panties caressing her curvy bottom. She became instantly wet. What was he doing to her? His hand followed the outline around to the front, pushing her panties aside ever so gently his long middle finger found her aroused. She spread her legs ever so slightly for him, inviting him in where his finger found her folds slick and it made him hard. He desperately wanted to be inside her.

Suddenly there was a loud noise at the end of the corridor, and they broke apart but just barely. They could see the other couple but they were pretty sure they themselves were hidden in the dark. The couple wasn't even looking their way and Julie was glad to see that they appeared entirely too involved with themselves, laughing and having a good time to notice the couple all but ripping each other's clothes off. Cooper pulled her across the hall to a little alcove, he leaned her back against the wall and he kissed her again. His kisses trailed down her neck and across her collarbone.

His hands were gentle as he kissed his way across her chest. Kneeling in front of her, Cooper took her dress in his hands twisting it up then he tucked it between her and the wall. Julie looked down at him, raking her hand through his hair. She thought she might lose her mind, as

147

the passion rose inside her making her tingle with antici-pation. He kissed the tops of her thighs and she thought she might explode. She looked desperately for something to hold on to. There was a fire extinguisher and a floatation ring on either side of her head, it would have to do.

He kissed her through her baby blue lace panties, her head rolled back, and her hips rocked eagerly forward. His mouth opened, cupping her womanhood, his tongue tasting her through the lacy material, and she moaned her pleasure. He helped her out of her undergarment and put them in his pocket. Then ran his hand down the back of her thigh, when he got to the back of her knee, he lifted her left leg and rested it on his shoulder. The scruff of his beard scratched the inside of her thigh exciting her even more. His lips touched her again with no panties as a barrier and she almost came undone. She whimpered craving his touch.

He toyed with her at first, little flicks of his tongue grazing her, causing her body to quiver. One of his hands grasped her hip the other covered her smooth round bot-tom and pulled her closer to his hot mouth. Cooper stroked her with the length of his tongue, ravishing her thoroughly enjoying the sweet taste of her.

She gasped and moaned his name, "Cooper, I can't keep quiet. We are going to have to stop." Her hand went back to his hair pulling him away from her. He stood slowly her leg sliding off his shoulder and down the length of his muscular arm. He kissed her again, she could feel the cool breeze across her naked lower half as he pulled back. He gazed knowing he had never seen a woman as beautiful as Julie was, especially aroused by his touch. Her eyes had glazed over with desire and her arms came up around his neck drawing him back to her. Cooper's fingers found her again and slid slowly inside her, teasing her clit with his thumb. He knew he was driving her passion to the edge when she groaned a low, almost animalistic moan into his mouth.

He knew she was feeling a little self-conscious but he also knew that no one would be able to hear over the thumping beat of the music and damn how he wanted to make her moan like that again, he wanted to hear it over and over again. It was exhilarating to know he was the one bringing her to the height of pleasure. He pulled away from her and she stumbled forward wondering where he was going, embarrassed she had become oblivious to her surroundings yet again. Cooper pulled her skirt down and took her hand.

"Are we going back to the party?" she asked still breathless.

He kissed her gently, "No, Sweetheart. I have one more place to show you."

"Oh," was all she could manage still feeling tipsy from his lovemaking.

His hand cupped hers and he pulled her along the edge of the boat's corridor, away from the party. They turned inwards then down another hall and came out to the front of the yacht. She couldn't believe her eyes, "Is that what I think it is?" she asked incredulously. In the darkness, she could see his grin, "Yeah, that's the family helicopter." She could see the outline of it. He flicked on a light switch that illuminated small round lights on the floor in a circle surrounding the helicopter. They could still hear the thumping of the music, but they were secluded from the rest of the party and no one was allowed up here.

He ushered her over to the door and helped her climb inside. She glanced around the cabin, two plush leather bench seats were facing each other. She sat on the one facing the front of the helicopter. He got in shutting the door behind him and taking a seat opposite her. They sat for a silent second gazing into each other's eyes, sexual tension building between the two of them.

"Do you think anyone will hear you in here?" he asked softly.

She shook her head slowly, "Why," she asked coyly, "do you think there is going to be a reason I might be making noise?" Feeling more confident they wouldn't be interrupted made her want to turn the tables on him just a bit. Deciding to show him he wasn't the only one who could seduce, she dropped her shoulder and the strap of her dress slid down her arm. She turned to look at it then looked up innocently at him, knowing his gaze had followed the descent of the strap. Gratified that her skills as a seductress hadn't been missed as she saw him swallow, hard.

He nodded his head slowly, this time it was his eyes that were glazed over with anticipated passion as their eyes locked again. Julie uncrossed her shapely legs, every movement deliberate, intending to drive him mad for her as she had been moments before. She rose slowly crossing the short distance to him. Lifting her skirt, she exposed her long tan legs and gave him a little reminder that he still carried her panties in his pocket with a quick glimpse before she straddled him. Resting her naked ass on his lap she combed her hand through his hair. Julie could feel the evidence of his arousal through his shorts. It was making her already wet center ache to end this game and take him deep inside her. Instead, she asked, "Did you like that?" referring to her strap falling.

Sure, his tongue had swollen to twice its normal size he merely nodded his handsome head. She took the hand that was in his hair and crossing herself gently slid the other strap slowly off her lightly tanned shoulder and down her toned arm. "What about that?"

"Yes," he whispered almost choking on his desire for her.

Her hands rested on his chest, she could feel the strength of him beneath his shirt, and her desire to feel him overwhelmed her. She tugged at his shirt, and he leaned forward so she could help him out of it, eager to dispel anything blocking contact with their skin. It was quickly discarded on the floor behind her as her hot tongue stroked his warm skin, kissing his collarbone, tasting him.

Simultaneously, his hands worked their way under her dress rubbing her thighs getting dangerously close to her center then working his way back down. Julie kissed and licked his neck, and nibbled on his ear as his hands came back up and grasped her bottom and squeezed. She moaned, "That feels good," she told him in a whisper.

He licked and lightly nipped her neck with his teeth, "I'm glad."

She let out a sigh, "That also feels incredible."

"Everything you do is amazing."

She rocked her hips, grinding in his lap, "You think so?"

His hands tightened on her hips, "Most definitely."

She reached down and unbuttoned his shorts, "Let me help you out of these." He was more than willing to help her and together they removed his shorts, boxers, and shoes. He pulled a condom out of his pocket and held it up for her to see. She took the foil packet from him and opened it putting it on for him, rolling it down the rock-hard length of him.

Cooper helped Julie pull her dress over her head. She hadn't worn a bra today, and now freed of the dress her breast stood perky awaiting his assault. Cooper was more than happy to oblige, and his strong hand came up to her bare back, pulling her erect nipples closer to his face. He breathed in the scent of her. His tongue flicked at her nipples making them tingle in their hardness. She arched her back pushing her breasts towards him begging for more. Obliging, he took each one inside his mouth and suckled hard. She inhaled sharply but didn't pull away. Her arms wound their way around his shoulders and held him close. His teeth raked across her nipples, she whimpered and rocked her hips against him. Cooper was rock hard between her thighs as her moist warmth cradled him, she was slick, and he was rubbing against her but hadn't yet penetrated her.

She tugged on his hair pulling his chin up so she could meet his wet lips for a kiss. Their tongues swirled together. Her tender breasts pressed against his chest. Their lips were brutal in their desperate need for each other. Her hand slid down between their bodies and she guided him inside her. Cooper's hands ran down the length of her back to her curvy hips and down her thighs then back up again. Her hands gripped the headrest behind his head and used it to pull herself up and glide back down on his long shaft.

Julie's sighs became throaty moans, which were followed by cries of passion. The sounds of ecstasy filling the cabin of the helicopter were sweet music to Cooper's ears. He picked her up and laid her out on the opposite bench seat. He hovered above her gazing into her eyes. She reached up and brushed his hair aside then pulled him down to her. Her legs wrapped around his hips.

He drove his hard manhood deep inside her, kissing her feverishly. Her arms went up his back and held on tight as he thrust inside her pushing her across the seat. Julie had to put a hand up to brace herself against the door panel. One of his elbows was braced next to her head his other hand found its way into her hair cradling her head.

Her hand roamed down his backside while she licked his neck followed by a light nibble. The windows of the helicopter were fogging up around them, neither noticed nor cared. His hand traveled down the side length of her body ending at the crook of her knee and held her. Each thrust was becoming more purposeful than the last until both of them were panting and climaxing. Julie shuddered with her completion, Cooper holding himself above her. He leaned down and kissed her sweetly then just held her tight, still inside her.

She kissed his neck, "Hmmm," she purred into his ear, "you know how to make a girl feel satisfied."

He pulled back to look down at her again he seemed to be searching her soul. Satisfied? He was glad and he would take it, but did she feel loved too? He wanted desperately to tell her that he loved her, that he had always loved her, had never loved anyone but her, but he didn't dare push his luck with her. He knew how fragile she was. He eased out of her and scooted to the side of the bench seat, still holding her close. He stroked her bare back and she curled a leg over his hip. They lay there for a while, basking in each other's embrace.

When they were getting dressed, she panicked, "I can't find my underwear."

He grinned, "I have them in my pocket."

She waited expectantly.

"I would like to keep them for the rest of the party. I want to know you are walking around with no panties and I could just..." he let her imagination fill in the blank.

"Oh," she said breathlessly because she could envision several different scenarios that were all steamy.

"I have something for you," he told her. Cooper reached for his shorts, and she reached up to receive her present. She didn't know what to expect but she was pleasantly surprised when he fished out a bracelet. It was the one they had looked at so long ago after their fishing trip.

"Cooper! Thank you. I love it. When did you?"

Cooper laughed, "You're welcome. I went the day after you spotted it and picked it up for you. I've had it for a while. I've been waiting for the right time to give it to you."

She got to her knees and put her hands on his thighs. She leaned in for a kiss which he gladly gave her. "It's perfect. Can you help me with it?"

"I would love to."

He took the bracelet out of the box and clasped it around the delicate wrist she offered to him. Cooper lifted her wrist and gave it a light kiss with a seductive look in his eye. I'm in big trouble, she thought. At that moment she knew she was falling hard and fast for the boy next door.

Chapter Twenty-Seven

The next day Cooper took her to her apartment and she had him help her log back onto her computer. "What's my password again?" she asked. He came into the room and logged in for her.

"Let me write it down for you."

"Thanks."

"You're welcome."

Julie opened up her email as Cooper was walking out of the room but came up short when he heard her say, "Oh boy."

"What?" he asked curiously.

She was staring at the computer and began to rub her temples. "I forgot about this kid," her hand pointed to the screen. "I have a dozen messages from Andrew."

"Who?"

"Remember the kid that was in my office? I saw him again at the mall before our first date. I still haven't reread his paper. I'm not even sure what I can do at this point."

"Just read it then tell him there is nothing you can do. I'm sure the grade you gave him in the first place was accurate."

She sighed heavily. "Alright, well I could be a while."

"I'll just hang out downstairs and watch something on TV."

"Thanks."

"No problem."

She opened one of the emails because they all had an attachment and began to read.

Fifteen minutes later the doorbell rang, she got up to answer the door, glad to have a distraction. Running down the stairs she came up short, Cooper had the front door open, and Blake was standing there. He looked pitiful.

"Can I talk to you?" Blake asked.

What was the right answer? She looked at Cooper. He shrugged. Blake watched the exchange between the two and his shoulders slumped. She finished her way down the stairs. "I'll be right back," she told Cooper as she stepped out onto her front stoop and closed the door behind her. She sat on one side, her arms folded across her chest, and waited for him to speak.

"You look great, Sweet-" he stopped himself.

"Thanks, Blake."

"Are you with Cooper now?"

"Is that what you came here to ask me?" she wanted to know.

He shook his head. "I miss you. What happened to us? We were supposed to be husband and wife."

Julie felt bad that he was devastated, and she had happily moved on. Her heart broke a little for him. "I'm sorry, Blake. I am. I don't know what I can do to make it better for you."

He moved close to her, and she leaned back. "I want you to marry me." His voice cracked and a lump began to form in her throat.

"I wish-" what? That she had never got amnesia? She would be married to him and not with Cooper. Was that how it was supposed to be?

"I can't eat, I can't sleep." He told her. "I wish you could see how much your decision is affecting me. I can't get any work done. They sent me home today."

It felt like there was a knife in her chest. What was she doing? She hadn't thought much about how this was affecting him. Had she made the right decision? She had questioned it numerous times after finding happiness with Cooper she hadn't allowed her brain to search the dark recesses of her mind further.

"I understand you're hurting. I don't know why I didn't fall back in love with you. I wish I had known. Maybe someday I will know, but right now I just don't have it in me to fight for us."

"I have enough fight for the both of us," he vehemently assured her.

She took his hand and said softly, "I know you do Blake. I'm just-" she heaved a big sigh, "I'm sorry." She leaned up and kissed him on the cheek quickly. "Goodnight, Blake."

Releasing his hand, she left him out on her front stoop and went back inside. He didn't try to stop her. She closed the door softly behind her and half expected Cooper to be standing right there, but he wasn't. She found him in the kitchen. Julie stopped when she saw him, and he rushed to her side when he saw her face. He swallowed her up in his embrace. Her arms went around him and up his back holding him close. She felt utterly miserable. Ten minutes ago, she was on cloud nine, now she was in the depths of despair. Her body felt drained, weak and vulnerable. She needed time to think. She pulled back from Cooper. "I think I'm going to spend the night here."

"Okay," he said misunderstanding.

"Alone."

She saw the moment registration crept across his face, "What did he say to you?" he wanted to know.

"Does it matter?" she asked frustrated.

So was he, "If it means I'm out and he's back in then yeah, it matters." His voice was rising slowly.

"I don't know what it means. I just know that it isn't just you and me, but he was involved too."

"Are you kidding me? He isn't in the equation anymore. Remember? You gave him back the ring that means, no longer involved!"

She gestured with her arm outstretched towards the door. "He is still showing up at my front door I would say that puts him in the equation!"

Cooper got eerily calm, "Only if you let him."

Her hands dragged across her face, and she let out a frustrated growl. "I just need time to think."

"Are you considering going back to him?" he demanded.

"No." She let that sink into his brain before continuing and before he got too excited, "I do think, however, maybe we should cool it for a while."

Oh, he was mad. Fuming mad, she didn't have to know him for a lifetime to see it on his face. Honestly, she didn't blame him. She was kind of pissed off herself.

"I'm sorry, Cooper." She was apologizing a lot tonight, over things that were out of her control, well to an extent.

He walked to the door, and she stood in place, unable to face him. His hand was on the door "I'll see you-" he stopped himself, "when I see you." He hadn't gone a day without seeing her this entire summer, not one single day since the accident. He didn't know how long this "cooling off period" would last so he had no idea what to expect.

He shut the door behind him with some force and she jumped. She hadn't been able to turn around because she had fat hot tears streaking down her face. Falling to her knees she put one hand to her mouth trying to hold back the sobs that were escaping, and one arm wrapped around her stomach trying to ease the pain she felt in her chest. Doubled over she rocked herself back and forth.

Her cell phone rang, and she instantly thought, Cooper. She wiped her tears and sobered up for the call, "Hello."

"Hey, Sweetie. I was just wondering if you and Cooper were going to be home for dinner?"

She started crying again, "Mom." She wailed into the phone, "I don't know what to do."

"Julie, my baby, what's wrong? Did something happen? Are you hurt? Are you okay?" She was firing questions off at a rapid pace.

"Blake showed up and I had a fight with Cooper."

"Okay, honey this is what you are going to do. Are you listening?"

"Yes," she sniffled wiping her running nose again.

"You are going to go upstairs and draw a bath. You are going to get in it and soak. I will be over shortly with a bottle of wine and Chinese. Can you do that for me?"

She nodded her head then said into the phone pitifully, "Yes."

"Okay, I will see you shortly. I love you, Julie."

"Thanks, Mom. I love you too." She clicked off her phone and did exactly what her mom had told her to do and went upstairs to take a bath.

Sandy Hart found her daughter in a bubble bath when she got there. She had brought up two glasses of red wine. Julie sat up and took one of the glasses. Her eyes were swollen and red, "Thanks, Mom."

Sandy stroked her daughter's hair. "You're welcome. Now get out, put on some comfy pajamas, come downstairs, and let's talk this out over food and wine. I brought extra wine." Her mom smiled warmly at her then got off the side of the bathtub where she had perched and waited for Julie downstairs.

Julie had to admit she did feel a little better after soaking in the tub and crawling into a pair of cozy pajamas. She found her mom sitting on the couch holding a hairbrush. "Come sit," she told her.

Still holding her wineglass, Julie walked over and plopped down on the floor in front of her mom. "Why don't you tell me what happened," Sandy asked gently.

Julie took a sip of wine and gave a deep sigh. It was easier not to face her mom to recount everything that had happened. She told her everything, the kiss with Cooper

when she was still with Blake, breaking off the engagement, the party, the camping trip, and even if she had
thought better about it, she told her mom about the yacht.
Her mom stroked her hair with the brush soothing her
further into the submission of her confession. When she
was done her mom had her hair in a neat French braid
down her back.

Her mom refilled her wine glass and went to get
the Chinese from the kitchen. Meanwhile, Julie stood up
and stretched before she settled herself comfortably on the
couch. Her mom returned with containers of food and
wooden chopsticks. She pulled the coffee table closer to
them and laid the cartons out while Julie opened some of
the containers and took a deep sniff of food. It all smelled
delicious.

She took the chicken lo Mein and began wrapping
the long noodles up on her sticks and shoveled it into her
mouth. After a couple of bites, she asked her mom, "What
do you think I should do?"

Her mom took a really deep breath, "I'm afraid I really
can't answer that question for you. Only you can. I know
it is really hard for you to do because you don't have all the
information. You will just have to go by what you know at
this moment.

I love both of them. Cooper has been a part of our
family forever and you two grew up as best friends. I think
that is an important foundation.

On the other hand, I've known Blake for years.
He is also someone, like Cooper, who is kind, smart, and
funny. You were planning on marrying him. The date was
planned, there was a ring on your finger, bridesmaids were
in dresses, and we were on the way to the church when we
got the phone call that you had been in a car accident.

Sweetie, you've hit a bump in the road and, under-
standably, you are confused about your options. I wish I
could help more but in the long run, this is your life, and
you need to make the best decision for you. Never mind
how it is going to affect Blake or Cooper. Clearly, they

will both be devastated if you don't choose them. Who wouldn't be? You are a smart, beautiful, talented young woman that any man would be lucky to have."

Julie listened with great intensity as her mom spoke. She was hoping to gain some golden nugget, some perfect "ah ha" answer but what she was looking for wasn't there. She understood what her mom was saying she just wished her mom could decide for her. Putting down her food she laid across the couch putting her head in her mom's lap. "Can we just watch TV for a while?" she asked.

Her mom stroked the side of her face, "Of course we can, Sweetie." Sandy reached for the remote and flipped on the television.

CHAPTER TWENTY-EIGHT

The next day she didn't hear from Cooper or Blake, not that she expected to. Well, she had hoped. She still felt rotten, it was even worse when she had found the diary she kept here. This was a current one she found under her pillow, and she had stayed up reading until the early hours of the morning. It was filled with descriptions of her dates with Blake and what a great guy he was. ☐

She didn't know what to do with herself. She wandered around her empty house, looking through drawers and closets. She flipped through books in her study when she remembered the email she was looking at when Blake had shown up the night before. Oh crap, she really needed to finish reading that paper. Andrew had sent her a dozen messages and had seen her twice this summer. She woke the computer up by moving the mouse. What was her password? Was that just last night, when she was happy, before her whole world had come crashing down, again?

Her hand spread across the paper that had Cooper's handwriting on it, she missed him. Typing in the password her computer came alive. There was Andy's email sitting there staring back at her. Taking her time, she read line by line through the paper. It was a good paper. The information was accurate, but something nagged at the back of her mind. What was it? Getting lost in the paper she decided to research the subject matter. She began a Google search to find the answers. She spent hours engrossed in the subject matter. It was her stomach that reminded her that she needed to eat.

Getting up she went downstairs to the fridge. It was empty except for old pizza and last night's Chinese, "Score." After microwaving the Chinese, she brought it back upstairs with her and settled back in at the computer. It was late when she found what had been nagging her. Andy's paper was plagiarized. It was as clear as day when she found it.

Julie sat back in her chair. Unbelievable. She wasn't sure of the college's policy on this, but she would guess it was expulsion. Her mind chewed over the information. What should she do? She picked up the phone, then realizing she didn't know who she should call she put it back down.

It was after nine. How had the day gotten away from her? She was surprised and hurt that Cooper hadn't called her. She knew what she had said, and she did need time to think but she missed his presence in her life. She decided to leave the email until tomorrow, what was one more day going to do?

She crawled into bed and fell asleep.

CHAPTER TWENTY-NINE

C ooper was devastated, pissed, and unbelievably scared. His insides were twisting and felt like they were going to explode inside his body. He wasn't sure what to do. He wanted to find Blake and beat him to a bloody pulp. If he was being honest with himself Blake should want to kill him. Cooper had taken advantage of Julie when she was vulnerable. She had broken off her engagement because of him.

He thought maybe she would come running out to stop him. Tell him she had made a terrible mistake. She didn't need any more time or want to think anything over. Tell him that she has fallen in love with him. Cooper walked slowly to his car, but she didn't come. He drove home slowly hoping she would call him to come back but she didn't. When he'd returned home, and it didn't seem promising that Julie would call he picked up his phone.

Jack answered on the second ring. "Hello," boomed through the phone.

"Nothing's wrong," Cooper prefaced by saying, "but we have a problem."

"Sandy just left here in a hurry so, I'm assuming it has something to do with that."

Cooper cringed. He didn't like his girlfriend's parents knowing about the fight they just had but he needed to keep Julie safe. Even though they hadn't had any more accidents there was still someone out there that wanted to hurt Julie. Raking his hand through his thick hair he sighed, "Yeah, she wants to spend the night alone at her place."

Letting the implications of his words seep in, Jack's response was not what he was expecting. Hearing the other man's sigh Jack told him, "I've had an undercover police detail on you two since the brakes in the Jeep went out."

Cooper was shocked and relieved at the same time. "I had no idea," he confessed.

"That was the idea, Cooper. I'm not taking any chances, with my baby girl."

"I don't blame you. Thanks, Jack."

"Goodnight Cooper." Both men hung up.

That night Cooper didn't sleep, tossing and turning in his big empty bed. Should he give her space, or should he fight for her? If he did either, would he lose her for good? He punched his pillow and rolled over, frustrated.

The next morning, he was awakened by his cell phone ringing. Cooper dove for his bedside table. "Julie?" he asked into the phone without looking at the caller ID because his eyes were still closed but he was awake. He sat up in bed when he realized it wasn't Julie. "Sorry, what was that?"

The caller repeated his request. "Yes, this is Jeff Olson. I'm calling on behalf of Elizabeth Lucas. She is building a new home in California. Ms. Lucas has requested you come and work up a landscaping design for her."

"Of course," Cooper agreed.

"I have set you up with a ticket for this morning. That won't be a problem, will it?"

He rubbed his eyes. He wanted to see Julie but maybe this was the break they needed. He would go. He would only be away two days, tops. She would have time to think then they could talk. "No, no problem at all."

Jeff gave him the rest of the information and Cooper hung up. He checked his phone to make sure he hadn't missed any calls or messages from Julie, sadly none. He got up and showered then started to pack.

As he was going through his closet pulling clothes out, he wondered if he would require a nice suit. Probably he usually took his clients out to a nice dinner to show them his proposal. He pulled out one of his suits and set it out on the bed. When he went to pack his suit, an envelope fell out, realizing what it was as he picked it up. Perfect, he thought, he set it aside and finished packing.

Cooper wrote a quick note to add to the letter and drove to the Hart's house. Sandy met him at the door, gave him a big hug, and whispered in his ear. "Everything will work out the way it's supposed to."

He hoped so. It also made him think she was on his side.

"Julie's not here," she added.

"I figured," he told her. "I was hoping you could maybe give her this?" He handed her the envelope.

"Of course, I can." She took it from him.

"I'm leaving town for a couple of days. I have a work thing out in California, but I will be back," he said.

"Okay, we will see you when you get back."

"Thanks," he told her and hopped down the front porch steps.

CHAPTER THIRTY

J ulie had to call her parents for a ride the next morning and Megan showed up to give her a lift. Arriving in time for breakfast she helped herself to her mom's French toast casserole with pecans. She was drinking a tall glass of milk washing down the delicious goodness when her mom put an envelope in front of her. Wiping her fingers on her napkin she picked it up, "What's this?" she asked.

"Cooper dropped it off for you yesterday," her mom said nonchalantly walking back behind the stove.

She stopped, her heart thudding, should she open it here in front of them? She didn't know what the contents would be, she was also afraid of what it might say. Would he tell her she wasn't worth the aggravation? The only way to find out was to open it. She took a deep breath and broke the seal on the envelope, inside she found a note covering another sealed envelope. She read the first note.

Dear Julie,

I wanted to give this to you in person, but I got called away for work. I will be home in a couple of days. I don't like how we left things yesterday. I can't even begin to understand what you are going through, and I shouldn't have yelled at you. I can only tell you that I was scared. Scared of losing you all over again and I'm sorry.

I know that you found out that once before we had tried to be more than friends and it didn't end well. I was coming to you on your wedding day, not the best timing I know, but I wanted you to know that I hadn't given up on us and you shouldn't either.

I want to give you time to think but I also want to talk to you when I get back.

Sincerely,

Cooper Jackson

She took a deep breath when she finished reading the letter. Yeah, he hadn't given up on them. He was going to fight for her at her wedding? She ripped open the second envelope and began reading.

Dear Julie,

Today is your wedding day and sadly it is not mine too. Growing up I always envisioned us together. When I was little, I wished we would be neighbors forever so we could see each other daily because I loved playing with my best friend next door. You were always so fun and adventurous. You always made up games we could play, and I was never bored.

As we grew older, I began to realize I didn't want you to be my neighbor anymore. I wanted you in my life, in my home, with me forever. I knew you weren't there yet, and I was fine waiting for you. All through high school I waited, I told myself, that high school flings don't always work out, wait a little longer. When I went away to college, I told myself, to wait until after graduation. When you moved back and broke up with your college boyfriend, I let out a huge sigh of relief thinking I had almost lost you.

Then one day, you kissed me and my whole world fell into alignment. I was where I was supposed to be and you were where you were supposed to be, with me. Then disaster struck and you thought the impossible of Melissa and me. I didn't know if you were scared of what we could become so again, I waited. I gave you time to figure it out. I know now that was the biggest mistake of my life.

I should have fought for you. I am done waiting. It's now or never Jewels. It should be me and you forever. I love you. I have always loved you and I will always love you until my last breath.

Forever Waiting,

Your Cooper

With tears blurring her vision she finished the letter. She couldn't believe how moved she was, not only by the fact that he was coming to fight for her on her wedding day but by the words that she too felt but hadn't yet fully understood the depth of her emotion. She couldn't wait to see him now. She excused herself from the table and opened the French doors going out onto the deck. Taking out her cell phone she called him.

"Julie," he answered on the first ring.

"Hi,"

His voice softened, "Hey," it sounded so sexy over the phone. "Did you get my letter?" he asked.

She nodded her head, then realizing he couldn't see her she said, "Yes!"

"Did you like it?"

Still nodding, her head she laughed, through tears of joy that were finally falling, "Yes!" She desperately needed him home so she could show him how she felt even if she wasn't ready to declare it.

"Oh good, listen I'm so glad you called but I'm in the middle of something right now. Can I call you tonight? I want to talk to you."

"Sure, I'll talk to you tonight."

"Bye, Jewels."

"Bye, Cooper."

That night Julie decided she wanted to stay at her place again, she wanted the privacy of her own home without her family overhearing her conversation. She got dressed for bed and took her phone upstairs with her to lie down.

Watching a little TV, she got sleepy and ended up falling asleep.

Her ringtone startled her awake. The TV seemed to be blaring loudly. Reaching for the remote and her cell phone at the same time, she shut off the TV and answered the phone, which said it was two in the morning. "Hello?" she said groggily into the phone before collapsing back down on her covers.

"I'm so sorry! I forgot about the time zone change and I just finished dinner with my client, Elizabeth Lucas." □

"The actress you were telling me about?"

"Yes, she loved all my ideas, and she wants to meet you."

"What? How does she even know about me?"

"She saw my face after getting your call this morning and wanted to know who the lucky lady was. I told her I was the lucky one."

Julie smiled into the phone, "You're sweet."

"I know it's only been two days, but I miss you so much."

"I miss you too," she confessed. "When are you coming home?"

"I need another day or so. I have to set up a few things here. I need to get a crew together and order some things. I wish I was there with you right now, though."

"Me too, I'm all alone at my place."

"Really? What are you wearing?"

She giggled. "Seriously? You're trying that cheesy line with me?"

He chuckled. "Sorry, I can just picture you lying in bed, and I want to crawl next to you." She looked at the bedroom door and she could almost picture him walking through it.

"Oh really, and would you be fully clothed or naked?"

"That depends. I can undress quickly but if you want, I can crawl into bed fully clothed and hold you."

What fun would that be? "Can I help you undress?" she asked.

"Of course," his voice was smooth and seductive.

"I can picture myself getting up on my knees when you walk in the room and you strutting over to the bed. I would slide my hands up under your shirt and slip it up over your head. My fingernails softly graze down your chest down to the waistband of your pants. I scoot forward so that I'm close to you at the edge of the bed and rise slowly, licking and kissing my way up your sexy abs to your hard chest. My nails will trace the wet path my hot mouth just traveled to give you a long slow kiss."

"What are you wearing?" Cooper croaked, and then cleared his throat, "I want to take it off of you."

"A see-through nighty." She lied as she looked down at her tank top and cotton pajama shorts, which were cute enough but not the sexy she wanted him to picture in his mind. She heard him groan over the phone as he envisioned what she looked like and she grinned with womanly satisfaction.

"I want to put my hands on you. I want to caress the backs of your thighs while pulling you tighter towards me, my hands cupping your sweet ass."□

She purred, "Then I would undo your belt and slowly ease your pants down."

"Lift your arms," he commanded, and she obeyed by putting one arm up that wasn't holding the phone, "I'm pulling your nightgown over your head. Your breasts are beautiful." Picturing her in his mind he let out a ragged breath.

She let out a seductive laugh, "Thank you."

"I want to suck on them," he said and she sobered immediately.

"Yes please," she whispered hoarsely.

"My hands are on your back and I'm going to take each nipple in my hot mouth one at a time. I'm going to use my teeth to make them hard."

"That feels amazing," she told him. "Your hard cock feels so good in my hand like velvet stretched over steel. I'm stroking the hard length, up and down your shaft."

She heard him suck in a breath. Her hand slipped under her tank top teasing her breast imagining that it was him touching her. On a breathy sigh, Julie said, "I want to kiss you."

"I want to kiss you too," he told her. "My hand is between your thighs."

Julie bent her knees and her hand not holding the phone moved across her breast to the band of her pajama bottoms. Slipping under the waistband and past her panties she touched herself.

"Are you wet for me?" he asked.

"Yes, I'm so wet for you. I want you on top of me. I need you inside of me."

Enjoying the sound of her voice getting husky with passion, a passion that he knew all too well could swell and devour him whole, he raggedly whispered into the phone. "Slow down sweetheart, we have all night. Do you like what I'm doing to you with my finger?"

"Yes!" she breathed, "I'm kissing your neck and touching you, running my hands down your back." Julie's eyes were closed picturing the scenario they were playing out, feeling her ministrations with her finger and picturing that it was him who was pleasuring her.

"I want to suck you," Julie said.

"Oh, God, yes," he agreed with her suggestion.

"I'm bent over on my hands and knees while you stand next to the bed and I'm sucking you into my warm mouth. My hand is cradling your balls as my soft pouty lips are going to glide up and down on your dick. I start slowly sucking you deep inside my mouth, up and down, up and down." She tortured him. "My tongue swirling around your head then I'll take all of you in again, over and over."

"Julie," Cooper's breath was ragged.

"Do you like your balls licked, Cooper?" she asked huskily.

There was silence on the other end. "Cooper?"

"I think I almost passed out," he confessed.

171

She giggled. "I'm going to lick your balls Cooper and suck on them gently."

"I am picking you up by your arms and throwing you down on the bed."

"You are?" she sounded surprised, "What are you going to do to me?"

"I'm going to part your thighs, spread them wide for me, Jewels. I'm going to pull you to the edge of the bed by your ankles, till your ass is at the edge. I'm going to get down on my knees and I'm going to kiss and lick your inner thigh. I'm slowly making my way to your hot, tight center. I'm not going to touch you at first but you're going to want me to. Aren't you Sweetheart?"

"Mmmm, yes."

"You are going to feel my hot breath on your wet sweetness, not touching you but so close you writhe...aching for my touch. You want my tongue to touch you?"

"Yes."

"Do you need me to touch you?

"Yes!"

"Are you going to beg me to touch you?"

"Cooper! I need you to touch me. I want you to touch me. I'm begging you to touch me! Now, please I need it now!"

"My tongue is happy to oblige. You taste so sweet. I'm stroking you with my tongue. Do you feel it?"

"Oh, yes! Yes! Don't stop."

"I won't Sweetheart. I'm flicking your nub with the tip of my tongue as I slip my finger inside your hot, sweet wetness and it's driving you wild."

Julie's head was thrashing back and forth on the pillows. "Cooper," she breathed.

"Yes? Tell me what I can do for you."

"I feel myself coming and I want you inside me. Now, Cooper now!"

"You ready for me?"

"Yes, yes, I'm ready."

"Okay, I'm standing up. My hands are on your hips and I'm guiding myself inside you. You're so hot and wet for me. I'm thrusting my rock-hard dick inside you and I can feel you pulsating around me. Oh, God, Jewels, you feel so damn good!" He ground out.

"Oh! I can feel you." Her hips were rocking back and forth her fingers sliding in and out of her body then rubbing her clit until she wanted to scream. Her neck arched forward, and she moaned into the phone, "Cooper."

"Ahhh...yes Jewels?"

"I want..."

"Tell me. I'm deep inside you. I'm pumping into you so hard."

"Oh," she bit down on her lip.

"Tell me," he urged.

"I want you to fuck me," she said shyly.

"I want to fuck you," he assured her. "Julie?"

"Yes?"

"Can I come inside you?"□

"Yes!"

"Julie, I'm coming."

"Come for me Cooper, I'm right there with you." She cried out then sucked in a breath as she reached her climax, and she heard him groan his orgasm into the phone. There was a long minute of heavy breathing on both sides of the phone as they composed themselves.

"Was it good for you?" Cooper asked.

Julie giggled, "Oh my God. I can't believe we just had phone sex. That was amazing. You're good at that. Have you ever done that before? Wait I take that back I don't want to know."

"No never," he answered her honestly.

"Good, me either. I'm pretty sure." They stayed up talking on the phone until they both fell asleep with their phones to their ears, neither one wanting to break the connection by ending the call.

Chapter Thirty-One

Julie needed to address the history paper with Andrew, so she emailed him and asked if he could meet her for coffee later that day. He responded immediately. She drove into town and parked outside of the coffee shop he had recommended. It was not the coffee shop she had seen in the town square but one close to the college. Inside, there were trendy couches and chairs placed around the room on oriental rugs. There were eclectic tables of different shapes and sizes with mismatched chairs of multiple colors and back heights placed around the room. There was a small one-step stage that had someone playing guitar softly in the background.

Andrew wasn't there yet so she went to the bar and placed her order with the barista, a caramel macchiato. The woman behind the counter had a long flowing dress that was made of several patchwork floral patterns. Her hair was a dirty blonde and hung straight down her back. She paid for her coffee and took a seat by the window.

She watched as Andy came in, and bought himself a coffee, then he spotted her, and his face lit up as he walked towards her. He sat across from her at the table she had chosen. "So, you read my paper?" he asked.

She pulled it out of her purse and put it on the table. "I did."

He paused, "So what did you think? It was a good paper."

"It was a great paper." He beamed at her. Reaching into her handbag she pulled out another paper and placed it on the table next to his, "When Stan Jennings a Harvard history professor wrote it twelve years ago."

The smile he had on his face froze. She could see the fear in his eyes from getting caught. He swallowed hard and sat back in his seat.

"Want to tell me what's going on?" she asked calmly.

He sat back in his chair. Leaning forward, his elbows rested on his knees and his head fell into his hands. He was rubbing his face and then pushing back his hair. He straightened letting out a long steadying breath. He looked at her. "I'm really sorry. I have a lot of pressure on me from my parents. I heard about..." he looked at her, "your accident and I thought maybe if you didn't remember you might give me a better grade. Please don't say anything to the school or my parents. I've already lost my scholarship this would send them over the edge and if I got kicked out of school, I would be cut off."

He looked at her pleadingly. She could feel herself softening a little like she was sure she had done previously. "Listen, I don't appreciate you taking advantage of my situation."

"I know! I'm sorry, it won't happen again."

"You got that right. It won't happen again because if you do and you get caught and it comes back that I let you slide with just a bad grade I could lose my job."

"I promise Professor Hart. I'm on the straight and narrow. You can count on me to keep my word. I know what a serious infraction this is," he swore vehemently. "I want to make it up to you. I know you are looking for a research assistant next year and I need an internship, I could help you out with that."

She sat back in her chair studying him. "Okay, consider this your job interview. Tell me a descriptive history of this town." She took a sip of her drink, it was quite delicious.

"Well, Willows Cove, Massachusetts was established in 1722. The population is just under 7,000, but it fluctuates when college students move into town. It's roughly thirty-five square miles. There were three founding families, the Pembrookes, the Suttons, and the Cassams. The original town square is called Pembrooke Park where it is said to have the original willow tree in its center. The original meeting house is where the college now sits and there's a marble marker to mark the site. The college was built by William Casssam, a descendant of one of the original founding fathers in 1846.

The town hall, church, and a couple of houses are all still around the park. There used to be a saloon there but has since moved. The Sutton family home is still in existence across the park and the church is now a living museum still owned by the family's descendants.

Willows Cove is an old logging town. They would cut down trees and throw them in Berly Lake, the logs would float down the river to the old warehouses and Sutton Mill where mill workers would fish them out of the water and work them into finished lumber. It is also an old farming community with several big farms on the outskirts of town.

Sutton Mill burned down in 1898 and was rebuilt the following year. Twenty years ago, the property was bought and turned into a restaurant.

St. Vincent's Hospital was built in the early 1900s and has gone through several remodels and two additions." He went on to talk about the schools and businesses in town. When he was done, she gave him the internship.

CHAPTER THIRTY-TWO

J ulie thought her front door was going to come down. Someone was banging on the wood and wasn't letting up. Running to the door she checked through the peep-hole and saw who it was. Throwing open the door she was swept up in Cooper's strong arms. He was so eager to hold her, kiss her that he had stormed through the threshold slamming the door behind him as he took her in his arms.

Picking her up off the ground, she bent her legs at the knees, and his lips crushed hers. Her arms wound tightly around his neck her hands digging into his hair. Their tongues smashed together it was rough and neither one cared. She bit and held his lower lip pulling it towards her slowly before letting go, realizing that she never wanted to let him go. This moment felt so right, his homecoming, his coming home to her.

He looked down at her, devoured her with his eyes like a man starved, "God, I've missed you."

"Show me," she commanded.

Groaning he captured her lips in his again. She tugged at his hair and his arms crushed her to him, he never wanted this moment to end but needed to feel more of her. Needing to be closer to her, he set her down on her feet and hiked her shirt up over her head. As frantic as he was to remove all barriers between them, Julie began unbuttoning his shirt and he assisted her by ripping it off, sending buttons flying across her hardwood floors. She reached for his belt, and he tugged at her short buttons, Cooper unzipped her fly and peeled it off of her revealing her black undies. Shaking her hips, she helped him wiggle them off of her. She was barefoot so she was left standing there in her bra and panties.

Julie had managed to get his shorts and boxers off of him. He kicked off his flip-flops and pulled her into his arms again. He kissed her neck, removed her bra straps from her shoulders, and expertly unhooked her front clasp exposing her breasts to him. His hands slid down her sides across her hips and under the panties, easing them off her body.

She easily stepped out of them and finally naked they came together, arms entangled, tongues intertwined. He moved her towards the stairs, and she took them backward, neither wanting to break contact that seemed a lifetime coming, while he followed her. Not even halfway up the stairs, anxious to feel her body fully against him again he lifted her off her feet, her legs circled his waist.

Gently Cooper laid her down on the hard wooden stair treads and entered her. She gasped because it was so sudden, and she wasn't quite expecting they wouldn't make the bedroom but she was so aroused his sudden entry almost made her orgasm on penetration. Reaching out she held on to one of the banisters. He kissed her and she held on to him, her hand grabbing a fist full of thick hair. His hands reached under her trying to protect her from the bite of the stairs, not that she could have felt them with all her nerve endings focused on the hot core of her. One arm went under her back and the other pulled her ass closer to him as he thrust vigorously inside her.

Unexpectedly he rolled over, roles reversed. He was sitting on the stairs she was on his lap. She had to let go of the banister on one side and now reached for the handrail.

Her knees were on the stairs and with his help his hands guiding her hips she rocked up and down on his shaft. Throwing her head back, his arms went up her back and brought her breasts to his mouth. Rolling her hips, she ground herself against him. While he sucked on one breast his hand came down between them his thumb found her center and rubbed.

Julie moaned huskily as he sucked on her other breast. Her arm draped across his shoulder and down his back. Digging her nails into his shoulder she raked them across his skin and he sucked harder. She could feel her climax building as she ground his hard cock deeper inside her. She briefly thought phone sex was nice, but no way could it replace this. "You feel so good," she purred.

"Shit!" he exclaimed.

"What?" She was alarmed by his outburst.

"I forgot to put on a condom." He pointed to his shorts lying on the floor, "I brought one."

She turned back around having looked down at the shorts, "Just one?" she asked with a sly, seductive smile.

"More than one," he grinned at her.

"Oh good," she said, "well what do you think we should do?"

"Stop?" he seemed pained by the thought.

She rolled her hips again, still aching for release and not at all in the mood to change from her current position. "That would be a shame. Do you have any other suggestions?"□

He thrust inside her once more, "I could pull out?" He seemed uncertain about this option and shrugged as he said it.

"Yes, let's do that." She leaned down to kiss him. He continued to rub her, and she began rolling her hips against him, riding him at a pace that soon had his heart racing. As she raised and lowered herself on his throbbing cock, her hard nipples rubbed up and down on his chest with each stroke. Julie flicked her tongue over the lower lobe of his ear, bringing it into her mouth she raked her teeth over it. Her hot breath blowing in his ear was nearly his undoing, sending shivers through his body.

"Julie," he ground out.

"Yes, Cooper."

He licked her neck, his teeth nibbling on her giving her goosebumps making her nipples that much harder. His hands caressed her breast and then down her stomach while he continued to nibble both sides of her neck. It tickled and felt amazing, she wanted him to stop, and at the same time, never stop. His hand went around her back and down to her bottom manipulating her body, willing her to come.

She screamed out his name her body convulsing, pulsating around his shaft, and squeezing him in her orgasm. He pumped into her one more time then pulled her off of him. Cooper hated not being able to come inside her. He kissed her once more then stood up to go clean himself off. She followed him down to the downstairs bathroom. She waited naked for him in the doorway. When he was done, he went to her.

"What?" he asked.

"I like it when you're inside of me and we come together."

"I know. It won't happen again. I promise I won't forget a condom next time." He kissed her gently on the lips. "I didn't hurt you on the stairs, did I?"

"No, that was hot."

"You liked that?" he asked.

She nodded. "I also liked our phone sex session."

His hands rested on her hips, "We should find other things you like."

"What I like is your thinking." Julie smiled seductively, giving him her best, come-hither look and he was more than happy to indulge her.

CHAPTER THIRTY-THREE

"Cooper!" Julie shouted excitedly. Cooper flew down the stairs of her townhouse his heart pounding in his chest.

"What's the matter?"

Julie was oblivious to the fact that she had just scared the living daylights out of him. "Um," she was waving a piece of paper in the air in one and holding the empty envelope in the other hand, "I just got a class schedule. I have classes I'm going to have to teach in two weeks!"

"Oh," he stood in place at the bottom of the stairs. His mind raced. He hadn't thought about her return to school yet. Julie would be among thousands of people a day and he wouldn't be around to protect her. He wondered if the college would mind him escorting her across campus and hanging out in her classes until the mystery of who was after Julie was solved. Cooper knew Jack had pulled some strings with the police department to have a detail on her but with no other attempts on her life they may have no choice but to bring it to an end.

"Earth to Cooper," Julie brought his attention back to her. He was going to have to tell her to protect her.

He ushered her to the couch, "Please sit down."

"What's going on?"

"I need to tell you something and I don't want you to freak out."

"Too late," she laughed but quickly sobered as he began to tell her in detail everything that had happened since leaving the hospital including his and Jack's suspicions.

"Wait!" Julie had already interrupted him several times and he had patiently answered all her questions. "So, there's an unmarked police car outside of my house?" Jumping up she raced to her front window and peeked out from behind the curtain. "Which one is it?"

"The dark sedan across the street facing us." She could barely make out a dark figure sitting in the front seat.

"Oh no," she said as she saw her parents walking up her front step. "I forgot Mom and Dad were coming for dinner."

Cooper had already made it to her side as she swung the door wide to let them in. "So, Cooper tells me someone's trying to kill me," Julie said trying to sound casual and upbeat. To her, this was pretty much par for the course. She had no memory, a broken engagement, and a potential psychopath after her. Julie wasn't sure how much more she could take of this. Had her life ever been normal?

Apparently, no one had bothered to inform Sandra Hart either because her purse instantly hit the floor and her hand reached out desperately clutching Jack's shoulder. "Please, tell me you are kidding. I need a drink."

"I'm on it!" Cooper practically ran from the room to get her the desired drink. Jack closed the door and walked Sandy to the couch. Julie and Cooper joined them in the living room with a drink for everyone.

Cooper explained to Jack that Julie had received her class schedule and that was the reason he had spilled the beans. "I understand," Jack reassured him. To Julie and Sandy, "I didn't want to upset you ladies. We thought we would have this figured out by now. The police department has looked into my past convictions everyone is accounted for."

They continued talking about everything that had happened over the summer and ended up ordering take-out Thai food.

CHAPTER THIRTY-FOUR

Oh, God, this felt good. She had her eyes closed and her head thrashed back and forth on her silk sheets. She was still wearing a red lacey bra, which was his favorite color on her, and she knew it. She was wearing a short black skirt that he had lifted, and he had pushed her matching thong to the side to get inside her quickly. He was holding her black high heels he had not allowed her to remove as he thrust in and out of her.

He was standing next to the bed as she lay on her back with half of her bottom hanging over the edge. He released her heels, and she slid them around his neck as he continued to pump his hard cock inside her. His hands slid down her long legs and across her flat abdomen, his fingers played over her bra then slowly wrapped his big hands around her neck. He applied gentle pressure, choking her just enough to get her lightheaded which allowed her heightened sensation.

She never wanted this to end but she could feel her climax getting closer and welcomed the experience like no other. Her body convulsed and contracted around him. Her muscles began to relax but his fingers tightened more around her neck. She smiled realizing he was still trying to reach his climax and she tapped him on the wrist to tell him to ease up. When he didn't respond her eyes flew open.

She watched as his orgasm hit, sweat on his brow, he closed his eyes and threw his head back as he released his seed inside her, but his grip just got stronger around her neck. She couldn't take a breath she was literally gasping for air her nails raked his hands. She managed to gather enough strength to pull her feet back to her and shove her high heels into his chest. She was gratified to see she had managed to break a heel on one shoe and stab him with the other. He lost contact with her neck as he stumbled back, seeing this as her chance to escape, she flipped over and began crawling to the other side of the bed. She stood up when she was on the other side but there was nowhere to go as he was blocking the only exit.

She knew then she was going to die. She could see it in his eyes. He smiled at her when he saw the fear and recognition on her face. Quickly she removed her broken shoes, knowing she would need to make a run for it. Desperately looking around she knew that if she wanted to survive this, she had to escape but she didn't know how and started to back up, but he only followed.

She screamed at the top of her lungs, but no help came. He ran around to her side of the bed and when he did, she leaped over the bed and through her open bedroom door as fast as her feet would carry her. She knew he wasn't far behind her; she could hear him crashing through her home like a raging bull. She ran past the living room to her kitchen where her keys and cell phone sat on the countertop. She grabbed them in one swooping motion heading towards the door. Just a couple more steps, she could see freedom, could feel it.

Fast on the heels of that thought, she crashed into the ceramic tiles of her kitchen floor. The bastard had caught up to her and tackled her. She landed hard on her knees her phone skidding across the floor and away from her. She rolled over to face him and he was on top of her instantly.

She used the only weapon she had and put the keys in between her fingers as she had learned in a self-defense class she had taken and tried to deck him. Much to her dismay, she was too slow. He grabbed her wrist and twisted until she felt her wrist snap her grip loosening on the keys. She tried to bring her knee up in between his legs but he was sitting too far up on her body she only managed to knee him in the back which didn't seem to faze him. So, she reached down and in one quick motion grabbed his balls and squeezed with everything she had. He yelled out in pain and rolled over calling her a "Bitch."

Typical, she thought as she rolled over and made another attempt for the door.

"Stop" he yelled from the floor.

"Like hell," she said her fingers on the door when she heard the distinctive click of a gun being primed. She froze in place refusing to turn around. She wasn't so much scared anymore as she was royally pissed. She slowly turned around to assess the situation. He was still lying on the tiled floor of her kitchen one arm pointing a gun at her the other still clutching the family jewels. No way was she going down without a fight. She slowly lifted her hands in surrender as she looked around.

"That's a good girl. Now slowly come away from the door."

She took one step as if in compliance before diving out of sight of the kitchen and into the living room, his view greatly blocked on the floor. She ran around to the bar, looked into the kitchen, picked up her favorite cobalt blue glass vase, and hurled it into the kitchen which she believed was closest to his head. She heard the glass shatter and was rewarded by his swearing. She picked up another from her collection from around the world and chucked it with all her might at him in the next room. She heard him grunt from the other side of the wall. She was hoping one of her neighbors would hear the commotion and hopefully call the police. Her cell phone was still on the kitchen floor.

She had to do something. The next time she hurtled something breakable over the counter she noticed her knife rack. He had a gun she wasn't sure what good a knife would do, but she pulled the biggest one from the wooden block. Before she could crouch back down, she was grabbed from behind. She let loose the most blood-curdling scream ever heard.

A dog from next door started barking but neither one of them was listening to that as the struggle for life and death resumed. She fought with all her might, twisting and turning in his grip, thrashing wildly hoping to hit anything that would cause him pain or to release her. Not giving in easily he held her in a death grip.

She tried one more thing she had seen on Oprah and that was dead weight, she dropped like a sack of potatoes to the floor. He came with her, but his head slammed into the countertop in front of them. Blood began trickling down his face and he was forced to let her go.

Scrambling quickly on her knees still holding the butcher knife in one hand she tried to get up and flee. He found her ankle and dragged her back to him. She spun around the knife ready. He was on her instantly, his hands wrapping around hers which held the knife. This is not going well. She fought hard. Tears began to blur her vision as she realized this was the end. There was nothing else she could do.

The sound of police sirens in the background gave her a surge of hope but he took advantage of her slight hesitation and plunged the knife into her chest. She looked up at him startled, her hands slowly falling away from the blade and his hands. He leaned over her and kissed her on the lips, "It's too bad you fought the plan so hard. I would have liked to keep you around." He licked her lips as she drew in her last breath, "You were the best lay I've ever had." And with that, he was staring into her lifeless green eyes.

Hearing the sirens, he ran out the back door and kept running for his car three blocks over.

CHAPTER THIRTY-FIVE

T he day had finally arrived for the Annual Labor
  Day party held on the Hart's Estate. Everyone was
outside enjoying the food and company when the skies
opened up and rain began pouring down instantaneously.
Everyone sprinted towards the house seeking refuge from
the heavy rain. Cooper and Julie opted for the library's
French doors as everyone else went through the kitchen
doors.

They entered the quiet room laughing and panting slightly at the sprint for the house. Their hair and
clothes were dripping wet. Julie's white shirt clung to her
breasts. They were in each other's arms instantly, unable
to get enough of each other. Cooper was unbuttoning her
shirt exposing her taunt nipples through the lace of her
bra. He took her into his warm mouth as Julie's hands
cupped his head, her own falling back in pleasure. Cooper's hand began sliding up her thigh under her skirt when
they heard laughter coming from the hallway. They broke
apart quickly like they were in high school and could get
detention if they were caught.

Cooper took her hand and dragged her to the side
of the room hidden from the doorway. He pushed her up

against the wall and started kissing her again. Julie kissed him back, her tongue stroking his, her hands sliding up and down his back. The door to the library opened and they could hear people spilling into the room.

Julie looked up at him wide-eyed. Cooper smiled, lifted his hand above her head, and pulled on a mounted candlestick making the wall give way to a hidden room. It was dark in the room, well hallway, that they entered but Cooper just flipped a switch, and it illuminated a stairway to the second floor. She thought it would be dark and dank and filled with cobwebs, but it was just the opposite. The walls were finished off and painted, with no light bulbs hanging down but nice sconces on the wall. The floors were carpeted so there would be minimal noise within the walls, but she also bet that the walls were heavily insulated for that purpose. The bedrooms were up those stairs Julie thought.

"I'll race you," she whispered before taking off up the narrow stairs. There was no way he could pass her but he tried helping her along his hands on her bottom pushing her up the flight of stairs but that only slowed her down.

Julie turned around and being a couple of stairs above him, she was at eye level with him. Her hands were on the railing on either side. Julie wasn't touching him but with the look in her eyes, she may as well have been. Julie began the slow ascent up the stairs facing him every step she took he followed without breaking eye contact. They found her room upstairs and closed themselves inside.

They stood apart looking longingly into each other's eyes with the promise of what was to come. Julie stepped forward first, her hands extended out in front of her reaching for the hemline of his soaked shirt. Her touch was tender as she removed the wet shirt that was clinging to him outlining his gorgeous six-pack abs.

Cooper didn't move, he stood tall and proud as she studied his body. Julie's hands roamed over the muscles of his chest and down the washboard stomach. She undid the top button of his jeans and pushed them over his sculpted hips.

Cooper was busy feasting his eyes on the sight in front of him. Julie's shirt was still unbuttoned, and she still had drops of rain on her breasts. Her lacey bra fascinated him, and he couldn't take his eyes off the sight of her pink nipples straining against the fabric. Cooper came out of his trance when he realized she had fully stripped him, and she wasn't touching him anymore but slowly undressing herself.

Julie removed the clinging shirt and slowly slid the skirt down over her hips. She allowed Cooper to view her in her matching lacey lingerie. She kicked her sandals off and they flew across the room, and she reached behind her back unsnapping her bra. Julie smiled seductively at him when her eyes dipped below his waist, and she saw he was standing at attention. Cooper grinned when he saw her eyes widen at the site of his arousal.

He couldn't take any more of this sweet torture, he took a step towards her with a determined look on his face while Julie, in a playful mood, eluded his capture and ran for the bed. She was crawling across the expanse of her bed when he caught her ankles. Julie let out a shriek followed by a good-natured laugh.

"Now that you have me what on Earth do you plan to do with me?" Julie asked in mock innocence.

Cooper's hands on her ankles began traveling up her calves, Julie was still on her hands and knees as she looked over her shoulder at him, but Cooper wasn't watching her face, he was concentrating on her body. He bent over and kissed her hip, one hand holding on to her ankle the other hand roaming up her thighs and across her bottom. Cooper's roaming hand slipped between Julie's spread thighs and found her already wet. His fingers worked their magic on her body while his tongue did the same to her back.

Cooper crawled on the bed behind her, on his knees between her legs. Julie stretched out away from him and pulling open the bedside drawer she lifted out a whole row of condoms. Cooper let out a deep laugh. Julie grinned at him in return and tore one off, tossing it to him over her shoulder. He put it down next to him and pulled her ankles back behind him to bring her back to him.

Julie got up on her knees, but he wouldn't let her turn around to face him. One of his bronzed arms came around in front of her, cupped her breast in his hand, and pulled her back against his chest. His other arm came down around her hip and his hand went between her legs pushing her bottom against his erection.

Julie's head fell back onto his taut shoulder and his teeth began grazing over the skin on her neck. His finger began a slow rhythm against her body and her hips began working in rhythm with him. All the sensations were bringing Julie closer to a climax. Since she couldn't reach much of him, she grabbed the condom next to her knee, opened it, and with her hands behind her back put it on him.

Cooper took her jaw in his hands and turned her head towards him, kissing her deeply before pushing her down onto her hands again. Grasping her hips, he entered her from behind and she cried out in ecstasy. He pushed her body off of him then rammed deep inside her again she cried out encouraging him onwards. He repeated the motion. □

One hand still on her hip his other hand traveled up her back and tangled in her hair, clenching a fist full close to her scalp he tugged. Her head came back straining her neck muscle as he pummeled himself inside her. Her cries were getting louder and coming closer together. She couldn't stop herself even if she wanted to, which she certainly did not. She could hear the sound of him slapping up against her each time he thrust, filling her to the core and it turned her on even more.

She held on for dear life to the bed sheets in her hands, "Yes, yes, yes!" She screamed as her orgasm shattered her world. Mind-numbing sensations coursed through her body as she exploded from the inside out. She tried collapsing on the bed, but Cooper wouldn't hear of it.

"Oh, no you don't." Cooper laughed, "I'm just getting started." Without breaking the connection between the two of them he laid them down on their sides. Cooper was kissing her shoulder and neck when she turned her head to catch some of those kisses on her lips. Julie was the one who started the rhythmic pace with her hips and Cooper met her with a thrust of his own. Cooper's finger moved again reaching between her thighs and the more pressure he applied the more sensitive she became.

Julie cried out and Cooper silenced her with a kiss. Julie's hands wrapped around his head bringing him closer. She managed to pull him back on top of her. She arched her back to him and kept her face in her pillow to muffle the sounds of their lovemaking.

Cooper on his knees behind her grasped both her hips and began again this time faster and harder both of them trying to get as close as possible. Julie's cries of ecstasy were still heard through the pillow but this only aroused Cooper even more. With one final thrust, he felt Julie's orgasm with his own and he collapsed on top of her.

Afterward, they lay entwined in bed with the sheets pulled over their nude bodies. Julie's head rested on Cooper's shoulder his arm draped around her. Her leg was thrown over his and her hand playing with his soft springy chest hair.

"I still can't believe it took us so long to do this," Julie whispered.

"It was worth the wait," Cooper said snuggling her closer to himself.

"I wonder what my problem was that I couldn't see how great we could be together?"

"Maybe you were afraid of losing what we already had. I know I was."

"Really?" She lifted herself on her elbow to look down at him. Before he could respond the door to Julie's bedroom burst open. Julie sat straight up in bed. The sheets wrapped firmly around her. Her sister Megan seemed frantic and not at all shocked or concerned her sister was in bed with Cooper.

"You guys need to come downstairs, quick. Something has happened, the police are here." With that Megan raced away as quickly as she had entered, slamming the door so hard in her frantic retreat that it bounced back open and stood slightly ajar.

Julie jumped from the bed not caring if anyone saw her nakedness or not. Cooper was seconds behind as they desperately rummaged through the clothing on the floor sensing that something was wrong. Neither spoke a word to the other as they dressed, not knowing what to expect downstairs.

Julie rushed from the room first, having dressed quicker than Cooper. He reached her on the stairs and caught her hand in his as they continued to race down the stairs towards her family. She didn't acknowledge his gesture but was grateful for the comfort.

Downstairs was chaos, guests were being ushered through the front door with no explanation as to why. They had to wait a grueling ten minutes for all of the guests to disperse from the party. Everyone sat in the living room with two police officers, dressed in cheap suits, looking uncomfortable. One officer was typical, ate one too many jelly doughnuts type. He didn't look like he could chase a criminal one block much less apprehend the criminal after catching him. He had salt and pepper hair and was in his mid-fifties. The other officer was tall and lanky with short slicked-over hair.

When all of the guests had finally departed, Jack demanded of the police officers, "What is it you came here to say that has you sending our guest away in the middle of a party." He was hoping that they finally had a lead as to the threats to Julie's life. Could it possibly be over? The thudding in his chest told him the answer was no.

Sandy clung to her husband fearful of the coming conversation. The last time police officers came to the door it was to inform them that their oldest daughter had been in a car accident on her wedding day. In the pit of her stomach, a burning knot made her feel something was wrong.

The jelly doughnut cop introduced himself as, "Detective Sam Monroe, and my partner, Detective Roger Kowalski. I'm sorry to inform you that at approximately three o'clock this afternoon your daughter Shannon was murdered."

A startled gasp filled the room. Sandy immediately started sobbing, she had known after all. Julie went to her mother's side. Megan and Katie clung to one another crying. Jack stood reeling from the bombshell the detective had just dropped on his family, "You've made a positive I.D.? You're sure it's our daughter, Shannon?" Jack's voice steadied when he demanded, "Do you have a suspect?" His lawyer mode kicked into full gear.

"Sir," Detective Doughnut held out his hand as if that would calm down a grieving father, "I'm sorry, we can't comment on an ongoing investigation."

CHAPTER THIRTY-SIX

J ulie felt detached as she took note of everything on their way to the church. The day was bright and sunny, with a clear blue sky with birds singing harmoniously as if the world wasn't aware that people were in mourning. That a beautiful young woman's life had been taken too soon. Shannon's funeral was held at the same church their parents were married in, the same church where Julie was supposed to have been married. She hadn't been here since the accident.

Julie was dressed in all black as was Cooper who escorted her up the old stone steps of the church. They were led by her parents and sisters. She couldn't believe she was missing her sister. They would never be a full complete family again. Everyone had been so worried about her, why hadn't they put a detail on everyone in the family? She was suffering from survivor's guilt.

It had taken over two weeks for the Willow Cove's Police Department to release Shannon's body so they could bury her. Julie had been forced to take a leave of absence from the college until this was resolved and who knew how long that would be? Her family had been devastated to learn the details of Shannon's murder. They were informed she had put up quite the fight. Her apartment had been destroyed and there was DNA under her fingernails. They were disturbed to learn that not only had she been stabbed but had been strangled as well. The coroner was inconclusive on one point though. He had been unsure if Shannon had been raped or not. They knew she recently had sex before her murder. When the DNA from under her fingernails was matched, they learned the murderer had had sex with Shannon but was it consensual? The kitchen knife that was used to kill her was missing. They ran the DNA but came up with no matches in the system.

The entire district attorney's office was looking into all past cases Jack Hart had prosecuted. They researched known associates and tried to figure out if anyone had been paid to murder Julie or Shannon. So far, they had no leads so there was a police detail on the entire family.

Walking into the church she took in the cathedral ceiling and arched stained glass windows lining the outer walls. The altar was gorgeous, made of marble. Flowers adorned the whole front of the church. She noticed the casket in the center aisle near the front of the church and had to turn away. The wake had been emotional dealing with the loss of her little sister.

Leaning heavily on Cooper she asked him to find a quiet spot she could collect herself for a minute before taking their seats. Cooper turned her to a back room and what she saw made her gasp. Though it was empty now, she had a vision of herself inside getting ready for her wedding. This was finally too much to take. She collapsed and Cooper caught her before she hit the floor.

Chapter Thirty-Seven

Julie's Wedding Day

J ulie was at the church early on the morning of her wedding. She wanted a few moments of her own before the chaos of the day would overcome her. She was in the bridal suite in the back of the church. It was used by the wedding party to get ready and where the bride awaited the ceremony.

Sitting down in front of a vanity she put on the sheer stocking, folding them carefully up her pointed toes to the tops of her thighs. Hooking the lacey border to the straps attached to her garter belt, Julie slipped her feet into her sparkly high heels. Standing she puffed out her white satin gown. Her head snapped up when she heard something crash on the floor in front of the church. Julie realized the priest must have arrived, so she decided to go speak with him before the ceremony.

There was an old passageway that led from the bridal chamber to the front of the church where the priest and altar boys got ready. The door opened and revealed an old stone stairway original to the church. Lifting her long skirt, the long dark hallway led her under the church and up some more stairs to the sanctuary in the back of the church.

She heard noises before she reached the top stairs and began to slow down, almost crouched on the steps. The door was slightly ajar and the vision before Julie assaulted her senses. She let out a startled gasp and quickly clamped her hand over her mouth.

The occupants in the room didn't hear her as they were otherwise occupied. A man in a tux, his back to her had his trousers down around his ankles his legs braced apart. In front of him a woman also facing away, her arms braced on the wall, her legs spread wide, her three-inch heels giving her an advantage. The man had hiked up her gown exposing her shapely legs and rounded bottom.

They were having sex. He grunted as he pumped into her, and she was loudly moaning. He grabbed a fist full of hair and pulled her head back as she gasped.

"You like that Bitch, don't you?" he said before biting her neck.

"Oh, yes! Fuck me, Blake."

Julie sat, stunned, on the stone stairs. Her fiancé, the man whom she was to marry in two hours, was in the church screwing her sister. She knew her sister Shannon didn't like her, but to sleep with the man she was to marry the day of the wedding just to spite her was the last straw. She heard Blake groan as he shuddered and spilled his seed inside her. As he pulled out, she saw he wasn't wearing a condom. What an idiot. Well, it wasn't like it was planned or anything her sister had purposely come here to do this.

Julie was just about to barge into the room and let them both have it when Blake's words stopped her cold.

"You know I can't keep my hands off you when you don't wear any goddamned panties," he growled at her as he tucked his shirt back into his trousers. So, this wasn't their first time, Julie realized.

Shannon laughed wickedly, "That's the whole idea." She walked around in front of him, pressed her small breasts up against him, and stuck her hand down his pants. Shannon got a pout on her face. "I can't believe you're marrying my sister today." Julie could hear the venom in Shannon's voice when she said "sister." Julie wondered what she had ever done to deserve this obvious hatred. This kind of betrayal from her sister?

Blake sighed, "I know but it will be worth it in the end." What will be worth it?

"I wish her birthday was sooner than eight months away," Shannon whined. What the hell did her birthday have to do with anything?

"Well, I could always take care of it on our honeymoon, with some kind of accident. She signed the papers I drew up for her yesterday and put me in her will."

Shannon stepped away from Blake, "That wasn't the plan, you can't just kill her. We agreed you would divorce her after her twenty-fifth birthday and get half of the inheritance Aunt Gwen left her. I still can't believe the old bitch left her everything. If I would have known millions were at stake, I would have visited the old bat in the nursing home."

Oh. My. God. This was all about money? She was shaking her head trying to make sense of it all. Blake was willing to kill for it and her sister didn't care what happened to her.

"Why share half when I can inherit it all? We can run away together just the two of us." His hands cupped her bottom and tugged her close up against him. Blake started kissing Shannon's neck. "What do you say? I'll take you far away from this town and we will live like royalty in the Bahamas."

"Mmm... sounds tempting. Oh, Blake." she gasped when she felt his erection come back to life. "Do we have time?" Shannon was already unzipping him again.

"We'll make time," he stated as he hiked her skirt back up to her hips. Shannon shoved him down into the nearest chair, straddled his hips, and lowered herself down on his manhood.

Sickened by their betrayal, Julie was already running down the hallway back towards the bridal chamber. She was never more frightened than at this moment. She thought she heard one of them questioning a sound and stopped dead in her tracks, her heart racing, her back to the wall, as she listened for any movement. Finally, after what seemed an eternity, she heard Shannon say, "It was nothing."

Julie waited about half a second after she heard them in the throes of passion again before she took off running as her life depended on it because it did. She had to get to the police station, she would be safe there. Grabbing her keys off the end table she never broke stride on her way out the door. Julie didn't think she even touched the steps leading down to the front of the church. Jumping in her car, she started the ignition and gunned it. Her car lurched forward, not noticing that she'd pulled out in front of someone. Both cars jammed on their brakes but didn't have enough time to stop and the other car slammed into her car door.

Julie had glanced in the rear-view mirror as she heard tires squealing, that's when she saw Cooper standing on the church's entrance stairs. He looked so dashing in his grey suit and tie. Sharp shooting pain was what she felt on her left side. He's come for me! That would be her last thought, moments before Julie's world went dark.

CHAPTER THIRTY-EIGHT

Present Day

J ulie was becoming aware of her surroundings. At first, she thought she was in the hospital and the last couple of months had all been a dream. Concerned people crowded around her. Her parents, Cooper, Melissa, the priest, and her sisters were nearby. They were still in the back of the church, the same church where she realized that Blake and her sister, Shannon who was now dead, had betrayed her.

Her memory came flooding back to her in a tidal wave of emotion. Julie put her hands to her face and began sobbing. Cooper immediately swept her up into his arms and her mom was rubbing her back, but she couldn't stop the deep gut-wrenching sobs that wracked her body. Cooper held on and whispered in her ear, trying to soothe her but nothing could console her, and eventually, Cooper carried her out the backdoor and drove her home. Her family stayed to carry out the rest of the service.

Julie was curled up in the fetal position on her side of Cooper's jeep staring out the window, but she couldn't see anything because she had tears in her eyes that were flowing unnoticed and unchecked down her cheeks. "You scared the hell out of me Jewels. You just fainted. The second we walked into the church-"

Julie started to cry again. She didn't hear him swear or even apologize but she did feel his hand on her shoulder.

When they got home Cooper had to carry Julie inside and up to her room. He undressed her and put her in some comfortable pajamas that he found in her dresser drawers. She sat unmoving on the bed staring out at nothing. He picked up her feet, swung them around, and tucked her into bed. Her comatose state was starting to scare Cooper.

"I'm going downstairs to find that prescription your mom got to help her sleep and I'll be right back, okay?" Cooper asked but got no response. He ran downstairs as fast as he could and rifled through the vanity to find what he needed.

Cooper didn't quite know what to make of Julie's reaction at the church. Shannon wasn't the closest of her sisters, but he knew everyone responded to grief differently yet, somehow, he felt that it was more than grief that had caused her breakdown. He got a glass of water from the kitchen and returned to her room.

Julie had rolled onto her side with the covers pulled almost over her head with just enough room for her to breathe. She was sound asleep. Cooper put the pills and water next to the bed and slipped soundlessly from the room.

CHAPTER THIRTY-NINE

J ulie woke in the middle of the night. She couldn't believe she had slept so long. Her brain must have needed
the rest after all the realizations and emotional upheaval
of the day. She lay quietly, contemplating all that she now
knew. She was positive that Blake had killed her sister
Shannon and that he was the one trying to kill her. Proving
it would be another story. She didn't want her sister's name
to be run through the mud and she didn't want her parents
to ever find out about it.

She had broken off her engagement with him but, as
clever as he was, he had her sign the will before their vows.
Realizing he was still listed in the will he wouldn't even
have to marry her to inherit if she died before changing the
will. That was something she would need to rectify immediately if not sooner. She still struggled with the thought
that Shannon had been willing to kill her for money. Her
sister had everything she ever needed, what had made her
so greedy that she would be willing to kill her own flesh
and blood?

Julie's thoughts started to wander as she felt Cooper's
warm body sculpted around her. His bare arm was around
her midriff and his naked chest was pressed up against her

back. Her hand reached up to caress the golden hairs on his arm. She took his hand and lifting it to her lips pressed a kiss into his palm. Rolling over in his arms to face him she found herself utterly content in his embrace.

As Cooper slept, she studied his face. He had a strong jawline and an adorable dimple on his chin that deepened when he smiled. She liked his nose, not too big but not skinny either, it was nice and straight. His eyelashes swept in half-moon shapes across his cheeks. His forehead had small freckles near his hairline as a result of being in the sun all day. She frowned, she would have to make him wear sunscreen. Even though it looked cute she knew the sun could lead to health issues.

Most importantly when she looked at Cooper, she knew that he was hers. Her Cooper. She knew everything there was to know about this person. She remembered everything. She recalled him pulling her pigtails in the third grade and her pummeling him into the ground for it. She remembered them in junior high playing basketball and the competition between them was tit for tat. She remembered that first kiss, a dare in the garden that had carried her on cloud nine for ages. In high school, she remembered the hurt she felt with him going out with Courtney. She had buried herself in her schoolwork, came out as a straight-A student, and had gone on to college. They had both gone their separate ways in college, but they called each other often and saw each other during holidays and summers.

Julie had always been so comfortable around him. That was until they got older and her attraction to him became stronger. She could say anything to him on the phone but when they were together, and he would accidentally touch her she would jump away from him like she was on fire. It became increasingly difficult to not divulge her emotions. They told each other everything except how they felt about each other. She smiled to herself. They had been wasting all this time. They had almost made it there once...

CHAPTER FORTY

Eighteen Months Earlier

J ulie was hosting a Super Bowl Party at her townhouse that year. Her parents were there with Megan, Katie, and Melissa. Julie had invited some colleagues from work, and of course, Cooper was there. The New England Patriots were playing against the Dallas Cowboys in a battle to the death. The score was 10-3, the Pats were up, and the group was currently yelling at the television over a flag the ref had thrown against New England.

They had a friendly betting pool going to make the game a little more interesting to those who didn't follow football. Everyone picked a blank square, and numbers were assigned to them. Whoever had the numbers in the square at the end of each quarter won a pool of money. So far Joel, who currently was being good-naturedly accused of using his skill as a math professor to cheat, had won the first quarter.

Julie and her mom had outdone themselves with the food, laying out a fantastic Super Bowl spread. Chips with salsa, French onion, chili cheese, and parmesan artichoke dips were served with fresh bread. Chicken wings and meatballs were amid the veggie and fruit platters. Mozzarella sticks were a favorite as well as stuffed mushrooms hot out of the oven. Julie had made her famous bacon roll-ups with cream cheese and bread wrapped and baked in the oven. The first batch was almost gone before they reached the table. The laughter and alcohol were flowing, they had beer and wine, and Julie was in the kitchen making strawberry margaritas for the girls. Everyone was having a blast.

Cooper came into the kitchen to put his empty beer bottle under the sink, where she kept her recyclables. Julie was at the blender mixing away on the center island. Cooper came to stand beside her his hip, resting on the counter next to hers. "How's it going in here? Need any help?" Cooper asked as he opened his next beer, tossing the cap across the kitchen and landing it in the waste basket.

Julie watched, "Impressive." She sounded nonchalant, even to her own ears, but every time he was around, she wondered what it would be like to kiss him. Would he reject her? She didn't know and that's why she had always held back. Julie cherished their friendship more than anything else.

Inside the living room, they were booing and yelling. "Cowboys just scored a touchdown on a pick-six!" Came from inside the other room. Julie grinned at Cooper who was dressed in a New England Patriots jersey while Julie was sporting a Dallas Cowboys one in enemy territory.

"In your face," she said pointing a finger at him standing on her toes.

His face came down close to hers, "They'll come back."

"In your dreams." Julie saw the split second his eyes dropped to her lips before his warm brown eyes were teasing her again. The hand that was pointing a finger at him reached around his neck and pulled him in for a kiss, the moment their lips met it felt like a volt of electricity went coursing through her body. His lips were soft, and he tasted like beer. Normally she wouldn't like that but tonight she did, it felt and tasted intoxicating. She pulled away before Cooper even had a chance to respond to her kiss.

She came off her tip toes onto flat ground, her face was a look of utter shock. Cooper tried hard not to laugh because he knew it would scare her off, but he couldn't wait to tell her later how adorably frightened she looked.

Julie could see the humor dancing in his eyes and the small upturn of his irresistible lips and quickly turned around to concentrate her attention on the margaritas. "I want to watch the replay!" Julie shouted towards the living room and practically ran from the kitchen not even sparing Cooper a second glance. Pushing her way through the crowd, she sat down tucked between her mom and sister on the couch.

Cooper took his time coming back from the kitchen, he had poured the margaritas she had left behind and was serving them to the ladies. He bent down to hand her one. She didn't want to look at him but when he handed her the drink he wouldn't let go until she looked up and met his intense gaze. He was getting booed to get out of the way because he was standing directly in front of the T.V. so she glanced up at him and he let her take her drink.

He was smiling down at her his brown eyes warm and dare she say inviting. Oh, he can't wait to tease me about this she thought to herself. Why did you have to go and kiss him? You idiot, she mentally kicked herself.

"Okay, okay, I'm going." Cooper put his hands up in mock surrender as he was getting pelted with napkins and empty plastic cups as he backed out of the crowd and out of the line of vision.

Julie only made halfhearted attempts at cheering for the rest of the night. The Patriots came back in the second half and Julie turned to sneak a look over her shoulder to the spot where she knew Cooper was standing. Leaning casually with his shoulder against the door jamb, Cooper was holding a beer in one hand with one ankle crossed over the other and he wasn't watching his team win, he was watching her. Julie turned about five shades of red and spun her head around so fast she was worried she was going to give herself whiplash.

The night wore on and the game ended up in overtime, the Cowboys had come back to tie it up in the last few seconds of regulation play. The margaritas were starting to take effect and Julie was in desperate need of the bathroom. She had tried to hold off but just couldn't anymore, so she jumped up and bolted past Cooper. She fled down the hallway to the bathroom and locked the door. Feeling foolish she would have contemplated it more, but she had to go.

After washing her hands, she turned off the light and walked out of the bathroom. Lounging across the hallway was Cooper, waiting for her. She was tempted to go back inside the bathroom, shut the door, and hide but she stood her ground knowing she couldn't hide forever.

"Hey," she attempted instead.

"Hi," Cooper grinned. Julie attempted to push past him down the hallway when Cooper ushered her into the laundry room and shut the door. He flicked on the lights and looked down at her.

"You kissed me," he stated.

She reached over and flicked off the light not wanting to look at him.

"Yeah, about that, I'm...sorry. Heat of the moment thing...you know...touchdown! Excitement ...sorry." She attempted to explain. She rolled her eyes in the dark knowing that sounded pathetic, even to her own ears.

Cooper flicked the light back on, "So it didn't mean anything to you?" he asked.

Julie hit the light switch off again, she couldn't face him and lie, "No. Of course not. Why did it mean something to you?" She couldn't believe she got the question out and held her breath as she listened to utter silence in the dark.

"Yes." She heard him say. This time Julie flicked on the light, searching his face to see if he meant what he had confessed. She could tell instantly that he did.

"Oh," was all Julie managed in her shocked state. He's going to kiss me her mind raced seconds before his lips came down to meet hers. Her heart was slamming wildly inside her chest in anticipation of his lips touching hers.

Julie melted into Cooper's body, her arms instantly circling his neck to draw him closer. His strong arms wrapped themselves around her holding her upright to mold his body to hers. His lips sucked at her lower lip then his tongue touched her upper lip, and she opened her mouth to him. His tongue swept inside her mouth, and she met him with hers swirling intimately against each other straining to get as close as possible. Everything she had felt for him and had kept pent up for years exploded in this one kiss.

Her arms were touching the muscles in his back, and it wasn't good enough. Julie slipped her hands under his jersey and touched his bare skin, the firm muscles of his hips, sliding her hands up his back. He felt remarkable under her hands, all warmth and strength and sexy skin. She felt the scar on his shoulder blade where he had landed on a stick falling out of a tree when they were twelve then lost track of that thought as Cooper's lips left hers and started a trail down her neck.

"Don't stop touching me," he whispered in the dark. Julie realized Cooper must have turned off the lights and she was happy to oblige. Her hands ran down over his butt through his jeans, she had always admired his ass from afar. She pulled him closer and felt the full length of his arousal pressed to her belly. She gasped, shocked and excited at the same time.

Cooper took possession of her mouth again, his hands twisted in her hair slanting her head to the side to get better access. He pressed her back against the washing machine as his hand ran down the back of her leg pulling it up to rest on his hip. Cooper's thigh wedged in between her legs holding her in place.

Julie's hands went from his tight butt to his chest, her hands running down the length of him. She felt the sculpted muscle she had mentally drooled over for years. His golden chest hair curled around her fingers and Julie's hands cascaded lower over his washboard stomach, glorying in the feel of him under her fingertips. One finger trailed over the line of hair that led below his waistline. She then splayed her fingers over his stomach and dipped into the top of his jeans.

Cooper sucked in his breath and pulled away. "Ah, Jewels. We need to stop, or I will be making love to you on top of this washing machine."

"Oh?" Julie seemed to be considering it.

He chuckled, "Jewels your parents are right outside this door."

Disappointment swept through Julie, stunned she had so completely gotten lost in the moment that she forgot she had an entire house full of people including her parents, "Oh, yeah. Do you want to go out first?"

Cooper smiled. "I need a moment to compose myself."

Julie grinned. She meant to give him a quick kiss which turned into a not-so-short kiss before he shoved her out the door into the hallway and shut the door behind her. As she looked around the hallway, Julie was grateful to see everyone was still engrossed in the game, so she popped her head into the bathroom to fix herself.

Oh my God, everyone is going to know! Her hair was a mess of tangles, and her lips were bright red and swollen. Her cheeks were flushed and the look in her eyes would give her away for sure. She locked herself in the bathroom and brushed her hair out and tried to calm herself.

Julie did the best she could before walking back into the living room. Cooper was already in the room holding his beer again. She was just in time for the Cowboys to score the winning touchdown.

When she was near Cooper she joked playfully, "Ha, ha. You lost."

He leaned down and whispered in her ear, "No Sweetheart, I won."

She gave him a foolish grin before sauntering away. Cooper ended up having to give Melissa a ride home, but he winked at Julie before leaving.

The next two weeks were full of stolen moments and excitement. Then one Saturday she called Cooper's house to see what he was doing, and he sounded kind of weird saying he had a work emergency that he had to attend to.

Since she couldn't spend the day with Cooper, she called Melissa. Melissa told her she was sick and was just going to stay in bed all day. Julie decided to make her friend soup. When it was done, she wanted to pop in for a quick kiss with Cooper before heading to Melissa's house. So, she swung around Cooper's office and his secretary said she didn't know of any emergency, but it didn't mean that there wasn't one. She said clients sometimes called Cooper at home.

Julie went on to her friend's house and discovered Cooper's Jeep in her driveway. A sinking feeling swept Julie as she got out of the car. Maybe he had heard she was sick and dropped by to see how she was doing. She heard their laughter before she reached the door, Melissa didn't sound sick. She pressed her ear to the door and heard Melissa say, "Julie will never find out. I'm good at secrets."

She gasped as she pulled her ear away from the door. Running back to her car she slipped and fell on a patch of ice and almost slid under the vehicle. The soup remained intact in its container, but she felt like hurdling it through Melissa's window.

Tears were streaming down Julie's face. He had never said he loved her, not once in the past two weeks. He had never said they were exclusive, but to be involved with their mutual friend. Obviously, this didn't mean as much to him as it did to her. Well, if he didn't care then neither would she.

She drove to her parents' house looking for someone to vent to and she slid off the road into a snowbank. Blake happened to come along to the rescue, he looked so handsome in his suit, and he was so cute when he asked her out. That's when Julie began playing a dangerous game she couldn't win.

CHAPTER FORTY-ONE

Present Day

Julie was in Cooper's arms now, feeling the rise and fall of his naked chest as he breathed softly in his sleep. She had her memory back and she realized what a fool she had been with Blake. How stupid she was for falling for Blake's scheme to marry her and get her money. She was angry, angry at herself for almost ruining her life. She had never been in love with Blake, she knew that now. She had cared for him, sure, that was until she found out he was willing to kill her for money and was sleeping with her sister.

Deep down Julie had hoped Cooper would step in and declare his love to her but when he didn't, she felt bad for deceiving Blake. She found that she liked Blake and if she couldn't have Cooper then why not try to make a life with someone, she thought loved her? Not a smart idea as it turned out and Julie regretted every minute of it. She had inadvertently gotten Shannon killed.

Julie kissed Cooper's neck. This was her best friend in the world and now her lover and she wasn't planning on ever letting that go. She had always wondered what it would be like to be with him. Would it ruin their friendship? What if things didn't work out, would it cause a lasting wedge between them? She prayed to God it wouldn't. Julie had dared to take a chance and now she was planning on seeing this through. She felt so comfortable in his arms like this was where she was supposed to be.

She eased from his embrace and slipped out of bed then shivered, feeling the warmth of his body evaporating. Glancing at the clock she realized it was five in the morning. Grabbing some clothes from her dresser drawer she slipped into the bathroom, stripped out of her pajamas, and turned on the shower. Reaching inside she felt the warm water splash on her hand and turned it up making the steam rise, she wanted a hot shower. When the temperature reached her satisfaction, she climbed into the glass-enclosed stand-up shower.

Julie stood still under the pelting drive of the water letting her hair get soaked. She tried to get the images of Blake and Shannon out of her head. They had betrayed her. Was it planned from the beginning? Did they know each other first? How had Shannon found out about the money when Julie herself didn't even know?

She absentmindedly washed her hair as she thought of what she should do. The gun in her dad's safe came to mind. She was going to confront Blake. She turned around to rinse her hair and let out a startled gasp, her hand clutching her chest as Cooper stepped into the shower with her.

"Mind if I join you?"

Julie tried a smile, "Sure."

Cooper took her in his arms and Julie's head instantly rested on his chest. He was her safe haven. He tilted her chin up, "Do you want to talk about it?"

Julie shook her head no. She didn't plan on telling him that she remembered everything yet. She didn't want to look him in the eye either, fearing he would read her like an open book. Closing her eyes with her face still upturned to him, he leaned down and sweetly touched his lips to hers. Pulling away Cooper didn't get far as her right hand wound around his neck pulling him back to her.

What had started innocent enough on Cooper's part, Julie turned steamy. Her left hand curved around his tight rear end and pulled him to her. His strong hands slicked over her wet hair and cupped her face. Her lips parted and her tongue flicked over his lips, in turn, he mimicked her actions. Their breathing hitched, gasping at the sensations that coursed through every nerve ending.

Steam rose around them and hot water pelted their bodies unnoticed. Her tongue pressed against his, her head pushed towards him then pulled away and he followed her, chasing her kiss. His big hands started a slow descent down her body grazing his knuckles down the side of her breast with one hand and the other hand lightly caressing her midriff down to her hip with his fingertips.

Their bodies swayed together, pushing and pulling towards one another. Her hands began exploring up and down his back. One of her dainty hands reached between them, she found him hard and straining for her. Stroking him, encircling him with her soft hand she showed him what she wanted from him. She told him without saying a word that she needed him.

Cooper's hand cupped her womanhood and she moaned into his mouth. He pushed her back against the tile wall of the shower and broke their intense kiss their bodies still pressed together. He held her gaze as his finger teased inside her folds. Leaning her head back on the wall she watched him. Her breath was hitched in her chest coming out in small gasps. Julie could see his shoulder muscles flex as he coaxed her into wanting more.

She was practically panting, her thighs spread further for him, and he watched her intently as his long finger plunged inside her. She clutched his shoulder and bit down on her lower lip. While he clung to her, his arms wound tight around her. Cooper's strong arms lifted her feet off the ground, his arousal pressed against her belly and his strong hands slid down the back of her thighs and bent her knees.

Her feet could reach the glass on the opposite side of the shower, and she planted them there. Cooper lowered her onto himself, impaling her as he drove home. Her nails raked his back as he pushed her up and down on the wall. One of his hands cupped her breast. Looking into his eyes was the most intimate moment, she felt the love pouring from her and into his soul.

He recognized it for what it was and kissed her with everything he felt for her, and she put everything into that kiss. It was an unbreakable bond. His groan mixed with her moans. Her hands cupped his face desperate to hold him. Julie surrendered herself to him. Her climax rocked her to the core trembling around him. He pumped inside her three more, slow, deliberate times then shuddered as he spilled his seed inside her. They stood there, still wrapped in each other's arms as he kissed her again, his tongue swirling with hers his hands caressing her face. Pulling away, he looked down at her. She brushed her fingers across her forehead gently pushing his hair away. Leaning down he rubbed his nose against hers then softly kissed the tip of it. They were both so overcome with emotion it was hard to find the words to express their feelings.

Easing out of her, he gently lowered her feet down to the shower floor but did not let go of her. Reaching for the soap he lathered her up, covering her entire body in bubbles then did the same to himself. With one arm around her waist, they stood under the water to rinse off. Cooper asked, "Are you ready to get out yet?"

Julie nodded her head, so Cooper reached behind her and shut off the water. He dried her off with a thick white towel from the warming rack then used the towel on himself. Julie quickly slipped back into her comfortable pajamas and headed towards the bed once more. Cooper followed her, having pulled back on his boxers. They slipped between the sheets, and he pulled her close.

Julie pretended to fall asleep while waiting for the steady rhythm of his breathing to assure her that he had fallen back to sleep. Easing herself out of bed, she was careful not to disturb him. Pulling dark clothes from her dresser, she stealthily dressed in the dark and slipped out of the room undetected.

It was six in the morning no one was awake yet. Julie was able to sneak out of the house with no one the wiser. This time, knowing where all the furniture was and which floorboard had a squeak in it, she avoided them all.

Chapter Forty-Two

Cooper's eyes fluttered open as he stared across Julie's bedroom. His heart ached for her and the loss of Shannon. This morning in the shower, something had changed between them. It was more intimate, more loving. Smiling, he rolled over eager to wrap her up in his arms and feel her warmth. He wanted to tell her, confess his feelings for her. He thought she knew or at least suspected that he was madly in love with her, but he wanted to say the words. He didn't know why he had waited this long already, but that he had been afraid of losing her or scaring her. What he found when he turned her way was an empty side of the bed.

He could smell Sandy's cooking wafting up to him from downstairs. It put a sad smile on his face as it registered. Sandy hadn't cooked one morsel of food since they had found out about Shannon's murder. It was good to think she had started the process of healing, which he knew would be a long hard road.

Julie must have been lured downstairs to eat breakfast with her family. He quickly got out of bed and pulled clothes from the duffle bag he had packed. Cooper had practically moved in with Julie and her family, wanting to stay close by her side and protect her as best he could. He had Skyped with Elizabeth Lucas rather than having another meeting in California. □

He walked into the kitchen to find it a somber place. Katie and Megan were pushing food around on their plate and Sandra had mounds of food baked on the center island. Jack was sitting at the table flipping through the paper looking older somehow, worn, and disheveled. He looked around but didn't see Julie.

"Where's Julie?" Cooper asked, taking a piece of bacon off one of the plates on the island.

The family as a whole looked up as if they had just now noticed his presence. Jack lowered the paper to look at Cooper, slight concern on his face. Julie's mom instantly panicked.

"She wasn't in the bathroom upstairs?" Sandra asked.

Cooper was shaking his head when Jack jumped up from the table.

"Maybe she fell asleep in the library." The whole family was fast on his heels in the hopes of finding Julie asleep in one of the overstuffed chairs like she had done countless times. What they did find shocked them into stunned silence. Jack and Sandy had stopped in their tracks, the two girls bumped into them, and Cooper walked around them to see what they were staring at. The room was empty but over the mantle was a large painting on hinges that were swung wide, behind that was an open safe.

"Julie has her memory back," Jack whispered but everyone heard. They all turned around to look at Cooper.

"She was up at five this morning." He left out the part where he had made love to her in the shower, "I just thought she was having trouble sleeping." Cooper raked his hand through his hair. "What's missing?" Cooper asked.

Jack walked over to the safe. "Looks like everything is still here..." his voice trailed off as he picked up the gun case. It was empty, the code had been used and it stood open, and rounds of ammunition were gone as well. "She has a loaded weapon," he confirmed their fears.

"I'll call the cops." Sandra headed for the door.

"And tell them what Sandy, that our daughter has a loaded gun? I don't think so. Girls, give me and Cooper a minute."

Katie and Megan practically ran from the room. Sandra gave her husband a pleading look, "I won't lose another daughter, Jack," and followed her girls out of the room.

Jack slumped down in the nearest chair and Cooper began to pace. "I think she knows who killed Shannon," Cooper stated, fear seizing his heart.

Jack nodded, looking grief-stricken.

"We need to find her before she finds the killer."

Jack was in full-hearted agreement, "But how do we do that?" We don't even know where to start looking.

"We need to start pulling some strings. No cops, yet. Call her cell phone company for starters and see if we can't get a location."

Jack had his cell phone in his hand and began dialing.

CHAPTER FORTY-THREE

Julie had managed to elude the cops stationed outside of her house. They were on high alert after several attempts on her own life, especially now since her sister's murder. She had slipped out the back door and managed the maze with no problem now, knowing every nook and cranny. She punched in the four-digit code for Cooper's three-car garage and took his nana's black Lincoln, feeling extremely guilty in the process.

She drove to Blake's apartment but parked two blocks away, feeling oddly comforted by the gun in her pocketbook. Her dad had made sure all of his girls knew how to handle a gun with deadly accuracy. Blake lived on the third floor, and you needed to be buzzed in, but Julie still had his key. She let herself in and because it was so early in the morning no one was in the lobby. She took the stairs two at a time to the apartment. She let herself in quietly pulling the gun out of her purse as she walked slowly to the bedroom.

When she confirmed her hunch, she was going to kill the son of a bitch. No one was ever going to find his body, and no one would ever know what type of person Shannon had been. Shannon would remain the victim and not the woman who had betrayed her family. If Blake did not cooperate with her plan and go easily with her, she had a Plan B, self-defense in mind.

Blake was lying in bed face down, naked as far as she could tell. The sheet barely covered him, and she could see why she and Shannon had been attracted to him. He had used both sisters and resorted to murder when he didn't get what he wanted. She kicked the bed and waited for him to roll over, the gun aimed steadily at his head.

"Julie, what are you doing here?" he asked pulling the sheets up over his waist. There was bruising over his right eye. The cops had said there was blood at the crime scene that was still unidentified.

"I remember everything, Blake."

He dared to smile, "Julie that's great. Do you want to get married now? I knew if I just waited you would come around." He noticed the gun and then stuttered out, "Julie...what...what's going on here?"

"You see Blake, it's not good for you that I remember everything, now, is it?"

"Julie, what in God's name are you talking about? I thought you remembered how much you loved me. How much I love you."

Julie scoffed at him. "I remember how much you loved my money and my sister. I saw you two at the back of the church on our wedding day, plotting to kill me and-" □

Julie felt a sharp blow to the back of her head and a blinding light flashed before her eyes before she crumpled to the ground.

CHAPTER FORTY-FOUR

C ooper ran back into the library. "Julie has taken
Nana's car. She had to make it through the maze and
punch in the security code to do it. She has her memory
back. Any luck?"

Jack was shaking his head before holding his hand
up and speaking back into the phone. "Yes, I would like
to speak to your supervisor this is District Attorney Jack
Hart this is an ongoing investigation and unless you want
a lawsuit on your head you'd better-"

Cooper heard Jack mutter a swear word under his
breath. "They put me on hold again. Being District Attorney used to mean something before-Yes, hello? I need a
trace on a cell phone number..."

Cooper stopped listening to him as his thoughts took
over. Why wouldn't she say something to him? She knew
that she could talk to him and trust him. The thought
hit him like a ton of bricks. What if she didn't trust him?
All the old feelings of betrayal she had felt, maybe she still
felt that. Did she want to break things off with him? He
couldn't handle it if that were the case, he'd waited too
long for her to be his. He possessed her body and soul,
and she would always have his. When had she regained her

memory? Was it before they had made love this morning? Was she saying goodbye to him? They just needed to find her. He had a sinking feeling they were running out of time.

"Thank you." Jack was just getting off the phone.

"The address is 376 Spencer Street. Do you know where that is?"

Cooper let out an expletive, "That's Blake's place."

Jack and Cooper bolted for the door in unison.

CHAPTER FORTY-FIVE

Julie had a splitting headache. As she came to, she realized that she had been bound, gagged, and blindfolded. She struggled to get control of her senses and take stock of her surroundings in the dark. She tried to become aware of what was going on around her. No voices could be heard but there was a steady sound of something, she wasn't quite sure of what yet.

Her mind scrambled to fill in the blanks. Where was she? Who had hit her over the head? It wasn't Blake, he was sitting in front of her when that happened. Did he have a partner in crime? Was she completely wrong? No, she knew what she saw in the church.

Her arms were sore from being twisted behind her back and she was beginning to lose circulation. She must have been in this position a while, she concluded. Suddenly she was tossed in the air and hit metal before landing again on a short carpet, getting a little rugburn on her arm. Julie suspected she was in the trunk of a car. Where are they taking me, she wondered, as she fought back the panic welling up inside. Knowing she'd need to stay calm to have a chance of survival she took a slow steady breath.

Maybe going after Blake on her own hadn't been such a good idea. Julie felt around for anything she may be able to use to help her escape this situation and found her purse at her feet. It took her several long minutes to maneuver it to her hands behind her back. Her assailants had taken the gun away from her but hadn't taken her cell phone out of her purse.

First, she needed to deal with the tape across her mouth. In high school, she and Cooper had gone to the movies to watch an action flick where the leading lady had been bound and gagged. Julie had bet Cooper she could get out of the tape. Cooper had tied her up and put tape over her mouth, Julie had used her tongue to unstick the glue off the tape and then bit the tape to remove it from her face. She did it again now wondering why no heroine had yet figured out this trick then she dealt with the blindfold, putting her face against the short carpet in the car trunk and rubbing until the blindfold pushed up over her head and off her face.

Exhausted but knowing she had to push herself on, Julie prayed she had a signal and that her battery was still charged. She pressed the button on the phone and pressed where she thought the icon for the phone was. Then she ran her fingers over the screen, unsure of the outcome she could only hope she could reach someone who knew she was missing and recognize this as a call for help. Seconds later the car came to a screeching halt sending her flying into the spare tire, she landed hard on her phone and her tied arms causing excruciating pain from her numb wrists to her shoulder blades. Fear had Julie's mind reeling, she had yet to figure out how to free her arms, and regardless of the progress she'd made, she was essentially helpless. She couldn't do anything other than wait for the trunk to open.

Julie was blinded by the sun when the trunk lid was raised, Blake stood over her saying, "Nice try. You just called me." He flipped her over yanked her purse from the trunk and wrenched the phone from her grasp.

She watched as he threw the phone on the ground and stomped on it, then flung her purse into the ditch on the opposite side of the road.

In the brief time the trunk was open, Julie tried to gauge where they had taken her. She could see trees lining the road, she thought they were on a back road because she didn't hear any traffic and the potholes in the road indicated neglect. That plus what were the chances he would stop on a highly traveled road and risk the chance someone would see her tied up in the trunk of a car?

"I hate to do this, but I can't risk it." Blake raised her dad's gun over his head and brought it down, striking her temple causing her to welcome the darkness once more and escape the pain.

CHAPTER FORTY-SIX

J ack had to flash his District Attorney badge to be allowed into Blake's apartment by the landlord. Cooper
and Jack rushed into the apartment not knowing exactly
what they would find but knowing Julie had a few hours
head start on them. They found the apartment empty, the
bed unmade, and a small pool of blood on the floor at the
foot of the bed. Cooper fought back the sickening feeling
welling up inside him at the sight of what he assumed was
Julie's blood on the floor, instead he let the anger that was
hot on the heels of his panic take over. He'd kill Blake when
they caught him, kill him with his bare hands!

Jack whipped out his cell. "This is Jack Hart District
Attorney. My daughter Julie has been kidnapped."

Cooper raked his fingers through his hair and blew
out an unsteady breath as he listened to Jack give their location. Jack had more pull at the police station than he did
with the cell phone company because no one questioned
him once. They pulled up the GPS on the Lincoln Julie
had taken from Nana's garage and found it was parked two
blocks away. They also tracked the GPS for her cell phone,
and it gave coordinates that showed her phone was several
miles out of town.

Jack and Cooper didn't wait for the police to arrive but headed back downstairs to Jack's sedan. Cooper punched in the coordinates they had received, this time from the police department, into his phone and it gave them directions to get there. Cooper started to worry they were going to get to Julie too late when they left the last town and headed for the hills. An hour later they were pulling over on the side of the road, it was a two-lane road, not a house or business in sight. □

Cooper was the first to hop out of the car and began searching the right side of the road while Jack took the left scanning the ground for clues. Cooper had a sinking feeling when he didn't spot anything that could be considered shelter, he prayed they just found her phone and not her body lying next to it. He had to remain hopeful that they would find her alive. However, knowing her sister Shannon hadn't been as lucky didn't help his anxiety at all. Cooper's chest was constricted with fear, and he was having a hard time breathing normally. He knew he would have to remain calm if he was going to be of any use, not only in rescuing Julie but helping Jack as well.

Cooper looked up when he heard Jack swear under his breath. Jack was standing over what he could only assume was Julie's cell phone smashed on the ground. There was nothing out here but mountains and trees. Where could Blake be taking her and why?

Chapter Forty-Seven

A t ten thirty that night a ransom demand was made to the Hart home in the amount of thirteen million dollars. Not surprisingly, the exact amount left for Julie by her Aunt Gwen.

Jack and Cooper had arrived home shortly before, shoulders slumped with a huge feeling of loss and failure. They had been out all day searching the countryside for Julie. The police had advised them several times during the day to go home and let them do their job, but the men continued to assist in the search. They had done a grid search where they had found the cell phone and later her pocketbook. The police brought in a canine unit. That nearly killed the two men right there, praying the dogs would pick up a scent but not the scent of her dead body. Finally, when they found nothing at all at nightfall the two men returned home.

Jack found his girls Katie and Megan sitting on the couch with their mother staring at a blank TV. Patrol cars waited outside, and the FBI was inside setting up phone taps and camping out, the whole scene felt so surreal. One daughter was dead, and another was missing. What was happening to his family and why was he unable to stop it?

Cooper felt just as devastated. Why hadn't he seen the signs? Her breakdown at the church and her being up in the middle of the night not talking to him was uncharacteristic of her. He should have recognized instantly that something more than her sister dying was the cause of her odd behavior. Cooper just prayed that she knew how much he loved her. He had wanted to tell her early this morning when he was inside of her, but he hadn't wanted to tell her like that. He wanted no doubts. Cooper never wanted Julie to think that it was a heat-of-the-moment declaration rather than how he truly meant it, that he was madly and passionately in love with her, with every fiber of his being.

Cooper had been in love with her longer than he could remember. He had fallen in love with Julie as his best friend and confidant then again later when she grew into the beautiful woman she was today. He had lived his life without her already and the past few months were more than enough to realize he could not do it again without her. Julie was the one, always had been.

Cooper's parents had died in an airplane crash when he was three and custody was given to his grandparents who lived in the house behind Julie's. Nana was a young grandmother who took care of herself by going to the gym (the one they had built in their home) and was quite a social butterfly. So, she became quick friends with the young new family who moved into the house behind her with a young daughter Cooper's age.

Sandy was pregnant with Shannon when they moved into their new home. Nana had walked over with a store-bought pie and found her running after Julie while trying to make dinner one night. Nana offered to take Cooper and Julie for a walk while Sandra cooked dinner. Later that night, after dinner was eaten, and the children were sleeping on the couch together sharing a blanket the adults got to know each other. Nana made it her personal mission to introduce Sandra to her friends as the best caterer in the state. Even if it meant having to watch the children, which she secretly adored doing.

Cooper always believed his Nana would have signed a betrothal agreement right then and there if that was done anymore. His Nana and his grandfather, when he was alive loved Julie and her family as their own. They were always so warm and inviting. Cooper's Grandfather was partly responsible for Jack's success as a budding attorney. Henry Pembrooke had taken Jack under his wing at the club and introduced the young attorney around to all his influential friends, guaranteeing him high-end clients.

Cooper thought of his Nana, now such a different person she had become after losing her husband to a long illness. He hadn't had time to tell Nana about Julie yet and didn't relish the thought of telling her either. Nana, although a little addled in many of her memories, was still very clear in her love for Julie and her family like she loved her grandson. This news would devastate her.

The phone rang loudly in the background breaking the trance of Cooper's memories. Everyone froze staring at the phone then all chaos broke loose when everyone made a grab for the phone at once. The FBI agent in charge stopped them with the raise of his hand until his crew could get to their equipment in time then motioned for Jack to answer the phone. Jack looked at his anxious wife and gave her a reassuring nod before picking up the receiver. "Jack Hart," he spoke into the phone with a confidence he didn't feel.

"I have your daughter," the altered voice reverberated over the phone, "I want thirteen million in cash by this time tomorrow."

"I want proof my daughter is still alive," Jack demanded in his most stern voice.

A second or two of intense silence followed then, "Daddy, tell Cooper I like someone else and-" Then the phone went dead. Jack held it in his hand a long time, still up to his ear until the dial tone began buzzing in his ear. The crowd around him sat in stunned silence. They had heard the whole exchange. Then as if on cue they all turned towards Cooper, surely this was some kind of clue. A message only Cooper would understand.

Cooper felt as if someone had sucker punched him in the gut. His oxygen supply was limited as his whole world came crashing down on his head. Julie didn't love him and that was more than he could take. Was she in love with Blake who had supposedly kidnapped her? Was she being forced to say that? None of this made any sense. He had to clear his head and so without a word to anyone he walked out the back door and headed towards his grandfather's maze, where he could be alone in his own private hell.

No one tried to stop him, they knew he must be in shock, they were in shock. What was Julie thinking, saying that, when they all knew she was head over heels for Cooper? Always had been as far as anyone could see. Jack was the first one to speak. "She's trying to tell us something. We just need to figure out what it is."

"I'll make the coffee," Sandra said to no one in particular as she retreated to the kitchen. She needed a minute alone. Her baby girl was alive. Sandy sucked in a ragged breath. Yes, the shock of the statement had set them all on their heels for a moment, but Julie was alive! Relief overtook shock as the tears she hadn't dared allow to fall now streamed down her face unchecked.

CHAPTER FORTY-EIGHT

J ulie prayed that Cooper would get the message. She sat tied to a hard wooden chair, her arms were tingling, and her wrists were rubbed raw. She had dried blood caked from her temple down over one eye that was swollen shut. Not that she could see anyway, they had blindfolded her but not before she realized where she was. Julie knew that if her family demanded proof of life during the ransom call, she'd have to think of something quick and to the point without giving away that she knew where she was. If given half the chance, she needed to come up with a way to make her location known. She only hoped Cooper would understand what she was trying to tell him.

She could hear them discussing what to do with her through the closed door. Only Blake came into the room, but she knew there was at least one other person with him. He untied her from the chair and carried her to the bed, he cut off the bonds on her wrists and replaced them with metal handcuffs. One latched around her wrist the other secured to the bed post. He left her feet tied up and covered her over with a blanket.

"I wish this could've ended differently," he whispered as he bent over to kiss her forehead. She tried to whip her head aside, but he held her firmly. This man made her physically ill with his merest touch.

Listening, she heard him walk across the room and shut the door quietly behind him. She tried hard not to let the tears come. She rolled on her side and tried to go back to sleep. As she closed her eyes, she yearned to feel Cooper's arms holding her. Was it only this morning that she had felt the warmth and security of his embrace? Why the hell would she leave? It felt much longer than that, she longed to be home once more. Saying a quick prayer that Cooper would find her before sleep overtook her.

CHAPTER FORTY-NINE

C ooper was gone for hours. He'd wandered home and stood in the shower but that only reminded him of Julie. He still couldn't believe she wasn't there with him, how quickly things could change. Two months ago, Julie was going to marry someone else, three days ago Shannon was alive, and less than twenty-four hours ago Julie was in his arms. He put on sweats and a T-shirt and went for a run. He didn't know how long or how far he ran he just kept going, trying to shut his brain off, to shut off the emotions that had threatened to break him. Two hours later with sweat dripping down his face and a sweat-soaked T-shirt he stopped and collapsed on the side of the road. The rain started then, slowly at first then in sheets.

His mind raced as he remembered a day seven years ago. It had been raining then too. He and Julie were outside talking on the front porch of a log cabin when the rain started, and Julie was about to tell him something, he was positive. He grabbed her hand, and they ran into the nearby shed instead of going into the house. The cabin was full of people, and he was sure she didn't want them to know what she was about to divulge. He loved that he knew her so well. Inside the shed they stood on opposite sides keeping their distance from each other.

"Spill it," Cooper crossed his arms in front of his chest, leaned his back and one foot against the wall behind him.

Julie was looking down at the dirt floor, one foot kicking the dirt in half-moon circles. She proceeded with uncharacteristic shyness, "I umm...kind of like someone."

Cooper felt a thrill run up and down his spine. Was Julie going to finally admit she had feelings for him? It was just too good to be true. He almost couldn't bring himself to ask but he had to know.

"Really? Who's that?"

"He's totally wrong for me."

Shit, he thought this can't be me. Well, at least Cooper hoped she didn't think he was a hundred percent wrong for her. He almost didn't want to know at this point, but he forced himself to ask, "Come on... you can tell me."

"AJ Carlson," she said, finally looking up at him.

He could still see the look in her eyes. Cooper looked up from the side of the road, heart pounding but this time it wasn't from his run. AJ was a kid from their high school class, and she was right, he was no good for her. His head snapped up. He knew where she was! He jumped up from his position on the ground and began sprinting the long distance home. He was energized now, driven by adrenaline. He knew where the love of his life was, and he was going to get her. Luckily, on his two-hour run, he had begun to make a loop back towards home, so he was closing the distance to the Hart residence in record time. He fought through the pain of running and pictured Julie in his mind. He was never going to let her go again, once he found her.

Cooper collapsed on the front stairs of the mahogany porch. Megan and Katie were the first ones there. Each slipped an arm around him and assisted their long-time big brother into the house. Sandra filled a glass of water and handed it to Cooper when he was settled on the couch. Jack and the agents were hovering around him along with the girls as he downed the glass of water in one long gulp and handed it back. He tried standing up from the couch and was immediately met with resistance from everyone around him. Not to mention his damn knees gave out on him so he was forced to collapse back on the couch, "I know where Julie is," Cooper stated matter of fact.

That statement got everyone moving. Agents were grabbing pens while Jack was grabbing his keys and hauling Cooper to his feet in one swift movement. Jack practically carried him out of the house and redirected him to a waiting vehicle, a government-issued black SUV. He put Cooper in front with an agent and Jack, along with another agent, hopped into the back seat. Several cars followed them as Cooper directed them to get on the highway.

"It's about a four-and-a-half hour drive the way they went but they were using all secondary roads. If you get me to my boat, we can take my helicopter and get there much sooner."

The agent driving turned on his emergency lights and floored it. "We will see if we can't make that time even shorter."

The agent in the backseat was already on her phone calling in highway patrol. She arranged for the nearest landing zone and FBI vehicle ready for them. It was already two thirty in the morning, so they shouldn't have any problem with traffic.

Chapter Fifty

Waking up every twenty minutes or so, according to the digital clock she could see on the nightstand next to the bed, Julie dozed fitfully between nightmares. Handcuffed to the headboard she had only been allowed to lay flat on her back or her right side. She would give anything to lie on her left side, just because the option had been denied her. Exhausted and sore, she gave up on sleep. Julie started thinking about Cooper and how it used to be with them.

Eventually, she fell back asleep with tender thoughts of Cooper and dreamt of them making love. In her dream, she smiled wickedly with all of the fantasies she wanted to fulfill with him. She felt him nibble on her ear and caress her breast. She moaned as she felt his hand drifting down her abdomen and between her legs. Her mind was waking up a lot slower than her body.

"Cooper," she whispered.

There was a harsh laugh in her ear, and she instantly came awake, knowing this wasn't Cooper, but her worst nightmare coming true.

"Guess again, sweetheart," Blake whispered in her ear while he continued to fondle her.

She shoved against him with all her might and immediately realized he had removed the handcuffs. Blake didn't go far, in fact, he was on top of her instantly his hands pegging hers to the bed his face leaned in close to hers. "If you're not cooperative I'll have to gag you and put the handcuffs back on," he snarled. Then his face softened, "You don't want that do you?" As though he was concerned with what she wanted.

Julie shook her head vigorously. Think Julie, think. He smiled down at her. "I was really looking forward to our honeymoon, Julie." Blake leaned down and kissed her, but Julie turned her head and his kiss landed on her cheek. That's when she spotted the lamp next to her on the nightstand.

Blake's kisses were going down her neck, "See? I can be gentle, I can give you what you want, Julie. Your sister? She liked it rough, and I loved to give it to her fucking rough." Snarling, he bit her ear, and she gasped. He was encouraged, mistaking her response for desire. Blake began losing concentration as his mouth trailed down between her breasts. He had to release one of her hands to unbutton her shirt. It wasn't the hand she was hoping for. She couldn't reach the lamp with that hand.

Julie sucked in a startled breath as his lips closed around one of her nipples. She thought she was going to gag. She didn't want him touching her. She belonged to Cooper. Blake chuckled as he got a reaction from her and continued his narrative, "I could tell you would like it slow and sensual. I can give that to you." Blake's hand cupped the breast he had just kissed, his lips going to the other breast. Julie tried to get him to release her other hand, but he held her steady. Shit. She was going to have to make him think she was getting into this, or he wouldn't let go of her, or worse yet, he'd handcuff her again.

"You taste sweet like I remembered, I've been craving you." Her eyes squeezed tight, her head thrashing back and forth trying to get the image of Blake out of her mind.

His hand left her left breast and slid down between her legs.

"Oh, Blake..." Julie sounded false to her ears, but he didn't seem to notice. Julie swallowed hard, choking back her disgust before asking, "Blake?" He looked up with passion in his eyes. "Can you kiss me?" Her free hand tugged on his shirt to pull him back up to her. He grinned sliding up the length of her wedging himself between her thighs. Blake's head came up, his lips nuzzling hers. Julie tried with all her might to kiss him back her free hand roaming up and down his back trying to get him to release her other hand, but he resisted her futile attempts.

Julie broke away from the kiss, "I want to touch you." She looked straight into his eyes hoping she looked seductive. She must have been somewhat convincing, but his response was still not what she was looking for as he pulled her right hand down and put it on his hard arousal between their legs using his hand on the outside of hers to rub it up against him.

"That's how much I've been missing you, Julie." Blake's breath was becoming ragged with anticipation. Yeah right, me and a million other women. She wasn't buying what he was trying to sell but she was willing to bet there were plenty of women out there that did.

He released her hand, and though it sickened her to do so, she continued to rub him. His hands went under her bottom pulling her closer to him. She removed her hand and using both hands she grabbed his butt and moaned, continuing to play the part. Blake went back to kissing her neck when she slid her right hand up his back and in one swift movement grabbed the base of the lamp and brought it down hard on his head. Pottery shattered over the two of them, and Blake grunted and collapsed on top of her. At the same time, Julie heard an odd sound and one of the sliding glass doors shattered then a second later in rushed Cooper.

"I'm going to kill him!" Cooper roared.

Fear was instantaneously instilled in Julie's eyes. "It's not what it seems," Julie tried to get out from under Blake. God help her if Cooper thought she was betraying him.

"I know, Jewels." He shoved Blake off of her and scooped Julie into his arms, "I saw what happened. Let's get out of here."

"Not so fast," was heard from the door. Standing there holding a loaded pistol, legs spread apart to brace herself was Courtney Champlain.

Blake slowly started to regain consciousness on the bed. "Just couldn't keep it in your pants, could you?" Courtney sneered.

Blake never got a chance to give a bullshit line because Courtney turned her gun towards him and fired. Blake screamed, his hand held up in the air as if to stop her. She wasn't trying to kill him, just castrate him, which she did. She was an excellent markswoman.

Cooper had already pushed Julie behind him in a protective manner. When Courtney's gun swung back around to them, Cooper put his hand up.

"Whoa, Court. Calm down. You don't want to do this."

Tears started streaming down her perfect face. "I don't want to hurt you, Cooper. Julie, this is all your fault! You stole him away from ME!" she screeched the last, her eyes wild.

"Was Blake the boyfriend your parents didn't approve of?" Cooper asked gently, wanting her to talk to him until the cavalry could make their move. No one noticed or cared that Blake had passed out on the bed from the pain, in a pool of blood.

"Yes, he's a nobody in my parent's eyes. They loved you. You were perfect." Courtney all but spat, "Why couldn't you love me, Cooper?" Her gun lowered and she began to sob hysterically.

Doors flew open and FBI agents rushed into the room, taking a startled Courtney down to the ground.

"I need a medic!" One of the agents yelled out as he felt for a pulse on Blake's neck.

Julie felt weak and collapsed, falling on her hands and knees on the hardwood floor. She vomited until all she could do was dry heave. The events of the long day finally caught up to her and overtook her at that moment. Cooper continued to hold her as she bent over, he rubbed her back and secured her hair away from her face.

"Jesus," he swore softly when he saw her face, swollen and bruised. Rage welled up inside him, but he tamped it down knowing Julie needed him more than he needed to inflict pain, on the still incapacitated and bloody eunuch that was now Blake.

Cooper picked her up and carried her outside where the glow of the morning sun was just coming up over the mountains. They were at Courtney Champlain's parents' summer retreat. They had all come up here to party in the summer between their junior and senior year of high school. That year had been torturous watching Cooper and Courtney together. He was going into his senior year, the captain of the football team after having won State alongside his blonde cheerleader girlfriend Courtney.

Every time she got within breathing room of him, she thought she was either going to kiss him or go running for the hills, neither of which she did in the long run. Julie had toughed it out, acting indifferent and secretly crying herself to sleep some nights with the pain of not having him and the thought of him not wanting her. Looking back now she realized it didn't matter that they had never dated in high school, they were together now and that's what counted.

Cooper carried her around the front of the massive custom log home when she spotted her dad franticly pacing the front walk. "Dad," Julie cried out.

"Julie," Jack shouted, this night had aged him by a decade.

Cooper set her down gently, she ran into her father's arms which were wide open ready and waiting for her.

Bending his knees and holding his arms out wide like he had done thousands of times before when she was a child, she flung herself wholeheartedly at him. Jack Hart caught his little girl in a huge bear hug, tears of joy and relief streaming unabashed down his face.

Cooper stood back watching his adoptive family and his heart filled with emotion. Jack and Julie looked up and held their arms out for Cooper who had gone through this horrific ordeal by their sides. Both knew it was his understanding of Julie's message that had facilitated this joyous reunion. He gladly went into their comforting arms hoping he was offering some comfort of his own to them. They watched in unison as Courtney was led out in hand-cuffs followed by EMTs carrying Blake out on a stretcher.

A second EMT ushered Julie over to the back of his rig to assess her injuries. He bandaged her up the best he could, then cleared her to travel home to the rest of her family.

"Let's go home," Jack suggested to two people who couldn't agree more. "And call your mother, she's worried sick," he said handing her the phone.

The trio climbed into the FBI's black SUV and headed home.

CHAPTER FIFTY-ONE

When they reached home Julie jumped from the SUV and ran inside. Her sisters and mom rushed to meet her and the three of them collided in a tearful embrace. Julie kissed each one on the cheek in turn, "I love you guys so much," she wailed. "I missed you."

It was pretty much the same reverberated back to her with a bunch of inaudible declarations. The women swayed together as a whole. The men sauntered in, pleased with the sight that greeted them. They stood back and admired their family.

Finally, the women broke apart, not a dry eye in the house as they all wiped tears from their eyes. Sandy rushed to greet Jack, "Oh thank God you are safe! I was worried sick about all of you!"

Katie and Megan hugged Cooper, "Thanks for bringing her home."

Cooper seemed embarrassed by their praise, "I wasn't coming home without her." He was looking over the girls' heads watching Julie as he said it.

Sandy came over, kissed Cooper, and gave him a huge hug. "I love you, Cooper Jackson."

This time Cooper did blush, "I love you too." He told her.

He excused himself, took Julie's hand, and ushered her into the library. He shut the door behind them and walked her into the room. Releasing her hand, he stepped back and swiped a hand through his hair. Cooper let out a ragged breath and began pacing in front of her. Julie wrung her hands and waited for him to speak. It seemed like a lifetime passed as she waited, when the seconds became minutes and Cooper was still pacing, she demanded to know what was wrong, "Cooper you're scaring me! Say something," she pleaded.

He stopped pacing and faced her, "I'm scaring you!" he shouted. He had to take another breath to try and calm down. "You scared the living shit out of me!" His arms were flailing wildly. "Why didn't you come to me? Why didn't you tell me? We could have dealt with this together-"

A huge grin began to spread across her face.

"What!" He demanded to know what was so funny.

"I love you, Cooper Pembrooke Jackson." Her declaration deflated his anger. He had never heard her say the words and it left him breathless. He was on her in three long, fast-paced strides crushing her to him, lips grinded together and their arms wrapped tightly around each other. Falling backward onto the couch they inadvertently knocked over a floor lamp which went crashing down to the ground, neither one noticed in their feverous attempt to get closer to the other.

Instantly the rest of the Harts stormed the room interrupting their little interlude. Tensions were still a little high and the unexpected crash in the other room had sent them rushing to investigate. When what they witnessed was an intimate embrace between their daughter and Cooper, the boy next door, they all chose to immediately excuse themselves.

"Breakfast is in fifteen minutes," her mom called out to them as she closed the door behind her, a knowing smile unable to be hidden from her lips.

Cooper looked down at the woman underneath him. He had his Jewels back he could see it in her eyes. His hand caressed her face then held the tip of her chin "I love you too."

Tears filled her eyes, "I'm sorry I didn't tell you what was going on."

"I know. You terrified everyone. I was petrified I had lost you for good this time."

"It won't ever happen again."

"I would sincerely hope you don't have anyone else that wants to kill you."

"One can only hope."

"Not funny," he said to her before kissing her sense-lessly again.

CHAPTER FIFTY-TWO

T hat summer was the best and worst for Julie, she had found Cooper and lost her sister. A month after Shannon's death the family was informed that she had a safe deposit box and inside was a letter from Shannon addressed to Julie.

Dear Julie,

God, I don't know how this got so screwed up. Blake and I had been secretly dating months before everything started between you two. I was madly in love with him. Then one day I overheard Dad talking to Blake in the library. I was hiding in the secret passageway hoping I could sneak a kiss from Blake when Dad left. That's when I found out about Aunt Gwen and your inheritance. I was furious, enraged that the old bat would leave you everything and nothing for me, and immediately confronted Blake about it.

We came up with a plan for him to marry you and then divorce you a few months later after your twenty-fifth birthday when you would come into the inheritance. In the long run, I think it was mostly his idea from the beginning and he made me think I had some part in the plan. My bitterness towards you only got worse when you were spending so much time with my Blake. I wish I could take back the whole stupid thing. I never thought he was capable of murder. I swear.

The morning of your wedding we were in the church when he said he could kill you on the honeymoon and make it look like an accident. He told me that you had already put him on your life insurance policy. Then when the accidents started happening after the wedding was called off, I started to have my suspicions and I confronted him about it. He told me that if I didn't change your mind about marrying him, he would have no choice in the matter. He told me we could run away together and live happily ever after in some tropical paradise. As much as I envied you getting everything first, being Daddy's little girl, the money, everything...Jewels, I just couldn't do it.

As much as I want to believe in Blake, if something should happen to me, I have written my confession and implicated him in the process. Please forgive me.

Love,

Shannon.

Shannon's letter was allowed into evidence in Blake and Courtney's trial. Courtney's family wasn't able to bribe any judges and they were, in turn, prosecuted themselves for their efforts. Blake, along with being castrated by Courtney's gun, was given two life sentences without the possibility of parole. Courtney received twelve years for conspiracy to murder with no possibility for early release.

Nana passed away in early November and was mourned by all. She had told Cooper on her deathbed that she would be with the one she loved for the holidays and couldn't be happier about that. Cooper inherited all of his grandparents' real estate, and the country club, along with an insane amount of money.

Julie and Cooper continued to date. Each trying to make up for lost time.

EPILOGUE

I t was September, a full year after Shannon's murder and school was back in session. Cooper's work in the landscape business was winding down for the year but he was still busy with the running of the country club.

Julie had planned a weekend getaway for Cooper's birthday. They went into Boston and caught a Red Sox game, stayed in a luxury suite, dined in five-star restaurants, and made love frequently. When she told him she needed to pick something up from her parents' house on the way home he gladly stopped. Waiting inside was a surprise party that actually surprised him. They ate, drank, and were genuinely merry. Then, close to midnight when the party was winding down, Cooper pulled Julie aside.

"Come on let's go for a walk," Cooper said holding out his hand to her.

Julie smiled, "Sure." She placed her hand in his and felt his warmth. She didn't think she would ever get tired of the feeling. They walked alongside the pond between their homes, swinging their hands and listening to the critters chirp.

"Thank you for tonight," Cooper said.

"You're welcome but you know tonight's not over," Julie said suggestively.

"Oh, really?" he asked leaning over to nibble her neck.

She giggled, pulling away but not letting go of his hand. They walked through the arbor of the maze which was all lit up with lanterns at every corner and walkway lights lining the path on the ground.

"Truth or dare?" Cooper asked.

Julie started laughing as they meandered through the labyrinth. "Oh, no. You go first, truth or dare?" Julie asked.

"Ok. Truth." Cooper's voice was husky.

"Do you love me?"

"Yes," he said without hesitation. "I think I knew for sure since my thirteenth birthday party when I paid Cameron Miller 20 bucks to dare me to kiss you."

Julie's startled gasp caused him to chuckle. "You did not!" she tried to sound appalled, but it came across more as pleased.

He stopped in his tracks and turned towards her. She stopped and looked around her realizing this was the very spot where they had shared their first kiss. Julie looked into his eyes and saw the love he had for her. It had always been there, she realized that now, she just hadn't picked up on it before.

"Julie, I love you more than you will ever know. I always have and I always will. Okay, your turn now, truth or dare?"

"Dare," Julie spoke with a naughty grin, which instantaneously froze on her face when Cooper slowly got down on one knee.

"Oh, Cooper..." Her hand covered her mouth, which gaped open.

Reaching into his pocket, he pulled out a ring. No box because this wasn't just any ring from any store. She recognized it at once as Nana's ring. Platinum band with intricate detail on the band that had been custom-made in England almost a century before. The center stone was over a carat princess cut diamond flanked with two gorgeous emeralds. She had always loved that ring and the woman that had worn it.

She was having a hard time seeing the ring because her eyes were filled with happy tears. "Julie, I dare you to be my wife. Will you marry me?" He held the ring up for her.

"Challenge accepted," she said with a huge grin and tears streaming down her face.

Cooper hadn't realized he had been holding his breath until he heard her positive response. He jumped up into her awaiting arms kissing her with all the tenderness he felt towards her. "I'm never going to let you go."

"Good, because I don't plan on going anywhere."

Cooper slipped the ring onto her finger.

"I love you," Julie whispered.

"Music to my ears," Cooper replied in the same hushed tone.

They made love on a bench in the gardens, then made it to the grand staircase inside, and finally, lying sated in Cooper's bed, their sweaty bodies intertwined.

Julie held her left hand out, eyeing her ring. "I couldn't have planned a better evening," she said.

"What was your original plan? You had said the night wasn't over."

Julie propped herself up on her elbow, running her hand over his chest, letting the hairs curl around her fingers. She kissed him quickly before crawling over him to the nightstand and reaching for the remote. She snuggled back into bed with him, turned the TV on, and pressed play on the DVD player.

On the screen came baby pictures of Julie and Cooper separately, then pictures of the two of them from the time they were three years old right up to the baseball game that weekend. She had a collaboration of their favorite songs over the years playing in the background.

"Julie, that's awesome. I think it should be played at our wedding."

"I want to get married in the gardens."

"I think that could be arranged. Would you like the reception at the Country Club?"

"No, I would like it right here in your ballroom."

"It's our ballroom. What's mine is yours."

"My heart belongs to you," Julie told him, "Always has, always will."

"I'm glad you finally listened to it," Cooper said before kissing her again, looking forward to the life he had dreamed of with her. Cooper was unspeakably grateful for all the moments that had finally led them back home to one another. He knew without a doubt he would love this woman until his last breath.

Next in the Brides of Willows Cove Series

HONEY WITHOUT THE MOON

Chapter One

Honeymoon: a vacation taken by newlyweds.
The honey refers to the sweetness, whereas the moon
eludes the period of time.

Boston

Melissa Kline resembled a drowned rat. Her usually perfect curly black hair was plastered to her head, her impeccable clothes clung to her body, and her make-up was in streaks on her face. She was standing outside in the pouring rain in front of her apartment building as she waited for the Uber to come and save her. Just an hour ago, she had been on top of the world.

She had landed her dream job. Delaney Publishing had offered her the chance to move from Boston to New York City. Melissa had been so confident that she would get the job that she had given her notice at her current job and arranged for a moving company to pack up her belongings two weeks ago.

When she arrived home, she greeted the doorman by name as she took the elevator up. Walking into the quiet apartment she shared with her fiancé, she called out, "Hi, Hon." Their little King Charles spaniel raced into the living room to greet her. Kneeling on the floor, she scooped him up, rubbing his soft long, reddish-brown, and white fur, "Hi, Dart! Mommy got a new job today. Yes, I did. Where's Daddy?" She put him down, and Dart immediately raced down the hallway toward the bedroom.

Opening the door, Dart raced through her legs and bounded onto the bed. A bare-chested Chad was in the process of buttoning his jeans as he stood next to the nightstand. In their bed, a naked girl has wrapped her favorite 1200-thread count Egyptian sheets around her breasts. Her traitorous dog panted happily beside her as she absently stroked his fur. She wasn't just any girl. No! She was the perky 19-year-old college student they employed as their freaking dog walker.

"It's not what you think," Chad attempted, his hands outstretched.

A sharp, short laugh escaped Melissa. "Really, Chad?" She threw her arm towards the bed. "Because it looks like you are sleeping with Amanda, the prepubescent dog walker!"

"Mandy," the naked girl in bed dared to speak.

"What?!" Melissa turned the full force of her wrath on "Mandy."

"My name, I go by Mandy," the near adolescent had the nerve to say.

"Is she serious?" Melissa asked, incredulous as she turned back to Chad. Dart sensing something was going on with his parents, cocked his head to the side.

Chad walked towards Melissa, but she held her hand up, stopping him mid-stride. Dart jumped up and bounded to the end of the bed, his head swinging back and forth. He watched the interaction between the two of them with curious interest.

"How long has this been going on?" she asked, not wanting to know the answer but needing to know the truth.

"I swear this has never-" Chad started.

"Four months," the helpful Mandy offered from the bed.

"Shut up," both of them yelled at her in unison.

"Baby, just tell me what I can do. I will do anything."

"Anything?" she asked.

He brightened, thinking he had won, "Anything. I promise," he added.

She smiled, "Good. You will call every one of our guests and tell them why the wedding is canceled." The smile slipped from his face as she continued, "You are also going to call and personally apologize to my parents, and you will repay them every single cent they have spent on this wedding. Oh, and I never want to see or hear from you again."

She turned to Mandy, "Oh, in case you haven't figured it out yet? You're fired." With that, she turned suitcase in hand, head held high, and walked through the door. She whistled, and Dart jumped off the bed, sprinting after her, "And I'm taking the dog!"

Now, standing outside in the rain, Melissa's luggage next to her and her dog shivering in her arms. She squeezed him tight and promised him, "We are going to be all right."

Author's Note

D ear Reader,

I came up with the concept of "Amnesia at the Altar" when I was a teenager. Fast forward several years later. When I was a new mom for the second time, I stayed home with my two babies under the age of two! I confided in my husband that as much as I loved being at home with the kids, I needed something for myself. His first, immediate response was, "You always talked about writing a book. Why don't you do that?" Hmm, why don't I? I spent a year writing "Amnesia at the Altar," originally titled "For Better, For Murder." When I completed my masterpiece, my baby, I looked for a literary agent. I researched companies and their agents and handpicked agents I would love to work with. I was rejected seven times, all nice and polite, "You have a great imagination." "Just not what we are looking for." "Good luck." With each one, I was more and more discouraged.

Due to the recession, my husband lost his job twice in six months, and I needed to go back to work full-time. To make matters worse...my computer crashed, and I had NO BACKUP! Tens of thousands of words were gone. Life moved on, and just like that another eight years had passed. My husband asked me, "What happened to you writing a book?"

"When?" I asked him, "I work full time, have two kids, two dogs, and a house to take care of." Without saying a word, he gestured to the TV I was watching. He had a point. I did love watching my shows and movies. So, after that, I made a conscious effort to work on a book. I didn't give up watching my shows. I wrote "See You Never" in eight months. I published it three months later.

After that, I didn't stop. I found a copy of "Amnesia at the Altar" in an old email I had sent years earlier to a friend. I revamped the entire novel in between soccer and basketball games, a week's vacation in Punta Cana with 38 of my closest neighbors, and a crazy busy holiday season when my dog Toby spent a week at the vet (turns out he has a swallowing disorder, that of course is extremely rare), a six-week kitchen remodel that turned into a whole first floor remodel my husband and I did mostly by ourselves (and yes we are still married).

I also took a month-long James Patterson class that I would strongly recommend to anyone with an interest in writing. In the course, I came up with an entirely different novel that I would love to share with you. It's called "Shepard's Hook," and I hope to have that out next year as well.

I am still new to this whole process, and your continued support is greatly appreciated. Word of mouth is my best friend right now, so please, if you enjoyed this story, spread the word. I would love to know what you think of "Amnesia at the Altar," so let me know in a review on Amazon or Goodreads. You can also find me on Facebook (Misty Jae Ogert, Writer) and see what else I'm up to. Thanks for reading.

Sincerely,
Misty Jae Ogert